Handmaking
AMERICA

Handmaking
AMERICA

A BACK-TO-BASICS PATHWAY TO
A REVITALIZED AMERICAN DEMOCRACY

BILL IVEY

COUNTERPOINT / BERKELEY

Library of Congress Cataloging-in-Publication Data is available.

ISBN: 978-1-61902-053-5

Cover Design by Faceout Studios

Interior design by Neuwirth Associated Inc.

COUNTERPOINT

1919 Fifth Street

Berkeley, CA 94710

www.counterpointpress.com

Distributed by Publishers Group West

10 9 8 7 6 5 4 3 2 1

For Jackson Lears, Richard Sennett,
and
The Memory of Tony Judt

"A regime which provides human beings no deep reasons to care about one another cannot long preserve its legitimacy."

—RICHARD SENNETT

"That country is the richest, which nourishes the greatest number of noble and happy human beings."

—JOHN RUSKIN

CONTENTS

PREFACE

Late in his first Oval Office address to the nation—the one in June 2010 that talked about the out-of-hand leaking oil well in the Gulf of Mexico—President Barack Obama delivered this remarkable characterization of the American dream:

> What has defined us as a nation since our founding is the capacity to shape our destiny—our determination to fight for the America we want for our children. Even if we're unsure exactly what that looks like. Even if we don't yet know precisely how we're going to get there. We know we'll get there.[1]

What a striking statement! In the first place, how did such an offhand admission of vision vacuum and leaderly drift find its way into a presidential address? Speeches by our heads of state—especially those bounded by a sense of crisis and delivered from the draped solemnity of the Oval Office—are among the most massaged, most vetted, most thought-through declamations in human history. How could a crack communications team honed on the tight message control of the much-admired Obama presidential campaign let the leader of the free world say, in essence, that America's distinguishing feature is the willingness of citizens to aggressively journey along an uncertain path to an unknown destination?

And why wasn't this half-hearted assertion challenged by our pundits—print, TV, and Internet—who seem more than willing to parse every presidential sentence that can possibly be sliced, diced, and read like tea leaves to uncover hidden administration intent. Why didn't anybody notice?

And, most importantly, is this what President Obama really thinks? Is his sense of what America should look like really this unformed? Does he really believe we're on a kind of starship *Enterprise* adventure, "boldly going" we know not where? If rhetoric of this sort can find its way into an important presidential address, and if nobody—I mean *nobody*—finds it a bit unusual, what does this tell us about social democrats, progressives, and liberals and our capacity to lead? What does it tell us about expectations—what observers see in the progressive vision? What does it tell us about ourselves? How much, or how little, do we think is required to inspire Americans to join in crafting a society that advances social justice, a sense of meaning, and a high quality of life for all?

This is not a knock on our president—the softness of his rhetoric merely underlines the constricted state of today's Democratic imagination. But there will be a fresh administration and a new Congress in the winter of 2013, and while the economy, jobs, the budget deficit, and our exit from Middle Eastern entanglements will be the proximate subjects of legislation, televised interviews, and political posturing, beneath the churn of rhetoric and polls, the future will turn on vision, leadership, and a commitment to our American dream. As commentator Mike Barnacle explained on a *Morning Joe* telecast in June 2011, the American people want answers to two questions: "What are we doing?" and "Where are we going?"

Back in the summer of 2011, more than a year after the oil disaster Oval Office address, progressive discomfort with the president's dispassionate, tentative rhetorical style surfaced here and there. Obama "needs to be very careful to avoid leaving voters with the impression that his sphinx-like aloofness is all that liberalism has to offer,"[2] wrote Peter Baker in *The New York Times.*

More to the point, Drew Westen, in a lengthy opinion piece in *The New York Times*, explained exactly why the president needed to reshape—*dramatically* reshape—his vision of the future: "The stories our leaders tell us matter, probably almost as much as the stories our parents tell us as children, because they orient us to what is, what could be, and what should be; to the worldviews they hold and the values they hold sacred."[3]

Democrats resist sloganeering—a symptom perhaps of our charming residual attachment to the truth. But today we also shy away from big ideas, most likely out of fear, plain and simple. The liberal vision for America—of a healthy, prosperous society committed to social justice and equity—has been derided by right-wing critics for more than three decades. The notion of government-enabled progress has been demeaned to death. Progressives have retreated into a cautious incrementalism. Journalist Jack Hitt put it this way: "Democrats live one election at a time, one issue at a time, unaware that they've become electoral wallpaper in front of which daring conservatives delight in performing."[4] It's no surprise that, as pollster Stanley Greenberg points out, "Voters feel . . . estranged from government—and they associate Democrats with government. If Democrats are to be encumbered by that link, they need to change voters' feelings about government."[5]

For decades we have been warned that government is the problem; it should be no surprise that the message took. Today, the idea of engaging Washington to pursue shared national objectives has been pushed to the fringes of American political discourse. If you believe government can deploy public policy to enhance quality of life, you're dismissed as a tax-and-spend liberal. Suggest the extension of federal programs into health care, transportation, voting rights, or home ownership, you're not a mere liberal but, in today's conservative lexicon, a *European socialist* (heaven forbid)!

Perhaps it should be no surprise that, as historian Tony Judt put it, "Shorn of a story to tell, social democrats and their liberal and Democratic fellows have been on the defensive for a generation."[6] Or, as activist philanthropist George Soros argues, "Republicans have gained control of the agenda. . . . Democrats are forced into fighting a rearguard battle, defending the opposite position."[7] Instead of advancing our own big ideas, we fight back by deploying grab bags of facts—poverty levels, "food insecurity," income disparity—information severed from dreams. Today there seems to be a tacit understanding that it's somehow inappropriate for progressives to actually paint a broad-stroke picture of a better tomorrow. Our president is just projecting the de facto Democratic line.

There's no doubt that conservatives have driven home their own ideologically grounded narrative. *The Washington Post*'s E.J. Dionne shorthands the "Republican syllogism" this way: "The economy is a mess. Obama and the Democrats are for big government. Big government is responsible for the mess. Therefore the mess is the fault of Obama and the Big Government Democrats."[8]

This is simplistic, illogical, and wrong. But it's also a clear, straightforward, easily grasped argument that resists subtlety and elbows analysis to the side.

Such insubstantial assertions work because beneath these false associations lurk two generations of disingenuous right-wing argument about the dangers of government, the social benefits of unrestrained capitalism, and the virtues of a belligerent foreign policy. Incubated in conservative think tanks during the 1970s, nurtured by conservative pundits like Irving Kristol, and today hammered home by operatives like Grover Norquist, the Right's blunt-edged attacks on labor, the social safety net, women's health, and new immigrants have embedded a Republican conventional wisdom in the American consciousness.

Today our progressive vision, not much more than a motley collection of devolved New Deal and Great Society initiatives, crouches fearfully in the corner of America's political arena.

Recall the response to the 2010 congressional midterms. Swallowing hard after election losses, Democrats managed to advance a feeble rendition of a defensive nuts-and-bolts agenda. Paul Krugman and Robin Wells, writing in the *New York Review of Books*, came close to shouting "Abandon ship!"—arguing that it was important for Democrats to "try to draw the line," to fight "on economic issues," all the while "preparing to delink their political fate from Obama."[9] This sort of uninspired, defeatist, tactical thinking couldn't be further from what social democrats really need.

In fact, liberals have been handed an opportunity. It took the Right more than thirty years to marginalize progressive assumptions that fueled the New Deal and the Great Society. But today, as the United States wanders among the detritus of a disastrous economic collapse, the scaffolding holding up the Republican conceit of free markets, big defense, and shrunken government is beginning to sway.

In the United States, home prices show no signs of recovering to pre-recession levels, and despite a rebounded stock market, record corporate profits, and resuscitated banking and auto industries, unemployment hovers just below 9 percent. And the reality is even worse: one out of six American men ages twenty-five to fifty-four is likely to remain unemployed even after the overall economy recovers. Wages have not kept up with increases in the cost of essentials such as housing, energy, and education. While inflation-adjusted middle-class income has actually declined for more than a decade, compensation at the top has soared. In 1990, executive pay was 24 times greater than that of an average worker; in 2010 that multiple was 325. A palpable sense of unfairness pervades American society—a newly perceived absence of social mobility. The Occupy Wall Street movement decries the concentration of wealth among the top 1 percent of the population; there is an understandable belief that the system is rigged. Bailed-out banks retain profits while passing on massive losses to future taxpayers. As John Plender wrote in the *Financial Times,* it appears that financial professionals have tilted the playing field. "Through campaign finance and political donations," Plender wrote, "they have bought themselves protection from proper societal accountability."[10]

The thirty-year lies of the Republican era—that small government will open the path of opportunity, that an unregulated marketplace will distribute goods and services equitably, and that wealth aggregated at the top will magically trickle down to the rest of us—have finally been exposed. At the beginning of 2012, the *Financial Times* introduced a series of essays exploring "Capitalism **in Crisis**" (emphasis in original). The newspaper's concerns are well founded. In Wisconsin, unionized workers first took to the streets and then secured petition signatures sufficient to mount a recall election targeting antiunion governor Scott Walker; in the New Hampshire Republican primary campaign, a bruised Newt Gingrich attacked Mitt Romney for what amounted to excessive capitalist zeal—Romney's role in acquiring, streamlining, and ultimately cannibalizing troubled corporations through his work with Bain Capital. Texas governor Rick Perry, his presidential aspirations fading, piled on: Romney and Bain Capital were "vultures." The internecine dustup was reported by the *Financial Times* beneath what was undoubtedly for the paper an unprecedented headline: "Republican rivals label Romney a heartless corporate raider." Former treasury secretary Lawrence Summers's comment in early 2012 that "serious questions about the fairness of capitalism are being raised"[11] was something of an understatement.

Republicans in disarray might seem like good news for progressives. Not so fast. With liberal values marginalized and the false promises of a market-dominated society finally called into question, America's *value space* has been emptied out. That's what I talked about when I keynoted a D.C. conference on "The American Idea" in the fall of 2011. America's economic collapse and Great Recession have generated suffering and apprehension. When times get tough—when the distractions of spending and consuming and travel and wealth are taken away—society must fall back on central beliefs, central understandings, basic goals—*values*.

But right now that critical space is empty. As our president's tepid Oval Office words of inspiration reveal, liberals have played defense for so long that we no longer notice that values and vision have vanished. For a Right that has for three decades smugly run roughshod over the most potent symbols of progressive democracy, the Republican faith in capitalism and market fundamentals has suddenly been put in play. Occupy Wall Street may still lack a coherent program, but by first concentrating on the excesses of America's banks and then shifting to a more general exposé of the basic unfairness inherent when wealth resides with a top "1 percent," the movement has forced us to engage the truth—that if society and its citizens are to flourish, the hard edges of postindustrial capitalism must be smoothed to achieve shared public purposes.

Employment is stuck, and U.S. politics appear to have entered a "new normal" of prolonged gridlock. In this dismal environment, what do Americans want? MSNBC interviewer and analyst Chris Matthews, punditizing in the wake of the New Hampshire Republican primary, argued that we long for "a return to normalcy"; Americans want to "get back to what we had."[12] But, of course, that's the rub: While the economy will slowly recover and unemployment will tick down a little, we won't ever get back to the build and borrow, borrow some more, credit card mania that made the first decade of the new century feel like so much fun. If there's a kernel of truth at the center of Matthews's observation, it's that what we want to get back to is something hard to express—something older, more fundamental, more deeply American than simply the return of big homes and high credit card limits.

That's what this book is about. By revisiting the roots of progressive thinking, by identifying what needs to be undone to correct for the excesses of the era of "market takes all," and by outlining a vision for a society that's not just richer but *better,* I hope to replenish the liberal value space, bringing centrists in while challenging my conservative friends to offer not just tired slogans but a better plan. We need to think about this now; if we don't, fear and resentment will permanently displace long-standing ideals. As Martin Wolf observed, "There are darker forms of politics in the wings: nationalism, chauvinism, and racism."[13]

Handmaking America is not about solving our problems; it is about rediscovering the values that have made America an unmatched problem solver. I believe we must reexamine what we want from education and what we give up as technologies invade work and home. But I am just as convinced that citizens, through consensus and investment in government, can respond, nurturing the conditions of a high quality of life grounded in achievement, heritage, and participation. I promise to frame a liberal narrative that will inspire but will also make specific observations and proposals. There are things that we must change and things that we must do.

Right now we don't need facts, and we don't need a new message. Progressives need vision—the kind of vision that recovers core principles, one that inspires us to accept higher taxes, to defer debt-enabled gratification, and to even tolerate a few more years of high unemployment as we advance to a real destination—a new rendition of a high quality of life in a vibrant democracy. We must imagine a life of quality that is not mired in consumption and debt; we must again see taxation as the vehicle for achieving shared dreams; and we must push back against the entrenched Republican assertion that government is somehow the enemy of individual achievement and human progress. Americans must undo the policies and practices that stand between us and a life of creativity, connection to community, and engagement in politics. We must establish new rules to reset the balance between marketplace ambition and public purposes.

As I've listened to progressive leaders over the past few years, watched them on television, and read our best policy arguments in newspapers, magazines, and speech transcripts, I've become convinced that it is critical that social democrats rediscover core values and reinvest in the power of big ideas. What is our vision of a good society? What will quality of life look like if we never recover the cash, jobs, homes, and holidays that marked our just-ended Age of Consumerism?

Jeffrey Sachs has observed that economic stimulus measures have thus far "reflected a hope that a temporary fiscal bridge would carry us back to consumption and housing-led growth—a dubious proposition since the old 'normal' had been financially unsustainable."[14] Sachs is right. But if the old normal is gone forever, where *are* we heading? How did we move so far off track that the American dream came to mean nothing more than big houses, nice clothes, and gigantic Wall Street bonuses? How did our politics morph into a gossip-ridden blood sport? How were long-standing American commitments to meaningful work, thrift, and good government undone? Can Democrats, in an era of economic uncertainty, proudly advance a compelling new agenda that looks to the future while honoring lasting values?

In the summer of 2008, I became part of the Barack Obama presidential campaign, working as a volunteer in a confidential research effort called the Obama Transition Project. While this preelection transition initiative was secret, it was scarcely sinister; we were merely gathering public information about agencies and departments of the federal government to create action plans designed to ease the entry of political appointees into new postinauguration leadership positions. Secrecy was necessary only because, at the height of the campaign, the slightest hint that the Obama team was assuming victory could be all too easily turned against us. We couldn't appear to be "measuring the drapes" before we had actually been handed the keys to the victors' new offices.

I was tasked with assembling a report on the National Endowment for the Arts, the federal grant-making agency I headed during the second Clinton administration. Our thirty-page "Road Map" and two-page "Summary" were completed just before the election. Then I became part of the real Obama transition team, relocating to Washington to complete postelection transition reports on three agencies, the NEA, the National Endowment for the Humanities, and the Institute of Museum and Library Services. Although it had been seven years since I had left government service to return to Nashville to launch an arts policy center at Vanderbilt University, the issues that had engaged me during my years as NEA chairman still had my full attention. So I welcomed the opportunity to help with the exciting and ultimately transforming Obama campaign, and I eagerly took on the challenge of connecting some of my ideas about art, heritage, and quality of life with a brand-new Democratic administration.

Coincidentally, my book *Arts, Inc.: How Greed and Neglect Have Destroyed Our Cultural Rights* had been published in the summer of 2008, just as I joined the Obama team. *Arts, Inc.* assesses the health of the U.S. arts system, arguing that market forces and a cavalier attitude by mainstream policy leaders have pulled America's expressive life away from public purposes.

As I anticipated, the core ideas in *Arts, Inc.*—expressive life, cultural rights, the extreme power of media markets—found an immediate audience among leaders in the arts and entertainment. But by November, when I was relocating to Washington to work in the Obama transition, it was clear that mainstream pundits simply didn't see the cultural scene as an arena that held any significance for policy leaders. In the policy frame that sets the limits of discussion in the U.S. system, ideas about culture—even big important ideas—don't have a home.

I began to think there was a need for a second volume, one that was less about the way art and knowledge are created, distributed, consumed, and preserved and more about the challenges we face as American society settles into a new century. While the character of our nation's expressive life would be central to this broadened, more political argument, I also felt driven to consider technology, advertising, and the way changes in media and public policy have undermined representative government. Inspired by nineteenth-century pioneers of progressive thinking,[15] I set out to both critique the way we came to live in the late twentieth century and to propose changes that might give us a high quality of life—a quality of life independent of the treadmill of consumerism and empowered by revitalized representative democracy.

While cultural heritage and personal creativity would be crucial to my argument, this new volume would not be about the arts. Rather, I would talk about the frame of policy, corporate practice, innovation, and individual initiative that determines the character of our lives as workers, parents, and citizens, figuring out where we've gone wrong and offering suggestions as to how we can straighten things out.

My experience with the Obama transition, both inspiring and cautionary, only strengthened my resolve to write about our twenty-first-century democracy from a new, more policy-centric perspective. The atmosphere in our transition headquarters—three floors of a Department of Justice office building ten blocks east of the White House—was predictably giddy with triumph. We'd won! Success!

No surprise. After all, it is not at all unusual for hard-charging professionals to interpret an event as an end point when it's really a beginning. The intensity of successful political campaigns and the deep engagement of campaigners are especially prone to produce the view that the really heavy lifting is all in the past. I was struck by the persistence of "campaign think"—the insistence that the new government (like the campaign) must speak with one voice, a position that jibed with the *soto voce* assumption that career government professionals (or anyone not from the Obama campaign team for that matter) were not to be trusted. And while the transition's rhetoric and its participatory website seemed welcoming to comments from multiple stakeholders, in truth it didn't seem like any of us were paying much attention to outside advice.

The participants in our transition meetings appeared all too familiar. Not just names and faces from the campaign but dozens of old hands (like me) who had served the Clinton–Gore administration. Yes, there were a few reformers dedicated to single-payer health coverage or Internet access for all, but they were outnumbered by experienced, mid-level former federal appointees who had filled up their out-years working in think tanks or lobbying Congress. Our team of transition worker bees was assembled on the seventh floor. Go upstairs and there was John Podesta, former Bill Clinton White House chief of staff, and right across the hall was Betty Currie (yes, *the* Betty Currie), who had done her level best to keep "Miss Lewinski" away from the president. This was Bill and Hillary land lifted up and plunked down intact inside the Obama camp. No surprise that the voices of real change within the Obama transition seemed too weak to offset the business-as-usual platitudes of Washington's Democratic establishment. American voters had long believed that "the game is rigged and that the wealthy and big industries get policies that reinforce their advantage."[16] As the work of our transition team evolved, a bit of this reality showed, and I became less and less confident that our rendition of "hope" and "change" would overturn this preconception.

But I was most troubled by the absence of an overarching narrative. Where was the terrific Barack Obama story—the mixed-race child with roots in Africa and the American Midwest, reared in exotic locales, educated at the finest universities, trained in the grit of urban politics, and blessed with a secure, attractive family? This is the stuff of the essential American dream—a successful life dependent on the truth of our nation's finest instincts. Why had this compelling narrative been cast aside? And if we *were* all about change, what were we moving away from, and where were we headed? Of course, we targeted a laundry list of policies: the war in Iraq, health care, Guantanamo, torture, government support for the arts. But we seemed to operate without a big picture, content to build on the remarkable achievement of the Obama election by rolling out a set of narrow, Clinton-era-style initiatives. What should have been a great story seemed thin. As Richard Wilkinson and Kate Pickett put it in *The Spirit Level*, our politics, certainly the politics of the new administration, "had abandoned the attempt to provide a shared vision capable of inspiring us to create a better society."[17]

The shifting backdrop clouding politics in the closing months of 2008 cried out for a new vision. Even as our team of transition volunteers worked on the specifics of agency review in our seventh-floor offices, the economy appeared to be collapsing around the incoming administration. Markets lost a third or more of their value, and recession, perhaps even depression, loomed. We all held our breath; would we soon find ourselves in a replay of 1934, with bread lines, bank failures, and platoons of photographers, writers, and actors deployed in a modern-day reincarnation of the WPA? For a time it appeared that market fundamentalism and the related illusion of salvation through debt and consumption would be undone; that Americans would be forced to reconsider long-held assumptions, returning to core principles. This would be a catalyst for *real* change.

Reality has been less dramatic; the backdrop more ambiguous and less insistent on action. Thanks to a hefty but probably inadequate spending initiative, it appears that the United States avoided, or at least deferred, an apocalyptic economic collapse. Instead we have entered an uncomfortable holding pattern: Unemployment is high, millions of homes stand in or near foreclosure, banks fail, and government seems frozen by partisan wrangling. While household income decreased by about 3 percent during the Great Recession, it actually dropped by close to 7 percent in what has been labeled a recovery.[18]

It should be no surprise that instead of a healthy-though-forced reconsideration of basic American values, anger and distrust have come to the fore. In mid-2009, the Pew Research Center reported that 72 percent of Americans agreed with the statement "Poor people have become too dependent on government programs," up from 69 percent two years earlier.[19] China is on the rise, and American workers fear immigrants will take their jobs. Between episodes of sex scandal and celebrity excess, cable television and talk radio have descended into the poll-enabled election-year he-said/she-said finger pointing that only inflames fear and suspicion of leaders and government. As Al Gore wrote in the spring of 2010, "Some news media now present showmen masquerading as political thinkers who package hatred and divisiveness as entertainment. . . . Their most consistent theme is to label as 'socialist' any proposal to reform exploitative behavior in the marketplace."[20]

Adding to the accumulated ill will is the widespread view that Wall Street, enabled by Congress, ripped off the middle class. Even Toyota, Olympus, and Walmart, companies cloaked in an impeccable mantle of quality, fell prey to financial scheming and plots to dodge product recalls and regulation. In the run-up to the 2010 midterms, the Tea Party, with its weird coalition of uninformed constitutionalists, tax protesters, gun nuts, Sarah Palinites, and anti-Obama "birthers," became the media's metaphor for a disaffected electorate. A mentally disturbed college dropout armed with a thirty-shot semiautomatic handgun grievously wounded a member of Congress and murdered five others. American soldiers continued to die in Iraq and Afghanistan.

Looking back from the vantage point of spring 2012, the achievements of the 2010 lame duck Congress have almost disappeared behind the distracting fog generated by natural disaster, interminable military engagement, and an economy that can't quite find its footing. But taking a longer view, those of us who served the transition can take satisfaction in the achievements of the administration we helped launch. Despite Republican midterm electoral gains, it is clear that the reform of health care and finance and the reversal of the onerous "don't ask; don't tell" policy of the Clinton era topped off the administration's first two years with a successful flourish. But such individual achievements—even the death of Osama bin Laden—fade with the news cycle; progressives remain determined to avoid any overarching story that positions legislative change and progress in international affairs as steps along a path to social progress and a high quality of life for all.

In the forty months since the Obama administration took office, I have gradually come to the conclusion that progressives long ago simply stopped worrying about the need to tell a compelling story of how good government can marshal smart public policy to enhance quality of life in our democracy. Somehow, with all the best intentions, we have reduced our argument to nothing more than a set of facts—demographics, budgets, percentages of growth or shrinkage. Social democrats have owned the facts for decades, yet today we still have truth without vision, reform without empathy, the promise of change without a narrative of the way things would look if they actually got better. And while we tracked demographics, revenue, and educational achievement, Republicans repeated their self-serving mantra: government is bad, taxation is an unnecessary burden, regulation stands in the way of achievement. In fact, as Thomas Frank taught us in *Pity the Billionaire*, the Right has boldly converted the massive failure of its tiny government/powerful market agenda by doubling down, asserting that what America *really* needs is another round of cuts and a Wall Street even less constrained by public purposes.

But it's important to remember that in a deep sense, the Tea Party movement is a response to a real crisis; beneath the stated fears about jobs, immigration, and taxes, there lurks an abiding sense that the nation has lost its way. Government slavishly "serves" but never inspires the people; work has become a source of anxiety rather than a reservoir of accomplishment and satisfaction; and consumerism has been unmasked as an unsustainable quest to secure happiness by mimicking "lifestyles of the rich and famous." The Internet and its digital enablers have lured us into a rabbit hole of incoherent babble. The trappings of modernity no longer amuse us, and we suspect that despite the stock market's rebound, Americans might never recover the standard of living we enjoyed when unsustainable bubbles in real estate and credit paid the toll. Trust in government is near an all-time low, and economic inequality has hit levels not seen since just before the Great Depression.

By revisiting the nineteenth-century origins of a progressive society—a healthy suspicion of modernity, a critical take on the worrying social effects of industrial capitalism, and deep respect for craftsmanship, humane design, and nature—liberals can revitalize our values. Once we resuscitate the poetry of our roots, filling America's value space with progressive ideas, the basic, time-tested mechanisms of government can do the rest—securing a framework of policy sturdy enough to sustain a way of life more closely aligned with real American ideals.

Fair warning: I believe that government has a responsibility to pursue policies that increase the quality of life—yes, even the happiness—of its citizens. Our founding fathers believed that if government was organized in specific ways, Americans would simultaneously enjoy the security and connectedness of stable community life and individual opportunity for achievement and expression. By striking a fair balance between belonging and freedom, America would distinguish itself from societies that had come before, advancing democracy as a matchless mechanism for linking government to the public interest.

In the concluding paragraphs of his terrific study of nineteenth-century transcontinental railroads, historian Richard White explains his commitment to the idea of "contingency." What happened in the past was not predetermined but resulted from particular and often unexpected circumstances. For White, "the deep common ground of good history is that things did not have to be this way."[21]

I'm with him. And while a good historian might be content to explain the way a unique situation hardened into historical reality, explaining the past isn't enough. If we don't like the way things came together in the past, we should do our best to dismantle what hasn't worked and substitute policies and practices that can make things better.

The United States we live in today could not have been envisioned by our founding fathers. Industrial capitalism and its postindustrial offspring—modern advertising, weapons of unimaginable power, advancing technology, evolving notions of human rights, and the transformational ideas of Freud, Marx, and Darwin—have completely reconfigured the context in which our representative democracy was forged. Signs of caution are blinking red. Our world is complex and the dangers many, but commitment to collective action through democratic government remains our best way forward.

This book is about what has gone wrong and what we must do. To recover democracy's spiritual center, we must undo the effects of free market ideology that have dominated public policy for the past thirty years. We must reregulate media in the public interest and blunt the damaging effects of new technologies in the home and workplace. We must revamp education to provide every citizen with the tools of creativity and political participation and with the knowledge required to resist the refined techniques of manipulation that empower big advertising and right-wing messaging. We must give every young citizen the tools required to hold government accountable. We must reconsider democracy as a secular sacred space and consider how we can strengthen our nation's soul.

Americans are smart and hardworking. We will engage adversity, sacrifice, and work together when inspired. Americans believe in progress and in the unique character of the American experience and will elect leaders who can gather us into a shared vision. Facts are never enough. To recapture and advance the American dream, we must construct a compelling narrative of the way government, business, communities, and families can define and then craft a high quality of life in the postconsumerist democracy to come.

Finally, a word about the character and tone of this volume. *Handmaking America* is an extended essay in which I strive to build compelling arguments while acknowledging and sometimes incorporating the work of others. I am a progressive and a Democrat. Although specialists might object, I use the terms *progressive*, *social democrat*, and *liberal* as equivalents throughout the text.

As I developed my argument, two themes surfaced again and again: technology and education. Technology has significantly reshaped the way we work and has dramatically affected the way Americans absorb information and engage the marketplace. We instinctively like new devices, but it is disheartening to realize that the modern Internet has devolved even as its speed and capacity to amuse have grown.

The Net was once wide open and free. In a *New York Times* opinion piece, Virginia Heffernan lamented the disappearance of message boards, "key components of Web 1.0." They were online services, "built for people, without much regard to profit." Today, "Web 2.0 juggernauts like Facebook and YouTube are driven by metrics and supported by ads and data mining."[22] I have come to believe that any new screen media will in short order find itself deployed in the same business as your antique Zenith black-and-white: renting eyeballs to advertisers. Those ads that appear at the top of page 1 every time I visit the online *New York Times*, and the ones that startle me just before I click "Enter Salon," convince me that I am correct. Americans must hone a fresh set of defensive skills as new media increasingly serves the interests of the marketplace.

It is not enough for Americans to be productive, healthy workers; we must also be good citizens, participate in political life, connect with community and cultural heritage, and develop the satisfaction of personal creative practice. Absent relevant job opportunities, many 2011 college grads simply moved home. Craft work advocate Matt Crawford points out, "One of the fastest-growing segments of the student body at community colleges is people who already have a four-year degree and return to get a marketable trade skill."[23]

Actor-activist Richard Dreyfuss has launched the Dreyfuss Initiative to revitalize civics as a secondary school requirement, giving young citizens the knowledge required to make "effective use of the tools of political power."[24] Young people also must be taught to interpret and deflect marketplace demands projected through media and an increasingly sophisticated advertising industry. The content of education—history, literature, government, and engineering—has been pushed aside. But our fashionable reductionist focus on math and reading and our misplaced confidence in the capacity of multiple-choice exams to assess achievement have pulled our schools far off course. Just as we must reassess our devotion to novel technology, we must reconsider the purpose of education in our American democracy.

I have tried to write with the general reader in mind, imagining a youngish, college-educated mother who is concerned about how her two children will fare in our reset economy. *Handmaking America* is not framed around issues that leaders and public intellectuals think and write about—taxes, health care, the environment, infrastructure—although these subjects will show up here and there. It's easy to find mainstream policy books chock-full of well-researched evidence assembled by reform-oriented experts. Instead, I have tried to bring forward ideas, connections, and themes that have fallen into the cracks of public discourse. To me, these lost realms of engagement can be found first in the feelings of pride, accomplishment, and independence that arise from creating a painting, a poem, or a finely crafted piece of furniture; second, in the sense of belonging, security, and continuity that comes from a close connection with shared cultural heritage; and third, through meaningful engagement in our political process. If we are linked to the past through shared traditions, and if we can maintain respectful political speech and autonomy through personal creative practice, Americans have a decent chance of securing a high quality of life even after the false promise of debt-driven consumption has been convincingly laid to rest.

INTRODUCTION

The Center for American Progress—a left-leaning Washington-based think tank launched at the beginning of the Bush era—occupies four floors of a Washington office building a few blocks east of the White House. CAP's work space blends exposed concrete walls and floors with chrome-and-glass offices and a high-tech, digitally screened conference room. The metaphorical message is clear: We're contemporary, wired; tweeting and texting, but we're grounded in the hardscrabble strength of hand-built America.

Trustees of the center meet a couple times each year. The work is mostly ceremonial—reviewing issue-driven promotional campaigns, learning about special initiatives, and listening to reports from center fellows charged with creating position papers on issues such as health care, education, and national defense.

A few springs ago, I was seated at the shorter end of the center's big rectangular conference table, watching a rainstorm build intensity along H Street (*How will I ever find a cab back to the hotel?*), while two young CAP fellows seated opposite me presented a report on the problem of poverty in America. Their presentation was stacked with all the numbers: the current official poverty level and how much would be achieved if that figure were increased by, say, 10 or 15 percent. Perhaps because I was only halfway paying attention, distracted by the pounding rain streaking CAP's floor-to-ceiling windows, the overall mood conveyed by the report impressed me more than its content; the tone was cool, abstract, analytical. The numbers defined a situation, and the data suggested how things might be better, but nothing even hinted at why I should care. When it came to poverty in America, what were we trying to do about what, and how would things really be different were we to succeed?

Questions were invited. I raised my hand: "Where's the poetry? What are you saying about poverty that would make us care about your numbers? What storyline does all this information—all these facts—fit into?

And then I went further: "The Right has a story; they just say the same three things over and over: 'We will keep you safe; we'll keep government off your back; we'll keep Washington out of your wallet.' What's our story; what's our equivalent answer; what kind of America do *we* want? What three points can we throw back into the faces of conservatives who think the American dream is about unregulated commerce, low taxes for the rich, and cutbacks in Social Security and subsidized health care?"

My questions were basically rhetorical, intended to get our supersharp experts thinking about more than numbers. But I was also serious in my desire to see CAP's policy wonks stretch toward an answer. I looked around the room. My fellow trustees examined fingernails or paid fresh attention to the rainy street. A few looked up (possibly rolling their eyes), and for what seemed like five minutes but was probably a minute or so, nobody said anything.

"You are not alone."

Off to my left, Susan Thistlethwaite, CAP trustee and Chicago-based professor of theology, had spoken up.

"You are not alone." Everybody looked her way. There was another pause.

"Well," I said, "that's actually a good start."

But that's also where the conversation ended. Nobody weighed in with idea two or three to assemble a point/counterpoint response to the false promises of the Right. And nobody seemed to care. If our arguments lacked themes, frames, and metaphors, no one around the table saw it as a problem.

Now the Center for American Progress had already been accused of sidestepping the "vision thing." Founded by John Podesta, a former Bill Clinton chief of staff, CAP had demonstrated a flair for unifying disparate Democratic constituencies, breathing life into our progressive agenda during the Bush years, using technology and media to deliver our message. But while the think tank had "generated a mountain of policy ideas to buttress the party's core philosophy, what it hasn't done is to provoke any fundamental rethinking of how that philosophy works in a new century."[25] Just as our Democratic president, two years later, could refer to an undefined "destiny" arrived at by some unknown path, my progressive CAP colleagues didn't see the absence of a poetic vision for an American social democracy as an empty spot in the liberal agenda.

It was "Just the facts, ma'am."

But we'd owned the facts in the John Kerry campaign, and Al Gore had delivered facts and the truth four years earlier. If we have learned anything, it's that the truth is not enough. We need the dream, or to quote Tony Judt, we need "a moral narrative: an internally coherent account that ascribes purpose to our actions in a way that transcends them."[26] Thistlethwaite's suggestion "You are not alone" perfectly frames the traditional progressive arenas of reform—health care, wage minimums, the social safety net. It is the essential but ultimately insufficient heart of the liberal argument. We need more.

Over the decades, thinkers on the Left have rarely lacked a sense of where society should go and how we should get there. On the contrary, judged by the prescriptive visions of John Ruskin, William Morris, Thorstein Veblen, or especially Karl Marx, the liberal view of the future has been if anything too specific, too prescriptive, and at times—as in the case of Marx's fatally flawed communist dream—far too energetic.

Progressives have always believed in securing a basic level of material well-being for all citizens, including our most helpless; that's what "not being alone" is about. We must go further by reconsidering the "pursuit of happiness," advancing those features of public policy, political leadership, and personal responsibility that can secure the American way of life through an era of reduced expectations and lowered standards of living.

It can't be just a numbers game. Many smart progressive political observers have noted that income disparity is greater today than at any time since the 1920s—the run-up years that handed us the Great Depression. The comparison suggests a simple "Aha!" solution. To such experts, narrowing the distance between our haves and have-nots will trigger social change and produce a high quality of life, a faith-based idea that is mostly grounded in naive assumptions about economic determinism. Unfortunately, taxing the rich and shifting money to the poor and middle class isn't enough. For one thing, there's no way to know just how much equity is sufficient—what do you ask for and when do you stop? Like greyhounds chasing an artificial rabbit, social democrats instinctively pursue the redistribution of income. Sometimes we look a little foolish.

No, we cannot extract ourselves from the hole we've dug by adjusting taxation and wages or even by investing in education—the consensus proxy for rebuilding earnings and the economy. Instead, we have to begin at the beginning, describe the character of the society Americans deserve, figure out what has gone wrong, imagine what can be made right, and craft policies and practices that can help get us there.

There exists a real opportunity. The vision of the Right—"We will keep you safe; we will keep government off your back; we will keep Washington out of your wallet"—with its implied commitments to defense, deregulation, and low taxes, should have taken quite a hit in the last couple of years. Deregulation has handed America Enron, BP, Murray Energy Corporation, Bernie Madoff, toxic assets, and outsourcing. Low taxes on the rich have converted a late-nineties budget surplus into massive deficits—a transformation accelerated by an unprecedented expansion of American security and intelligence agencies and by the prosecution of two protracted wars. Occupy Wall Street taught us that "trickle down" had in truth defied gravity; wealth flowed uphill. And along the way, as economist Jeff Madrick writes, the positions and policies of Ronald Reagan "planted a visceral distaste for government in the American belly, justifying . . . runaway individualism and greed."[27]

An Open Door to Change

Late in 2010, Nicholas Kristof published a *New York Times* column entitled "Mr. Obama, It's Time for Some Poetry." It was true: America needed a new dream. We'd never needed it more. As we entered a presidential election season, U.S. unemployment still bumped against double digits. Unions stumbled in a recent effort. Traditional private-sector pension programs—once available to nearly half of retirees—now served only 15 percent of workers. Absent employer-funded retirements, baby boomers nearing the end of their careers were heavily dependent on 401(k) plans, home equity, and modest Social Security payouts. But the stock market had essentially been flat for ten years, and real estate values had declined; 22 percent of American homeowners owed more on their properties than they were worth. Middle-class income had been stagnating for decades, even as the cost of food and housing steadily increased; many Americans were paying more than 35 percent of their monthly income for housing alone. Social Security was under threat from a slash-and-burn, budget-cutting Republican Congress.

Further, more than two years after the U.S. financial meltdown, there existed solid evidence that the pace of any recovery would be slow at best, a sad truth underlined by the very real likelihood that we would never revisit the old dream, the one that had Americans cashing out of the endlessly appreciating value of homes, extending a half dozen credit card lines to inhale the intoxicating consumerist sizzle of bigger houses, fancier cars, new toys, and ever more elaborate holidays.

If our leaders are unable or unwilling to paint a compelling picture of a successful democratic society independent of the trappings of wealth, then politicians and their electoral fortunes are forced to ride the roller coaster of economic life, their elected offices dependent on whether a jaundiced electorate "feels better off." And when it comes to the economy, no leader is allowed to admit defeat, so it should be no surprise that elected officials have consistently characterized both the economic downturn and our currently stagnant economy as temporary, cyclical conditions. But years after recovery efforts kicked in, the unemployment rate bumps along, dropping to 8.9 percent, notching up to 9.1, then down to 8.6; manufacturing remains stalled; investors hold their money on the sidelines. At the same time, productivity (a cheerfully reported indicator that really means that workers are producing more in less time, for less money) is up. The six-hundred-pound gorilla in the corner that leaders dare not recognize is the simple truth that the wealth Americans displayed early in the twenty-first century never really existed. It was all debt that felt manageable only as long as the housing bubble continued to inflate.

Of course, everybody knows about the inflated housing prices, overly indulgent (and downright exploitative) mortgage lenders, and collapse of domestic manufacturing that defined the first decade of the century. What is not understood—not even discussed—is the likelihood that our new economic condition will be, for the foreseeable future, permanent. After all, you can't "recover" something that was never really there in the first place.

As economist Tyler Cowen put it, "It's unclear whether Americans have the temperament to make a smooth transition to a more stagnant economy."[28] Cowen is being generous. Lacking an overarching story that advances a vision of success and a high quality of life apart from wealth generation, Americans have retreated into confusion, frustration, and anger. As *New York* magazine columnist Frank Rich put it, "A desperate and angry country is facing the specter of a double-dip recession with zero prospects of relief from a defunct Washington."[29] Despair, xenophobia, and class hatred stand ready to overwhelm core values, adding urgency to our need to craft a new narrative for our national value space, a revitalized vision for life in a progressive market democracy.

The Search for Values That Aren't about Wealth and Consumption

The first task of *Handmaking America* is to breathe some oxygen into those core markers of the American way of life that do not ebb and flow with the economy. It will require a fresh perspective on the "pursuit of happiness." Happiness is ultimately about some sense of "the good life," and it is, of course, the task of government to secure the best possible life for all citizens. But this truth begs crucial questions: What is the "best possible life," and what public policies best take us there?

It is here that present-day discourse fails us. The rise of marketplace values, the endless War on Terror, deregulation, all accompanied by the drone of right-wing attacks on the credibility and competence of government—these relentlessly repeated conservative assumptions have shaped the thinking of a full American generation. The conservative narrative has pushed important moral imperatives like respect for the poor, affordable public education, and the vision of an egalitarian democracy completely out of the conversation. As Jeff Madrick put it, by the late 1980s Americans were "apparently comfortable with shedding their sense of obligation to the larger community." Our sense of mutual obligation, forged in the heat of the Great Depression, "the traditional sense of citizenship among Americans,"[30] was at an end.

"We will keep you safe. We will keep government off your back. We will keep Washington out of your wallet." The roots of this simplistic formulation go back a half century to the antigovernment, probusiness theories of Milton Friedman, to the individualistic stance of novelist/philosopher Ayn Rand, and to University of Chicago economists who quantified, theorized, and justified a financial sector free of regulatory constraint. By the era of Ronald Reagan, these philosophical and economic arguments had been condensed, as George Soros puts it, into a "Republican narrative" in which "the government cannot be trusted and its role in the economy—both regulation and taxation—should be reduced to a minimum."[31]

Circumstances helped the argument advance. Al Gore has noted that it was the defeat of communism in the late 1980s that led to "a hubristic 'bubble' of market fundamentalism that encouraged opponents of regulatory constraints to mount an aggressive effort to shift the internal boundaries between the democracy sphere and the market sphere."[32]

Social bonds and commitments crafted during the Great Depression were replaced by blind faith in materialistic individualism. For Tony Judt, "Fantasies of prosperity and limitless personal advancement displaced all talk of political liberation, social justice or collective action." From the 1980s forward, our national vision and conversation came to be dominated by

the obsession with wealth creation, the cult of privatization and the private sector, the growing disparities between rich and poor.

And above all the rhetoric which accompanies these: uncritical admiration for unfettered markets, disdain for the public sector, the delusion of endless growth.[33]

At the same time our democracy came to be dominated by the ideology of unfettered markets enabling unlimited wealth acquisition, media deregulation embraced a new style of partisan journalism, while at the same time increasingly sophisticated advertising fueled consumerism. Our desire for more and more high-priced goods has become a kind of mania, and "the strain of unbridled manic pursuit . . . is damaging to both health and happiness."[34] Smart phone technologies have even taken away *time*: the one commodity most valuable in crafting a life of companionship, community, and personal achievement. As Pico Iyer opined in late 2011, "The distinctions that used to guide and steady us—between Sunday and Monday, public and private, here and there—are gone."[35]

The rich, distant, and for the most part uncaring, remain objects of fascination, elevated as exemplars of personal accomplishment. Technologies increasingly shape our identities and define the ways we connect with the world and one another; we embrace every new device, though each requires that we give up our privacy and abandon control to distant software while binding us firmly to fees and subscriptions. As sociologist Juliet Schor puts it, "Somebody needs to be for quality of life, not just quantity of stuff."[36]

Today, despite recent critical reconsiderations of military adventurism and Wall Street excess, suspicion of "big government" remains the widely accepted conventional wisdom bequeathed by the Reagan years. Because our trust in government has been undermined, laws and regulations designed to align media, work, and the marketplace with public purposes are weak. Definitions of "success" and "quality of life" have been reconfigured to mean little more than "wealth accumulation" and "the things money can buy." The total failure of market fundamentalism and the myth of trickle-down economics have not been enough to reconnect citizens with government's role in protecting the public interest.

Capitalism—unfettered corporate, postindustrial, market-dominating capitalism—has come to be viewed as a defining component of American democracy. The truth that capitalism has no special democratic tilt (it works perfectly well within dictatorships and oligarchies) has not prevented Americans from conflating "free markets" and "freedom." The two must again be properly divided.

Rethinking Work

If *Handmaking America* can offer a new vision, and new strategies, for a high quality of life in a reshaped economy, we must take on a second task: a critical reexamination of capitalism in the twenty-first century—the way we work, the way we consume. Far from benign and distinctly aligned against the egalitarian aspirations of our democratic founders, modern capitalism has armed itself with technology and psychologically empowered advertising. Equipped with tools unimagined when critics of nineteenth-century capitalism decried the impact of assembly line production on the quality and character of labor, our industrial revolution 2.0 has again redefined work while elevating consumption to the level of a primary responsibility of citizenship.

American society has done a respectable job of crafting a system of government capable of preventing the concentration of political power, and—especially in the civil rights and women's movements of the 1960s and 1970s—we've used public policy to counteract the excessive accumulation of social power. But we have been unable—and in the recent past also unwilling—to push back against the concentration of economic power.

The nineteenth century was a time of great social transformation, much of it driven by technologies. The railroad, telegraph, and photograph reshaped concepts of time, distance, and the past.[37] Critics like Ruskin, Morris, and Marx—Veblen here in the United States—were dismayed by the effects of industrial production on society; these thinkers weren't focused on capitalism at all (Marx didn't use the word). Instead, their critiques zeroed in on the concentration of wealth and on labor and production—on the way workers were demoralized and talent squandered by the intentional division of the complex talents of an artisan into a sequence of simple tasks that could be easily performed by unskilled employees positioned at various points along an assembly line.

This assembly line approach to manufacture was a central feature of Henry Ford's imaginative concept of twentieth-century industrial production. Before Ford, automobiles were one-off products, manufactured by hand in small shops staffed by skilled workers capable in wood- and metalworking, leather craft, and so on. A cohort of two or three craftsmen might complete a few automobiles in a month—a pace grounded in the centuries-old process of carriage building. After Ford, it was the factory—a vast metaphorical machine made up of components positioned along a production line—that actually built Model Ts; a hundred cars could be built in a single day.

Ford's thoroughly modern approach to manufacture had two important effects, both of which are very much in play today. First, the technology of mass production made human action subservient to the demands of the machine. As technology critic Jaron Lanier puts it, "One persistent dark side of industrialization is that any skill, no matter how difficult to acquire, can become obsolete when machines improve."[38]

Once an artisanal skill becomes mechanized—once intuition and knowledge are replaced by software, push buttons, and pixilated screens—it can be effectively, and economically, dumbed down. The doctor is replaced by a nurse practitioner, the navigator shoved aside by the GPS, and the fighter pilot replaced by the unmanned drone. Comprehensive tasks engaging complex problems are reconfigured into a series of minor activities, none of which is very interesting in and of itself. These redefinitions of the character of work are advanced in the name of economy and efficiency (think less training, lower wages, and increased productivity) and enabled by a class of public intellectuals who argue that change equals progress, that new is always better than old, and that up-to-date technology is by definition good.

But something crucial to quality of life has been lost. As Matt Crawford puts it, "There is pride in accomplishment in the performance of whole tasks that can be held in the mind all at once, and contemplated as whole once finished. In most work that transpires in large organizations, one's work is meaningless taken by itself."[39]

The early auto industry's second most potent effect on the present-day economy was the elevation of consumption. Ford paid his workers enough to enable them to buy new cars, and it is the evolution of a consumer society that has enabled postindustrial capitalism to advance its reach and authority beyond anything that could have been imagined by nineteenth-century critics. Just as piecework has undermined labor, it is the vacuity of consumer values that has sapped our reservoirs of resilience, incubating the despairing envy that now characterizes our national mood in the wake of collapsed home values, financial markets, and industrial production.

Ford made it possible for workers to purchase the very automobiles they were assembling. Add to shiny black cars a bevy of newly minted labor-saving household appliances—refrigerators, washing machines, radio-phonographs—and one can see as early as 1920 the seeds of our twenty-first-century consumerist culture.

And let's not forget two additional twentieth-century innovations: credit and advertising. The "installment plan" made big-ticket items affordable; advertising made them desirable. And while novel debt instruments and increasingly sophisticated advertising advanced throughout the twentieth century, both accelerated from the 1980s on as economic and political power were deployed to glorify the marketplace as the only worthy arena of American expectation.

The Curse of Consumerism

Today our values are undermined by something early critics of capitalism could scarcely have imagined: the corruption of values by consumption. Veblen, writing decades after Marx, could see that buying things would define the twentieth century as much as industrial production had shaped the nineteenth. He coined the still-useful term *conspicuous consumption* at the turn of the century. In the 1970s, historian Harry Braverman extended Veblen's argument, observing that while industrial capitalism "began with a limited range of commodities," in the modern era it has "transformed all of society into a gigantic marketplace."[40] The breadth and depth of this ongoing process of commoditization cannot be exaggerated. Braverman's is not the usual complaint—that corporations control us with their advertising. Instead, we suffer from a malady of the sort described by French philosopher Michel Foucault when he writes about power. Americans have been converted; we've internalized market values. We experience consuming as a liberating activity, strong enough to at times present the illusion of social rebellion. "Freedom" is no longer a condition defined by the absence of debt and envy. Instead, modern-day advertising has transformed freedom into a central tenet of consumerist ideology. Crawford calls this "freedomism": the sentiment that allows buyers to somehow believe that the purchase of a new SUV is a ticket to the great outdoors, when the real effect is a hefty installment loan and the inevitable truth that to service the debt, one must work more hours, inside, at a desk.

Freedom, of course, is an overarching theme in the American narrative, but its essence has been corrupted by the marketplace. In fact, any idea—even one that from a distance might appear immune from capitalist co-option—will quickly be commoditized. *The New York Times* reported that annual spending in the United States on yoga totaled nearly $6 billion in 2008. For author Mark Singleton, "The irony is that yoga, and spiritual ideals for which it stands, have become the ultimate commodity."[41] Capital thrusts itself into every possible human activity. Everything is monetized; everything converted into product. It is in this spirit that the slightest hint of creativity is quickly transformed into a revenue stream; Donald Trump not only trademarked the phrase "You're fired!" but also laid legal claim to the specific hand gesture that accompanied each dismissal. The conversion of an (unfortunately) everyday phrase into intellectual property is symptomatic of America's nonchalant attitude toward commoditization.[42]

The transformation of every facet of human activity into marketable product in the end conflates money and meaning. Moral injunctions, inspirational sayings, the musings of artists and philosophers are replaced by slogans like "Poverty Sucks" and "The one who dies with the most toys wins."

The Corporation Is Strong

The face of modern capitalism is the corporation. An artificial legal construct necessitated by the business environment of the nineteenth century, the corporation has steadily gained influence within America's democracy. The modern corporation bears little resemblance to those of the industrial giants who generated dynastic power and wealth—the Fords, Rockefellers, and Carnegies. The distribution of power to shareholders and representative boards early on converted the monolithic corporation into a limited-liability company. Modern capitalists aren't owners but managers who derive power from their place in the flowchart pecking order. It's this kind of corporation and this kind of management that has dumbed down labor and reconfigured craftsmanship into mere piecework. It is this kind of corporation that has satisfied its expansive needs by fanning the fires of consumer culture while finding ways to make money by managing money.

When Dwight Eisenhower warned of a military-industrial complex, he was in effect cautioning Americans about the growing power of corporations. When presidential candidate Newt Gingrich attacked Republican primary front-runner Mitt Romney as a job-destroying venture capitalist, he was warning voters about the perils of entrusting government to a master of corporate success. But corporations are nothing if not resilient; neither President Eisenhower's well-remembered words nor Gingrich's less-considered intramural attack ads on a Republican rival have dented the corporation as a positively viewed fixture of America's democracy.

In fact, during the past three decades the influence of corporations has surged, in large part as a by-product of the lax regulatory environment introduced in the Reagan presidency (and maintained, on a bipartisan basis, by his successors). Coincident with regulatory reform and gentled enforcement, U.S. courts have energetically advanced corporate prerogatives. The right-leaning Supreme Court has consistently favored business interests. The place of corporations in politics has become a hot topic, and the willingness of courts to treat corporations as individuals—the assignment of human rights to an artificial legal construct—has been very much in play during the 2012 election cycle. The proximate point of contention is the Supreme Court's ruling in *Citizens United v. Federal Election Commission,* which equates money (read political contributions) with "speech" while empowering companies to participate in politics.

Government Is Weak

Only government maintains the standing and authority required to push back against the corporation and the reach of postindustrial, free-market capitalism. Only the government possesses the capacity to offset the advancing corrosion of work and the steady undermining of values through advertising and consumption.

But the U.S. Congress has become a noisy, money-fueled battleground in which companies design policy to gain competitive advantage without regard for broad public purposes. And America's government today has become ineffective—not weak in a conventional sense but undercut by Republican assertions that government is a drain on social resources and an obstacle standing in the way of individual development. Our budget has been overtaken by entitlements and a national defense agenda enabled by the War on Terror. The citizen's ability to work through government to redirect power and money to blunt market forces or advance quality of life has today been significantly curtailed.

For thirty years, policy makers have chipped away at the ability of government to regulate the marketplace on behalf of public purposes. Corporate interests complain bitterly about tax rates, but of course no company worth its salt pays full fare; a laundry list of tax deductions tailored to the interests of specific industries has made the effective U.S. corporate tax rate one of the lowest in the Western world (to say nothing of how U.S. law enables companies to move key financial operations to offshore tax havens). Lacking both resources and regulatory clout, the federal government can neither maintain essential infrastructure nor align the activities of corporations with modest public purposes.

Republicans cut taxes to deliberately starve the government. Then they point to the lack of revenue to justify even further cuts. Their strategy is as transparent as it is effective. The mantra of continual war, slashed taxes, and timid regulation has seeped into the public conscious-ness only to reemerge as deeply held conventional wisdom. Pared to its essence, the Republican view argues that if government just gets out of the way, everyone can participate in the same dream of success. But this is not true. As Tony Judt has written:

> The rich do not want the same thing as the poor. Those who depend on their job for their livelihood do not want the same thing as those who live off investments and dividends. Those who do not need public services—because they can purchase pri-vate transport, education and protection—do not seek the same thing as those who depend exclusively on the public sector.[43]

The notion that what benefits the rich will benefit us all perme-ates the right-wing political apparatus. It justifies low taxes, diminished services, failing infrastructure, and a regulatory environment subservi-ent to the interests of globalized corporations and Wall Street money handlers. The Republican view has infiltrated our legal system and has justified congressional gridlock around any tax-and-spend issue that isn't about war. It has caused observers in other countries (read the opin-ion pages of the *Financial Times*) to question the ability of America's democracy to engage and overcome the economic, social, and diplo-matic challenges of the early twenty-first century.

So government—what is wrong and what must be made right—is another central theme of *Handmaking America*. As the U.S. economy staggers and young Americans continue to die in wars drained of mean-ing, it feels as though our government has nearly ground to a halt. While it is tempting to blame it all on the Republican myth that a shrunken government and bloated financial elite constitute a vibrant democracy, Washington has instead been the victim of a "perfect storm": a conflu-ence of disparate forces that together have dismantled essential com-ponents of our democracy.

Media and the Allure of Direct Democracy

Right-wing ideology is one cause of stunted government, a truth partly enabled by timidity: the unwillingness of social democrats to mount an alternative vision of the way government can work for society. But government inaction—the gridlocked dance of Congress and the White House—has also been enabled by technology in the form of tweets, blogs, polling, and 24/7 ideologically driven television networks. The speed with which the smallest political act is reported and criticized has made it nearly impossible for leaders of goodwill to back away from party orthodoxy and campaign messaging long enough to collaborate on policy that serves the public interest. How can a legislator who's signed Grover Norquist's no-tax pledge quietly support a reasonable compromise to increase government revenue if she is certain to be 1) attacked on Fox News the next day; 2) immediately confronted with polls that suggest "58 percent of your constituents oppose any new taxes"; and 3) promptly dismissed by *Politico* pundits as walking wounded in any upcoming election.

I've headed a federal agency and worked for years in Washington. Believe me, on any given day, not all that much is going on. But polling produces a steady stream of what historian Daniel Boorstin labeled "pseudo-events,"[44] in this case information about in-the-moment public opinion that appears true because it is presented in numerical, "scientific" form. Polling compounds other trends in political life—term limits, sunshine laws, referendums, initiatives—to advance the idea, as columnist David Broder put it, that "the criterion by which any legislation or individual legislator should be judged is the readiness to carry out whatever is currently favored by the constituents."[45]

This sounds a lot like direct democracy. And I believe that America's drift toward direct—"everybody vote, every day"—democratic government is an insidious and corrosive, though mostly unacknowledged, feature of contemporary political life. Direct democracy has always appealed to our sense of fairness; it's just feels right that every American should somehow weigh in on every issue. But direct democracy ends up empowering a government of men, not laws. Whoever shouts with the loudest voice, trumpets the most polarizing argument, or retains the most skillful publicist ends up shoving opponents—even a healthy, smart majority—far into the corner. As John Avlon put it in *Wingnuts,* direct democracy gives us nothing more than, "groupthink in tiny platoons that can have a disproportionate influence on political debates."[46]

Scholar Cass Sunstein and others have argued that the fragmentation of news sources has handed us a set of personalized echo chambers, in which cable viewers and Internet explorers can select news outlets that reinforce their predetermined opinions.[47] The relentless slide away from representative democracy is abetted by the cavernous appetite of cable news and online news media. This deployment of technology through television and the Internet necessitates denial of the obvious truth that many issues—health care, taxation, war making, presidential elections—play out only over time; they cannot be meaningfully analyzed or even understood within the confines of daily or hourly news reports. Our current media environment is too distracted and too dependent on daily headlines to find space for the big, overarching themes that shape the character of politics and American society.

Technology, Education, and Responsibility

Working, governing, and consuming are critical arenas of modern-day dysfunction. But there are also broad underlying forces—specifically technology and education—that influence the way we work, govern ourselves, and pursue happiness. What we buy, what we know, and how we know it must be addressed if we are to craft a new liberal vision for America's democratic society.

Americans are optimistic and constitutionally modern; we seem hardwired to interpret change as good and to see new products and new ways of working as better than what was done in the past. So millions enthusiastically check e-mail on handheld devices before turning in for the night and do the same each morning, or even on the beach, where we imagine, while responding to the boss, that we're away on holiday.

This same enthusiasm for novelty places technology at the center of consumerism. It's television (by which I mean any device with a screen that combines information and entertainment with advertising) that has sold us on the idea that symbols of wealth are gateways to happiness and quality of life. In addition, today technology itself is often the product. Our openness to the new blinds us to the truth that the latest Kindle, iPad, or netbook will force us to rent content, purchase and renew software, and periodically (every three years or so) discard and replace aging gear. Steve Jobs and Apple perfected the science of marrying good design to imagined benefits to keep us buying versions one, two, and three of products, even when the basic utility of each device remains cloudy. But consider this: Despite advertising hype and the cheerleading of high-tech loyalists, the digital age has not produced a single product that can match the utility over time embodied in a Leica camera purchased a half century ago. In place of lasting quality, technology has handed postindustrial capitalism its perfect consumer good, and we've gone for it hook, line, and sinker; today we not only buy things, we buy the *same* things again and again and again.

Technology has also enabled the reconfiguration of politics and government. Of course, the effects of cable television have been felt for decades; the bias of Fox News is old news. But Facebook, Twitter, and the authority and pace of Internet blogging are something new. Social media in particular is like catnip for politicians desperate to maintain constituent links, but as Jonathan Guthrie observed in a *Financial Times* interview, "Twitter is . . . an elephant trap for the indiscreet."[48] Certainly former congressman Anthony Weiner would agree; his careless online interactions with female contacts gave America its first sex scandal that didn't actually involve sex and a circus-like resignation press conference in which forty cameras, one hundred reporters, and one heckler from satellite radio's *Howard Stern Show* converged to produce four minutes of bedlam sufficient to boggle the mind of any foreigner unlucky enough to tune in.

"You Are Not Alone." Maybe, just maybe, we can start here and craft a progressive vision for America sturdy enough to push back against the Republican mantra of war, constrained government, and low taxes. Maybe, just maybe, in a new, subdued economy, the value of community and connection will reenergize America's collective will and break the isolating selfishness endemic in the Right's go-it-alone society.

For eighteen months I've been asking sympathetic liberals to help me think through the key points of a new twenty-first-century vision for our progressive American democracy. Susan Thistlethwaite's starting point is a good one—when citizens are left alone in old age, in poverty, ignorance, or ill health, our nation has truly failed. Her formulation stands in stark contrast to the cold isolation projected by the Republican dream: "Everybody on your own." Her argument suggests movement toward a society in which we find ways to understand and care for one another. She projects the principle that a progressive vision for a successful democracy must offer distinct moral objectives.

Here's a second idea: "You can live with purpose through work, family, and community."

I'm most attracted here by what's missing, namely any hint of our current mania for wealth and consumption. The phrase leans toward policies that ground us in heritage and enable our voices to be heard. As someone devoted to the arts, I envision personal creative practice as one way to live with purpose; certainly, engagement with ideas that influence government and help shape policy are purposeful. We cannot attain such goals if we are just left alone. We will not in isolation enhance the character of family life, embody the pride of craft, or maintain community traditions and values. Instead, as Tony Judt puts it, "We have to decide what the state must do in order for men and women to pursue decent lives."[49]

And finally: "America is still a beacon on a hill."

I know, I know; the sentence paraphrases Ronald Reagan paraphrasing John Winthrop's "shining city" reference, but there's a kernel of an important idea here. If America is special, we need to seek the essence of our exceptionalism; it's not just wealth and power. If America is a great nation, we must step away from the militaristic bombast and smug confidence in riches that have shaped the image of America for outsiders over the past ten years. Remember, for decades after the end of World War II, America's generosity of democratic instincts effortlessly cultivated a unique, compelling image on the global stage: We were powerful but nonthreatening, welcoming to strangers, tolerant of difference, rich but generous, working diligently to minimize race, class, and gender as barriers to social justice and individual achievement. At home we often despaired of our shortcomings, but from afar, the American glass appeared more than half-full—the United States was a bastion of goodwill, blessed with an economy that spread wealth throughout society and a democracy that kept leadership accountable to the people, attuned to their shared aspirations.

Yes, if America is to again be a beacon on a hill, we must pull back from the contemptuous application of global power in the age of the War on Terror; we must replace "hard power" with the elements of "smart power" and "soft power" defined by Joseph Nye, the diplomat turned Harvard scholar.[50] He argues that effective international engagement requires not only the projection of economic and military might but also deep cultural engagement and respect for the values of other societies. How we behave in the outside world is important. But the United States is not attractive simply because we are rich and powerful. On the contrary, our stature derives from our capacity to offer an appealing vision of an opportunity for everyone to "pursue happiness." To again be a beacon to the world, America must rediscover the true source of our greatness and reinvent the way we live, work, and lead, balancing a vision of both economic opportunity and social justice. As former national security advisor Zbigniew Brzezinski has written, "The key to America's prolonged historical appeal has been its combination of idealism and materialism, both of which are powerful sources of motivation for the human psyche."[51] To again inspire global respect, we must reconstitute that balance by paying close attention to quality of life here at home.

In the spring of 2011, I was driven from downtown Beijing—the old embassy district—to a new fortresslike U.S. facility outside the city for a meeting with cultural officer Tony Hutchinson. Hutchinson was at the time an unusual if not unique government official, serving simultaneously as a senior foreign service officer and Episcopal priest. I brought out my three themes for a progressive vision of American democracy—connection; personal achievement; a society that inspires the world. Tony thought for a minute and added a new one: "We owe it to each other."

Tony's right. Democracy is ultimately about the common good, and the common good is cemented by mutual obligation. The Republican conventional wisdom that taxation is an inconvenient, unnecessary, unreasonable burden on workers and small businesses is a categorical denial of our commitment to one another. After all, it is through taxation that we redirect some measure of America's accumulated wealth to accomplish things that we can only do together. More importantly, the moral tone of society is defined by what we will give, not what we get to keep. As author John le Carré puts it, "My definition of a decent society is one that first takes care of its losers, and protects its weak."[52]

"We owe it to each other."

Progressives have always owned the very best facts. We understand income disparity, flatlined real income for our middle class, the traps ensnaring the working poor, the cost of endless war making, and the debilitating effect of incarceration rates on minority communities. It is honorable that progressives maintain what George Soros describes as "a lingering attachment to the pursuit of truth."[53] But truth is only potent when joined to vision. What must we dismantle, and what must we begin, if we are to advance a vision of a good society?

There are limits to the reach and impact of public policy, no matter how well formulated. We can reinstate regulation, reconsider limits on media ownership, and develop guidelines for what should or should not be forgiven when it comes to bad behavior online. But ultimately, columnists, bloggers, pundits, and politicians must recalibrate personal expectations and embrace a new sense of responsibility. This will require that we rethink our notion of the good life, stepping away from the conflation of wealth and happiness—the selfish corollary to the conservative conviction that we should all be left to our own devices.

A reconfiguration of American education will be essential. We must provide citizens with the tools required to interpret and deflect the many manifestations of power that come at them every day. With his initiative to restore civics as a high school subject, Richard Dreyfuss is half-right; young citizens do need a better understanding of government and politics, but they must also bundle a real grasp of campaign advertising, talk show spin, and political speech with the skills required to understand and perhaps deflect the manipulative power of modern-day corporate messaging. I argue that we need a "new civics" designed to equip citizens to engage and critique the sophisticated power of government and markets in the twenty-first century.

Education can also reinvent the relationship between Americans and work. Certainly President Obama was right in the summer of 2011 when he spoke of creating "pipelines right from the classroom to the office or the factory floor." America needs a new kind of vocational education that equips young citizens with the skills required by an economy grounded in high-tech manufacture and the generation of ideas. However, when linking schools with the marketplace, we must proceed with caution. Twenty-five years ago, business stuck its nose into the tent of education; now the whole camel is inside. But education is not only about jobs; learning is not only about working. We need to educate citizens first and workers second.

Education can provide the skills required to fill time away from the workplace with engagement in cultural heritage, community leadership, and personal creative practice. If our modern economy reduces all labor to the routine, then the classroom must equip us to secure the satisfaction of productive labor elsewhere.

"You are not alone. You can live with purpose through work, family, and community. We are still a beacon on a hill. We owe it to each other."

This will be our progressive vision for a revitalized American democracy. But it will only inspire, and only succeed, if we together agree that we must take a new path, reconstructing a policy frame in which commitment to one another, confidence in collective action, and resistance to the siren song of power produce a high quality of life for all.

Handmaking
AMERICA

1

WORKING

The outcome was remarkable: 150 passengers, five crew members, all safe when a bird strike killed both engines minutes after US Airways flight 1549 departed LaGuardia, forcing a dangerous water landing near the western edge of the Hudson River. Most passengers and crew were unhurt; a few injuries were serious but none life threatening. While nobody made it to Charlotte that day, real-time images of passengers lined up on the wing of the sinking jet and emerging tales of the steady-handed leadership displayed by the US Airways crew marked the flight a success.

Captain Chesley "Sully" Sullenberger became an overnight hero. He had made a smart, quick decision, carried out the water landing with aplomb, and walked the aisle of the downed airliner until he was absolutely, positively certain that everybody had gotten out. The outpouring of gratitude and affection directed at Sullenberger was immediate and enduring. Months after the event, as he recalled in his memoir, the US Airways pilot still seemed surprised and a bit unsettled by the outpouring of sentiment aimed his way. People were approaching him "with tears in their eyes. They're not sure why they're crying. Their feelings about what the flight represents . . . just cause a swell of emotion."[54]

Certainly Sullenberger had behaved responsibly, even heroically, and stories like this one—success snatched from the jaws of defeat if not sudden death—had become all too infrequent in the American narrative.

But I think there was something else.

Novelist James Salter, a former military jet pilot, describes the crash landing as "a bit of luck and a job perfectly done."[55] True enough, but that's not all. Beneath the responsibility, humanity, and concern that distinguished Sullenberger's determination to bring all 150 safely to shore was a consummate professionalism of the sort that today seems all too rare in the U.S. workplace.

What Americans witnessed that day was the work of a *craftsman*, someone, in the words of sociologist Richard Sennett, determined to follow "an enduring basic human impulse, the desire to do a job well for its own sake." Craftsmanship is a learned response to challenges: "Every good craftsman conducts a dialogue between concrete practices and thinking; the dialogue evolves into sustaining habits, and these habits establish a rhythm between problem solving and problem finding."[56]

Or, in the words of Sully Sullenberger:

> You have to know what you know and what you don't know, what you can do and what you can't do. You have to know what your airplane can and can't do in every possible situation. You need to know the turn radius at every airspeed. You need to know how much fuel it takes to get back, and what altitude would be necessary if an emergency required you to glide back to the runway.[57]

No pilot is trained to recover from the failure of both engines; the event is simply too unlikely. Fortunately, Sullenberger possessed the experience required to identify and solve (within a few minutes) a totally unexpected problem in the air. He was prepared. He had amassed more than thirty thousand hours of flight time in military jets, in low-speed, no-engine gliders, and in an array of airliners. His wife, Lorrie, describes him as "a pilot's pilot" who "loves the art of the plane."[58] In short, Sullenberger was on that day a modern-day rarity—a dedicated practitioner of a distinct trade armed with the knowledge, insight, and intuition required to bring flight 1549's short journey to a safe if wet conclusion.

Americans have no reason to remember that once upon a time, most labor had this character; "The worker was presumed to be the master of a body of traditional knowledge, and methods and procedures were left to his or her discretion."[59] That way of working has quietly but steadily been eroded; it has become something rare. While Sully Sullenberger deserves our admiration and gratitude for many reasons, part of the "swell of emotion" he still encounters arises from the tacit understanding that his performance epitomized a hallmark of old-time labor in America—real professionalism, real craftsmanship—that has been almost entirely pushed to the side. Today, jobs that once required the application of insight, intuition, and experience—teaching, lawyering, practicing medicine, or flying airliners—have been recast as tasks requiring little more than the application of a set of rules and procedures predetermined by experts. In the United States, the essential satisfactions of craft work have been leached from even the best jobs. Sully Sullenberger is the exception that proves this rule.

A Tragic Outcome

Barely a month after Sullenberger's masterful in-flight improvisation, commercial aviation suffered an incident that produced an entirely different, tragic outcome. In February 2009, a Colgan Air Q400 tur-boprop commuter jet crashed on approach to Buffalo, New York. No one survived. The aircraft stalled—that is, the wings simply ceased to support the weight of the aircraft—and it plunged to the ground uncontrollably. The airplane "slowed while on autopilot during a night IFR [nonvisual] approach." As a stall grew near, automatic systems on the Q400 intervened: "The autopilot kicked off; the stick shaker—and then the stick pusher—activated exactly as designed." But according to the flight recorder, the young Colgan Air captain pulled back on the controls, an action guaranteed to deepen the stall, dooming the flight. The commuter turboprop had been in danger for several minutes, but when the crew took manual control of the aircraft, their actions made things worse. One expert speculated that the pilot acted out of instinct, not experience or training. Trying to raise the aircraft's nose may well have been "a startled response to a completely unexpected pitch change, where the primal and completely wrong reaction was to pull."[60] Investigators cited many factors that contributed to the accident, including crew inattention and fatigue. The captain possessed relatively little experience with the specific type of aircraft, and both pilots were at the end of a long workday that had begun with commutes to their base of operations. Certainly, it is neither fair nor appropriate to blame individuals for the crash. As Sully Sullenbeger said of the Buffalo tragedy, "Something in the system allowed . . . well-trained, experienced, well-meaning, well-intentioned pilots not to notice where they were."[61] The "system" in this case includes the autopilot, the stick shaker, and the stick pusher—automated devices that first alert the pilot to an incipient stall and then actually force the controls (pushing them forward) into a position from which the aircraft can recover. But consider a deeper meaning: These automated components of modern aircraft extract certain decisions from the cockpit and replace them with procedures that have been figured out in advance by engineers and test pilots.

We all fly on commercial airlines, increasingly on commuter aircraft flown by young, relatively inexperienced, undercompensated, and frequently fatigued pilots—pilots more attuned to systems management, and to the complacency that automation can induce, than to the stick-and-rudder attentiveness that enabled a successful outcome to a water landing in the Hudson. In fact, aviation experts continue to grow concerned about the increased application of automated technology to commercial aircraft. When the crew of a Northwest Airlines flight bound for Minneapolis inexplicably flew 150 miles beyond their destination, it was ultimately determined that the captain and first officer were both manipulating personal notebook computers, apparently checking out personnel policies associated with the pending Delta/Northwest merger. In an effectively unstaffed cockpit, the pilots innocently flew on. Commenting on the incident, Robert Sumwalt, a member of the National Transportation Safety Board, observed (understatedly), "Humans are not good monitors over highly automated systems for extended periods of time."[62]

It should be no surprise that the Buffalo crash generated editorial concern and ultimately congressional action. A new bill (HR 3371) requires more total hours for commuter airline pilots, remedial training in stall recovery, and a greater focus on airmanship and pilot skills in preemployment screening. The legislation represents a tacit admission that automation, distraction, and the absence of a certain level of skill have undermined safety; the essential craftsmanship of aviation—the "rhythm between problem solving and problem finding" has been compromised.

It would be good for the safety of the traveling public if HR 3371 turns things around. I'm skeptical. While the claimed purpose of automated airline flight is safety—autopilots and related systems promise to eliminate human error—the real effect has been to convert pilots from aviators into systems managers. Systems managers can be trained more quickly and paid less than a top-notch pilot with deep experience. As

Sullenberger puts it, "Some of the smaller regional airlines have lowered the minimum requirements for pilot recruitment, and they're paying some pilots $16,000 a year. Veteran pilots—those who have the experience that would help them in emergencies—won't take those jobs."[63]

Labor Reconfigured

In the nineteenth century, the piecework and assembly line process that defined the nature of factory labor fragmented tasks that had once been whole. A worker no longer manufactured a wagon wheel, flintlock rifle, or rocking chair from start to finish—one person applying a complex set of skills to single-handedly produce a finished product. Instead, the elements of a wheel—hub, spokes, and rim—were produced by separate individuals who made only a single component part. The individual laborer no longer held a concept of the whole, finished product in his head; such an overall concept was now in the domain of management.[64]

The utopian and authoritarian alternatives to capitalism advanced by nineteenth-century critics all failed—in the case of communism, they failed quite disastrously. But the underlying critique of industrial labor has never been refuted: craft work confers pride and a sense of accomplishment whereas assembly line labor is dull and devoid of meaning.

Sully Sullenberger was the first American hero to emerge in the twenty-first century, and his achievement in large part derives from the exercise of old-style craftsmanship. Sullenberger represents the possibility that a skilled, experienced individual can overcome the dangers of failed technology. But today we treat and train doctors, teachers, and airline pilots as though the traditional attributes of craft hold neither meaning nor honor. Why would anyone imagine that this new-century way of working—executing rules and procedures set by distant managers, experts, and engineers—might appeal to the best and brightest?

Our technology-enabled drive for measurement, metrics, and efficiencies is a disguised throwback to "scientific management," a century-old business tactic intended to make workers more productive. Scientific management involves analyzing the flow of work—especially industrial production—with an eye toward increasing productivity and efficiency. Picture an expert armed with a stopwatch hovering over a factory worker as he performs repetitive tasks on an assembly line. That's the metaphor that defines Taylorism, the set of theories and practices attributed to scientific management's creator and principal advocate, Frederick Winslow Taylor. The popularity of Taylorism peaked in the 1920s; by then it had spread from the assembly line to the typing pool.[65]

As characterized by Harry Braverman, Taylorism relied on and advanced three underlying principles, each very much in play today. First, the process of labor should be disassociated from the skills of individual workers. Second, the conception or planning of a job or task should be separated from its execution. Finally, knowledge of conception and process must be redeployed from above to ensure that each step of the labor process and its mode of execution can be tightly controlled. As Braverman puts it, scientific management was "an essential effort to strip the workers of craft knowledge and autonomous control and confront them with a fully thought-out labor process in which they function as cogs and levers."[66] In this sense, a modern "knowledge worker" tethered to her computer, desk, and cubicle suffers a twenty-first-century version of the same stultifying fate as the stopwatched assembly line pieceworker.

Some external trappings of Taylor's scientific management have been abandoned or at least moved to the margins. After all, any process that involves on-site measurement and timing of repetitive manufacturing tasks runs counter to the facade of management–labor collaboration, so crucial to the mythology of modern-day capitalism. But the underlying essence of Taylorism—that efficiency depends on breaking a job into component parts, establishing a set of standardized, efficient performance practices that can be imposed on a task to ensure consistency, while using expert knowledge to control process and set goals—has embedded itself in the DNA of postindustrial capitalism.

Were Taylor to pop up today as an analyst of America's workplaces, the old-time management theoretician would be thrilled to see that his core ideas about how labor should be organized had moved far beyond the assembly line to redefine professions that had long been dependent on individual mastery of complex tasks. The introduction of iPhones, BlackBerrys, e-mail, tweeting, and continuous texting has enabled work to be sliced, diced, and expanded to fill our time; 24/7 is the new normal.

Teacher Craft and Medicine

My favorite class in high school was American history, taught by Floyd Brooks, a wise talented bachelor who assigned unconventional readings and used the past as a jumping-off place for lively discussions of contemporary affairs. He was droll and somewhat colorless; I remember thinning gray hair, a repetitious gray suit. I saw him Sundays in the ragtag choir mounted by the Presbyterian church in our shrinking mining town, but otherwise there was little indication that he had a life outside school and his classroom. Brooks was inspiring and encouraging. He set a standard of performance in written assignments and in-class comment that was challenging but achievable. He taught me that history offered an endless parade of interesting people working to solve intractable problems and was thus a powerful source of useful insight. Americans still envision teaching in this idealized way, and the desire to recruit and retain the very best young professionals is one of the most oft-stated goals of education reform. But this is another example of the kind of doublethink required when education comes to be the plaything of market forces. We claim to want bright, imaginative, inspiring teachers in every classroom, but all we want them to actually do is pump our kids full of specific facts and narrow skills so they perform well on standardized math and reading tests.

Equipping students with the limited skill set required by multiple-choice exams does not require inspiration, empathy, or any particular talent; it is an activity that can be implemented by the educational version of, well, *clerks*. And the task itself—the way in which young people are disciplined toward test outcomes—is managed scientifically, proscribed by the classroom equivalent of a teacher's autopilot.

Our focus on test scores has locked in a narrow definition of learning and of excellence in education. Vanderbuilt University recently completed a much-cited study of teacher merit pay, concluding that extra pay did not produce better teaching because the students of better-compensated teachers did not improve their performance on standardized tests.[67] Of course, there's an obvious problem here: If you define good teaching as the production of high standardized test scores, you've placed a narrow outcome frame at the very heart of the study. This kind of tautological research—measuring the quality of teaching only in terms of test results—will reward the wrong things and in the end push really talented teachers out of the system.

Today there is simply no room for a really excellent teacher like Floyd Brooks. My semester with him focused on one historical era: the Great Depression. The entire class read Frederick Lewis Allen's *Only Yesterday* and spent hours discussing the relationship between the 1930s and what was then our present—1960s industrial America. I went to college and majored in history, and I realized that Brooks's history class had made me smarter in ways that were still paying off a decade later, when I was in grad school. The terrific teacher made his students really think, but would this excellent class have prepared us for some generic multiple-choice quiz on American history? I doubt it. Would he be judged a good teacher today? No.

Teaching is by no means the only craft-empowered profession threatened with reforms designed to maximize the efficient production of predetermined outcomes. Three years ago I facilitated a planning meeting for a small, highly effective law firm in Nashville. The four principles had nearly been overwhelmed by growth in their entertainment-based practice, especially in the area of small clients—individual performers, songwriters, and start-up entertainment companies. After five hours of conversation they arrived at an inevitable conclusion: They would have to standardize some forms and contracts and interact with some clients using paralegals and interns. This new approach would depersonalize their work and guarantee that some subtleties of client circumstances would not be addressed in agreements or negotiations. Technology would help them construct documents that were standardized, impersonal, and easy for less trained frontline employees to manage. There was palpable discomfort in the conference room as these professionals realized that to remain profitable, the firm would have to compromise the character of its legal service, perhaps undercutting the very qualities of craft work knowledge that had made them successful in the first place.

Consider also the way psychiatry has been reshaped over the past half century. Once the bastion of interactive, one-on-one "talk therapy" reliant on the knowledge and insight of highly trained physician/analysts, the field was reconfigured over a few short years by the still-questionable determination that mental distress was the result of chemical imbalances in the brain. As Marcia Angell writes in the *New York Review of Books*, the introduction of psychoactive drugs designed to recalibrate brain chemistry has ironically coincided with an "epidemic" of mental illness.

Psychiatry has been transformed. Gardiner Harris, writing in *The New York Times*, recounts changes in Dr. Donald Levin's practice, launched in 1972. "Then . . . he treated 50 to 60 patients in once- or twice-weekly talk-therapy sessions of 45 minutes each. Now, like many of his peers, he treats 1,200 people in mostly 15-minute visits for prescription adjustments. Levin reports that the process makes him feel like nothing more than a "good Volkswagen mechanic." Where once "his goal was to help his patients become happy and fulfilled; now it is just to keep them functional." As in all modern professional efficiencies, price is a big part of the story; Dr. Levin finds himself in competition not with other physicians but with less trained psychologists and social workers, "who can often afford to charge less." As Levin explains, the profession tried to resist:

> At first, all of us held steadfast, saying we spent years learning the craft of psychotherapy and weren't relinquishing it because of parsimonious policies by managed care. But one by one, we accepted that craft was no longer economically viable.[68]

Advertising Values Invade Management

Writing in the 1950s, Braverman observed that certain job designations had begun to take on an indistinct character. He noted that "the designation of 'programmer' has become somewhat ambiguous, and can be applied to expert program analysts who grasp the rationale of the systems they work on, but just as readily to mere program coders who take as their materials the pre-digested instructions for the system or subsystem and simply translate them mechanically into specialized terminology."[69] This observation was both trenchant and prescient— Braverman anticipated a looming change that was only fully realized in the computer age: the ability of modern management to distract workers from the erosion of labor by elevating job titles while routinizing complex tasks.

Today, by labeling anonymous, cubicle-bound computer-code writers as members of a unique "creative class,"[70] managers employ top-down flattery to mask the truth that, even in a so-called knowledge economy, most jobs are repetitive and routine. As Matt Crawford puts it, being labeled "creative" "invokes our powerful tendency to narcissism, and in doing so greases the skids into work that is not what we expected."[71]

Similarly, highly educated workers can be reconciled to less-than-satisfying jobs if postindustrial production tasks can be framed by notions of altruism or self-improvement. David Brooks observes that "bobos" ("bohemian bourgeois") will "knock themselves out if they think they are doing it for their spiritual selves, for their intellectual development."[72]

This notion that routine jobs can be glamorized—and made appealing—by the application of a few superficial indicators of old-style craft labor marks the movement of consumer values into the workplace. Crawford, who has a PhD from the University of Chicago, had acquired significant experience in the construction trades before he entered graduate school. He notes that although once graduated he obtained a job that required his advanced degree and whose dress code (tie required) and other symbolic elements suggested that he "belonged to a certain order of society," the actual work (producing abstracts of academic publications) provided "a more proletarian existence than I had known as a manual worker."[73]

The widely promoted idea that workers are part of a labor/management "team" and that the production process depends on creative input from frontline staff is a "studied pretense." Richard Sennett points out that "many new economy firms subscribe to these doctrines of teamwork and cooperation, but . . . these principles are often a charade." The Walmart, Best Buy, or Apple employee who is asked to help select the best location for a product display is being offered nothing more than "the illusion of making decisions by choosing among fixed and limited alternatives designed by a management which deliberately leaves insignificant matters open to choice."[74]

In *The New York Times,* Susan Cain writes in "The Rise of the New Groupthink" that "virtually all American workers now spend time on teams and some 70 percent inhabit open-plan offices; by 2010 office space for workers averaged 200 square feet, down from 500 square feet in 1970."[75] While executives might brag about the "bullpen" layout of office work space, the ubiquitous cubicle—the doorless, one-size-fits-all, neutral-shaded labor cell—has become what author Ellie Winninghoff described as "a not-so-subtle reminder of the lack of stability and security in the corporate workplace."[76] Teams are not liberating; they instead encourage docility and enable control. Cain continues, "People in groups tend to sit back and let others do the work; they instinctively mimic others' opinions and lose sight of their own and, often, succumb to peer pressure."[77] Or, as Richard Sennett puts it, "Teamwork is the group practice of demeaning superficiality."[78] This is not management 2012 but camouflaged Taylorism 2.0; the team-directed cubicle office is merely one feature of the latest and most psychologically sophisticated application of scientific management.

While they don't provide employees with anything like real independence or autonomy, "teamwork" strategies require a whole set of behaviors new to labor. Among other things, "Workers in teams must make a show of friendliness and cooperation under the watchful eyes of the boss minders."[79] Modern labor—especially in office settings—requires the application of an elaborate set of other-directed social traits that would have been of almost no value in, say, an agrarian society. (If a nineteenth-century farmer was "moody," who aside from his immediate family would care?) By the same token, behaviors that would have once been seen as merely eccentric—shyness, attention deficit disorder, and even mild autism—rise as pathologies in an economy that demands continuous forced interaction and interpersonal manipulation.

Mental illness really *is* epidemic in the United States today. Ten percent of all Americans over the age of six take antidepressant medication. No doubt the commoditization of mental illness through the promotion and sale of psychoactive medicines is one cause; our mental health community has certainly been complicit in placing troubled patients on a prescription drug assembly line. But the nature of modern work, our need to perform under tight control while acting as though we are creative and independent, generates significant emotional pressure. As Harvard sociologist Daniel Bell puts it, "Modern life creates a bifurcation of role and person which for a sentient individual becomes a strain."[80] Nowhere is this tension more apparent than in the "happy team" cubicles of the modern factory or office.

The Perpetual Workday

Jill Andresky Fraser's book *White-Collar Sweatshop* details the movement of factory floor, scientific-management-style techniques into the office. Overall real wages scarcely budged in the 1990s, and earnings for college-educated workers actually declined by more than 6 percent. We might surmise that the lack of salary increases were offset, in part, by noncash benefits, but these too were extracted from the compensation package. "Lunch hour? An anachronism. Commuting time? A good chance to return phone calls. Sleep? Never mind if you were up until 2 AM on the phone with a client across the globe. Be at the office at eight. These days, workers are expected to be on call 24/7—24 hours per day, seven days per week,"[81] writes Fraser. Seen in this light, innovations like flex time or working from home are in fact strategies to bring new sorts of workers—think women—into the job market and to subject them to a new set of (frequently electronic) rules and controls.

Think about it. Fifteen years ago, would you have taken a job if you had to be available every day, respond to messages from your boss late at night, and maintain contact with the office while on vacation? You would probably have taken a pass. But today, of course, just about any job, especially the good ones, exhibit precisely this oppressive 24/7 character.

It's a corrosive double whammy: At the same time as technology has redefined labor by converting craft occupations into assembly line piecework, new gadgets have allowed our less inviting piecework tasks to follow us home, invading our bedrooms, filling family time, distracting us on holiday. This change in the character of work took place very quickly. As technology critic Jaron Lanier observed, "It's as if you kneel to plant the seed of a tree and it grows so fast that it swallows your whole village before you can even rise to your feet."[82]

Americans are suckers for new technologies. We cheerfully purchased the Sony Walkman (how quickly we forget!) and embraced digital cameras, cell phones, plasma TVs, smart phones, and now iPads. Just as we've consumed high-tech gadgets at home, we welcome electronic devices in the workplace; won't they save precious time by making us more efficient? Our enthusiasm for innovative machines obscures the truth that all they do is bind us more tightly to our jobs while forcing us to work longer hours.

"You can live with purpose through work, family, and community."

Easier said than done. For centuries, work has been the arena of accomplishment in which learning and insight combined skills of mind and hand to solve problems, bringing forward something useful, beautiful, or both. Back when women entered the workforce in big numbers at every level, it seemed the importance of labor as a source of meaning and identity only increased. But the financial collapse of 2008 produced profound, perhaps lasting, changes in American labor markets. As Clive Crook argues, there exists a real "likelihood that lengthening spells of unemployment [will] become self-perpetuating, as skills erode or grow irrelevant."[83] State governments are attempting to balance budgets by sacking teachers, nurses, and police officers, and underwater mortgages have made it impossible for millions of workers to sell houses to relocate in search of new jobs. As Tyler Cowen writes, "We need to be prepared for the possibility that the growth slowdown could continue once the immediate recession is over."[84]

We know that real wages have been flat for more than two decades. Technology-enabled productivity increased, but that hasn't helped workers. Productivity per person-hour increased by 5 percent between 2009 and 2010—postrecession—but productivity went up because the number of hours worked went down. So for the past ten years, workers substituted charge cards and home equity loans for stagnant wages to maintain what seemed to be a middle-class lifestyle. That era of self-delusion is over and has been replaced by doubt, disappointment, pessimism, and a deep suspicion of financial and political power. In an unprecedented development, millions of newly minted college graduates are moving directly from the classroom to the unemployment lines and sometimes to the encampments of Occupy Wall Street. American workers now compete in the much-touted global market; it is a distinct irony that not Marxists but corporate leaders urge the workers of the world to unite in a drive toward efficiency—efficiency that can be best defined as low wages.

America is stumbling into the abyss of unheard-of income and wealth disparity. The lack of jobs and the offensive distance between the wealth of Wall Street and the plight of the 99 percent are pressing down on a workforce that includes both displaced industrial labor and unemployed educated professionals who still feel entitled to lucrative posts in what Richard Florida calls "an idea-driven knowledge economy that runs more on brains than on brawn."[85] We're learning that while this "knowledge economy" exists, in reality it's present for only the few who can serve the esoteric and rapidly changing demands of high-tech industries. Facebook might ultimately be valued at $50 billion, but it makes no product and employs only a few thousand workers. As Richard Waters wrote in the *Financial Times*, "While the jobs of the future have yet to be revealed, the job losses and disruption to working lives from accelerating technological change are already apparent."[86]

Reconfiguring Work in Democracy

It is tempting to imagine—even to recommend—changes in the character of labor and the workplace that would restore satisfying, meaningful work as a central part of life: the way Ruskin, Marx, and Morris envisioned it a century and a half ago. But that would be naive. As historian Jackson Lears said in a recent interview, "Whatever the color of your collar, your job may still be 'proletarian' to the extent that management controls the pace, process, and output of your work."[87] Lears is right, and I think the march of management efficiencies in the direction of increased productivity cannot be rolled back. Apart from a handful of artistic careers, the sad truth is that deeply satisfying work for pay is squeezed-out toothpaste that can't be coaxed back into its tube.

My suggestion is this: that Americans recover the satisfaction of artisanship by stepping to the side, building the kind of meaning found in craft work outside the office, classroom, or factory. More than anything, the pursuit of meaning in the contemporary market-defined environment requires *time*. Technology in the workplace holds out the promise of more time, but as we have seen, increased productivity—more output; fewer hours—benefits only the bottom lines of corporate profits wrung from the decreased cost of labor. Unions and concerned, engaged citizens must press for public policies that enable workers to capture time, benefiting from efficiencies generated by piecework and automated devices. But I don't believe our modern workplace can be reconfigured from the outside, and the corporate world has exhibited little interest in resisting global pressures on hours and wages to give American labor a better quality of life.

Here's an alternative: A properly configured and fairly implemented four-day workweek would shift at least some of the time-saving benefits of high-tech devices to workers. And given an imaginatively assembled array of possibilities, the extra time attached to a weekend will offer a pathway to a life of quality and meaning.

Where the four-day workweek has been tried in the United States, results have actually been encouraging. Utah launched a four-day, ten-hour-day week for state employees in 2008. Seventy percent of workers liked it, mostly because the extended personal time facilitated volunteer work and closer contact within families. Although the statewide program ended in the fall of 2011 (anticipated savings on energy never materialized), cities such as Provo retained the policy. Google has established a four-day week for some engineers, specifically to enable opportunity for creative thought.

It's important to remember that experiments with short workweeks have to date been advanced only as money-saving strategies. (Are you surprised?) However, given the acceptance of these early efforts, it seems certain that a four-day workweek (perhaps featuring nine-hour days) focused not on cost cutting but on enriching quality of life would be even more welcome. And it's important to a handmade America; extra time in which to connect with politics, new knowledge, community heritage, religion, and family will lay the foundation for an American lifestyle less slavishly ensnared in consuming and debt.

Technology and Education

Our ability to live well in a progressive, handmade society depends on what we know and believe; much of that knowledge must be applied to placing the transformational impact of technology in perspective. True, Americans have enthusiastically welcomed new devices at home and at work. But today technology is generating powerful imbalances in society and government, transforming the place of Americans in a global economy. We have both a right and an obligation to challenge the effect of automation, software, robotics, and the Internet on how we labor and live.

Former U.S. labor secretary Robert Reich gets one thing absolutely right: "Modern technologies allow us to shop in real time, often worldwide, for the lowest prices, highest quality, and best returns." Unfortunately, "these great deals come at the expense of our jobs and wages, and widening inequality."[88]

Stated most simply, high-tech machines enable fewer workers to do more while transforming complex artisanal tasks into piecework. Americans love to shop for bargain commodities, of course, but corporations also shop for labor, and modern technology and communication force workers to compete with lower-paid counterparts in Singapore, India, and China. Even here in the United States, an auto assembly job that pays $28 an hour in Michigan will pay half that in South Carolina.

It's obvious that the average "working Joe" needs a better understanding of how the workplace is being transformed by technologies deployed by corporations in the pursuit of efficiencies, increased productivity, and increased profit. A couple years ago, *New York Times* columnist David Brooks worried about these effects in a piece cleverly and accurately entitled "The Outsourced Brain." What does it mean for society if we don't know where we are, where we should eat, or whether or not it's raining without looking at our telephones? And it's a special problem in the workplace; a cab driver who can navigate only with a GPS is a qualitatively different professional than the London artisan cabbie who's memorized streets from Paddington to Elephant and Castle. In addition, "Productivity Hits All-Time High" may be a mogul-pleasing headline, but less-in/more-out is scarcely good news for workers. And as we've seen, automation, digital devices, and software-driven menus not only displace jobs but change the very character of work itself.

Of course, technological change has been a feature of civilization since before the printing press, and the destruction of the old has always accompanied progress; illuminated calligraphy is pretty much a thing of the distant past. However, the digital age is unusual, if not unique, in that it has been advanced by the tag team of powerful corporate interests aided by massive advertising campaigns, supported by a cohort of intellectual apologists who praise every new device and vigorously attack any Luddite bold enough to question the *real* value of the newest netbook, iPhone, or online music service. This combination—big advertising supported by reasonably big minds—is something new, and it's enabled digital advocates to pretty much have their way in the workplace and at home. Who has critiqued computers in the classroom? Evidence of helpful results is scarce, but as one ex-marine teacher put it, "This technology is being thrown on us. It's being thrown on parents and thrown on kids."[89] Americans need a general understanding of the way efficient technologies affect the availability of jobs and the meaning of labor, and an understanding that society can rightly use the levers of government to blunt the most troublesome transformations in a defining human activity—work.

So here's the second, and more specific, point: American education must better address the needs of our present-day economy. Early in 2012, I heard an NPR *All Things Considered* piece on the burgeoning Montana firearms industry. The segment interviewed the president of Montana Rifleman, a small manufacturing firm that, responding to a U.S. firearms boom, was then shipping up to one thousand rifle barrels per day. He indicated that there "are plenty of workers, but he still struggles to fill certain jobs," adding, "Finding skilled machinists is one of the hardest things for us to do right now."[90] This problem is widespread. Tyler Cowen has identified a "fundamental skills mismatch"[91] in the relationship between school and the workplace. American secondary education has drifted toward precollege for all, an objective memorialized in a commitment to standardized testing. Yes, we need mathematicians and good readers, but we need high school graduates skilled in information technology, high-end machining, and a range of other technical manufacturing skills that fit the new economy. This is not rocket science; it's not test taking either.

President Obama has underscored the role of community colleges in providing high-end workplace skills. On its face, this seems a good idea; community colleges are affordable, are open to just about anyone, and are often hardwired into the demands of a local economy. But as Thomas Bailey has written in the *American Prospect*, community institutions are filled with first-generation college students who often work full-time while attending school at night. Their preparation for college work is frequently subpar; it's no surprise that graduation or certification rates after six years are well below 40 percent. Community colleges are also especially dependent on state funding and despite increased federal support are suffering as states slash budgets in this postrecession decade. Rethinking the high school curriculum may be smarter, more affordable, and more effective than a buck-pass to two-year colleges.

I do believe there's a need for a better match between secondary education and the apparent needs of the workplace. But to be honest, I'm uncomfortable with arguments that talk about improving education—especially public education—entirely within the context of the economy and America's workforce. The values and needs of corporations have thoroughly invaded the conversation about education, and you don't have to scratch the surface of most reforms very hard before a narrow agenda shows up: math plus reading plus multiple-choice tests produces graduates perfectly suited to technology-enabled, rule-following piecework.

Despite the desires of corporate oligarchs, education can't be only about popping out capable worker bees. Our very democracy depends on the maintenance of a citizenry capable of critical engagement with technology and change, society and democracy; an engagement with context and precedent—an understanding of history, society, finance, and power—sufficient to permit smart choices. We do not get the wise citizens we need if schools do nothing but train workers for our voracious corporate maw.

It's clear that we went too far back in the 1960s, when experts determined that every student should experience some version of a college preparatory curriculum. When I attended Calumet High School a half century ago, the program offered three tracks: academic, vocational, commercial. "Academic" was pretty much what secondary education looks like today. "Commercial" trained secretaries and bookkeepers; my recollection is that the commercial track was mostly populated by girls. "Vocational" was as distinctly male, its trainees spending half days sequestered in noisy wood and machine shops in the basement of the school. But vocational training at Calumet High was dead serious; the program was hardwired into the Calumet and Hecla Mining Company, and graduates could anticipate immediate employment in the (admittedly fading) multifaceted corporation that dominated northern Michigan's copper mining industry back then.

Now, Calumet's old three-track system was rife with real and potential inequity. Lip service was applied to the way eighth-graders were slotted according to test scores and individual aptitude and ambition, but there existed plenty of room for ethnic and sexual stereotyping, for making nonacademic tracks way stations for kids who just didn't fit in. Once placed, nobody ever "got out" by making the transition from commercial or vocational into the (somewhat) exclusive and (slightly) refined reaches of the academic path. But despite obvious flaws, the system wasn't entirely without value. While academic students were pointed toward college (and an inevitable extension of adolescence), our vocational and commercial peers were destined to grasp their diplomas and immediately head off to work. There existed more than a trace of envy, and an uneasy admiration, for these incubating carpenters, machinists, and draftsmen who were actually learning to *do* something. As Matt Crawford puts it, "The physical circumstances of the jobs performed by carpenters, plumbers, and auto mechanics vary too much for them to be executed by idiots; they require circumspection and adaptability. One feels like a man, not a cog in a machine."[92]

We must achieve a subtle, realistic balance between education for craft work and education for citizenship. Even if we rework both the intellectual and the vocational mission of secondary education to align learning with the demands of the economy and our twenty-first-century democracy, we can never restore the character of preindustrial labor in which "the worker was presumed to be the master of a body of traditional knowledge, and methods and procedures were left to his or her discretion."[93] If work is to enable a life of purpose, we must find meaningful labor outside the office and factory. If the independence, mastery, and satisfaction inherent in craft work have been lost, Americans must open up new opportunities to pursue labor of consequence. John Ruskin wrote, "In order that people may be happy in their work, three things are needed. They must be fit for it. They must not do too much of it. And they must have a sense of success in it."[94]

How do we respond to Ruskin's observations? First we must convert the gains in productivity produced by technology and innovative management into a four-day workweek. If our jobs—even high-end professions—are to be increasingly managed and routine, Americans must simply step aside into choice work that provides sufficient space to study and practice meaningful labor. Our workweek should extend from Monday through Thursday, period.

Second, we must go further in our efforts to reconfigure the way we educate citizens. It's fine to shift focus toward skills that will earn a living—to follow President Obama's initiatives linking community colleges with employers, providing college-level courses to some high school students, and outfitting young people with "industry-accepted credentials." But no matter how well a newly minted worker fits the needs of corporations, we have seen that the marketplace does not provide many opportunities to "live with purpose" through labor.

So we must provide citizens with skills that will enable personal creative practice and deepened engagement with community and cultural heritage. If our occupations have been corrupted by the demands of postindustrial capitalism, we must use extra leisure to engage in activities more meaningful than a modern-day job—activities that approach something like Max Weber's sense of "vocation." Richard Sennett characterizes *vocation* as containing "two resonances: the gradual accumulation of knowledge and skills and the ever-stronger conviction that one was meant to do this one particular thing in one's life."[95] Training that advances skills and builds commitment of this sort is hard to relate to today's cubicled workplace, but it's especially available in the arts—in music, creative writing, theater, dance, and visual arts.

Given what we now understand about the absence of meaning in most jobs, it should be no surprise that Americans today spend billions each year advancing informal mastery of artisanal skills. Right now, personal creative practice is served primarily by an array of companies providing art supplies, musical instruments, private instruction, and a mind-boggling variety of self-help arts instruction DVDs and downloads. Arts education in schools has been pushed aside by teach-to-the-test math and reading. If we are to fill a three-day weekend with activity that brings a sense of achievement, mastery, and the joy of creativity, arts training—in the broadest sense—must be relocated to the center of quality education.

Over the past three decades, Western capitalism forgot the lessons the marketplace had learned during the painful leftist rebellions of the early twentieth century—namely, that capitalism worked in society only if it was tempered by regulation designed to ensure that everyone got their share. Over the past thirty years, American business grew the unproductive financial services sector, pushed Washington to repeal or ignore nettlesome regulations, and failed to warn workers that the glories of globalization would be accompanied by the loss of millions of jobs here at home. The result has been widespread and nearly unprecedented dissatisfaction with our financial establishment. As the Carnegie Endowment for International Peace's Moisés Naím put it, "America's long, peaceful coexistence with income and wealth inequality is ending."[96]

The danger of our new and unique class of alienated workers and the unemployed is not some kind of revolt but instead the real likelihood that the unemployed—fearful and discontented—will turn toward authoritarian, simple-solution leaders touting isolation, xenophobia, and contempt for the basic workings of democratic government. This is already happening. State legislatures are bearing down on unions and immigrants and advancing bills that secure gun ownership and restrict women's health services while making it harder for the elderly and poor to vote. In the run-up to the 2012 Republican presidential nomination, Newt Gingrich sounded high-pitched "dog whistle" messages that stirred xenophobia and outright racism. One more shock—a terrorist attack; clear signs of a double-dip recession—and Americans could conceivably lurch so far right that infrastructure, foreign relations, and the cornerstones of what's left of our egalitarian social safety net could be permanently disabled.

In the summer of 2011, the *Financial Times* opined that when it came to solving America's continuing financial challenges, "Further short-term stimulus should be on the table."[97] Unfortunately, the obvious short-term fix for a flaccid employment picture—a government jobs program focused on infrastructure and education—is not only entirely off the table but, according to budget-slashing members of Congress, not even in the room. We're left with no real response to a three-year-old employment crisis that has morphed into a persistent low-grade flu.

We are living in the sad shadow of unfettered markets, of unquestioned confidence in an unregulated, little-taxed, corporate culture to provide a high quality of life for all. But the good life does not seem to be there for Americans today, and there exists a feeling that we have strayed from the very values that made our nation great. If character is what you are in the dark; real greatness is what you possess absent wealth and power. We cannot put the genie of craft work back into modern labor—powerful forces are pushing jobs in exactly the opposite direction. But now that we won't be as rich as we thought we would be, we can reconsider our commitment to serve commerce and reconfigure what we learn and value to give ourselves at least a chance to maintain a high quality of life.

Sully Sullenberger was surprised that wherever he went, strangers approached him with gratitude and congratulations. He described what he thought his good day at work meant to admirers: "It enabled them to reassure themselves that the ideals that we believe in are true, even if they're not always evident. They decided that the American character still exists, that what we think our country stands for is still there."[98]

2

GOVERNING

On page 116, deep in the landmark *Perry v. Schwarzenegger* federal court decision that revitalized the gay marriage movement in California, Judge Vaughn R. Walker advanced an important idea. Citing the authority of an earlier case, he affirmed the principle that "fundamental rights may not be submitted to [a] vote; they depend on the outcome of no elections."[99] Ted Olson, one of two lead attorneys who successfully represented plaintiffs in the case, put it even more directly in an interview with Chris Wallace on Fox News: "We do not put the Bill of Rights to a vote."[100]

Perry constitutes an important affirmation of marriage as a fundamental right. The incisive and deeply sourced decision offers the real promise that the opportunity for single-sex couples to marry will become settled law. At least as importantly, the decision also pushes back against the concept of the initiative (known as the proposition in California) and its underlying assumption: that Americans should duel over every government action however small and take them to real-time up or down votes.

In 2000, David Broder exposed the corrupting character of initiative movements in *Democracy Derailed: Initiative Campaigns and the Power of Money.* Focusing on California, Broder made a compelling case that well-funded minorities can easily secure signatures required to place tax policy, gay marriage, or English-only regulations on ballots, and that the process enables special interests to advance ideas that would be difficult or impossible to legislate through normal means. Broder correctly observes that the initiative runs counter to basic principles of representative democracy.

After all, the founding fathers envisioned a system that trusted selected leaders, "whose wisdom may best discern the true interest of their country,"[101] to act on behalf of other citizens for terms of two or four years. Of course, citizens would from time to time assess the performance of elected representatives, but for the most part we could all go about our business between election cycles. Representative democracy frees us of daily concerns about government's mundane responsibilities.

Our liberal vision—that Americans can flourish through work, community, and shared obligation—can be realized only if government works. But today representative democracy is threatened; the California proposition merely emblematizes our growing tendency to bypass legislatures to bring every issue to the people. Innovations like term limits and sunshine laws, implemented to increase government transparency and accountability, are doubled down by a hovering 24/7 cohort of news analysts, commentators, and bloggers. Deregulated media and spotlighted governing have all but overturned the character of America's democracy, replacing representative government with the cacophony of a perpetual town meeting.

Peter Baker, writing in *The New York Times,* bemoans the "fractious, backbiting, finger-pointing, polarizing, partisan, kick-the-can-down-the-road brinksmanship of Washington politics," asking the obvious question: "Is this any way to run a country?" Surprisingly, his answer is yes. "For all the handwringing about how the system is broken, this is the system as it was designed and is now adapted for the digital age."[102] Baker is wrong; the system is broken, in part because it has been "adapted for the digital age." Media and the online environment have enabled dysfunctional politics. Regulation has not kept up. If government is to frame and implement our progressive vision for America's twenty-first-century democracy, we must understand both how our politics rolled off the tracks and what must be done to realign leadership and legislation.

Polls and the Reporting of Polls

Consider this excerpt from a *Morning Edition* piece filed by NPR reporter Andrea Seabrook. The segment aired in February 2010 in advance of President Obama's televised bipartisan meeting on the pending health care bill.

SEABROOK: Republicans say, "It's right there in the polls." A *Newsweek* poll shows 52 percent of Americans disapprove of Mr. Obama's handling of health care. Another poll shows half oppose the current plan; and an ABC News-*Washington Post* poll says three out of five think it's too complicated and too expensive. But there's a pitfall for Republicans here, too.

Those very same polls I just quoted show other trends. In the ABC poll, respondents trusted the president to solve health care problems over Republicans by five percentage points. A Pew Research Center poll asked which party could do a better job at reforming the health care system; 45 percent said Democrats and only 32 percent said Republicans. And many recent polls have shown that people who are generally wary of President Obama's plan often show strong support of most of its individual parts.

So while Senate Republican leader Mitch McConnell says Americans have already rejected health care . . .

MITCH MCCONNELL: Fifty five percent of them oppose it and 37 percent support it.

SEABROOK: Senate Democratic leader Harry Reid says Americans want his party to keep working on it.

HARRY REID: Fifty-eight percent of the American people would be angry or disappointed if we didn't pass health care reform this year.[103]

This *Morning Edition* transcript is striking because it seems, well, so normal. TV, radio, or online—day after day—this is what political reporting sounds like. But what's really going on here? What possible meaning can we derive from such a gumbo of contradictory numbers? What did it mean when Donald Trump, and then Michele Bachmann, Herman Cain, Rick Perry, and Rick Santorum, each briefly topped polls in the early weeks of the 2012 Republican presidential primaries? A poll taken six months before a convention or nine months in advance of an election possesses no meaning at all.

Meaning doesn't seem to matter. Today representatives of the American people—including leaders of both parties—repeatedly invoke one poll or another to justify positions. It's hard to find those who know what they actually believe is the right course and why. Instead, our elected officials fall back on the slender evidence offered by poll numbers as though they possessed the authority of a ballot. Among other things, polling offers elected and appointed officials a handy device for shirking personal responsibility. "The numbers made me do it," they can say. The numbers make it right. The press enables officials, who avoid the hard work and risk of providing real leadership by setting a vision and pursuing it. Reporters build interviews around reactions to polls, proceeding from the premise that any politician acting contrary to a poll is engaged in something inherently irrational and fundamentally antidemocratic. Consider this exchange between Senator Dick Durbin and host Steve Inskeep from the same February 25 *Morning Edition* broadcast:

INSKEEP: Are you willing to say, flat-out, Democrats are willing to pass this bill that most Americans tell pollsters they don't want, even without a single Republican vote?

DURBIN: I hope it doesn't come to that. But I can tell you, at the end of the day if we end up doing nothing the American people have a right to be upset.

Paraphrased, Inskeep's question (you'll have to imagine his tone of mild astonishment) is essentially this: "Are Democrats crazy enough to try to govern contrary to what most Americans tell pollsters they want?"

In this case Dick Durbin *is* willing to say that Democrats will pass a health care bill without Republican help. He's an exception. Most of the time, flouting the truism that "polls tell you what people think about something they haven't thought much about," leaders of both parties believe that polls, if not God, are firmly on their side.

The initiative movement suggests that the public cannot trust its elected officials to govern, and polling provides the illusion that the public has at hand the knowledge needed to decide. We complain about money in politics and the lack of smart, in-depth analysis. But such worries gloss over deeper structural problems. Further, the thirty-year drip drip drip of conservative contempt for government has also extracted a toll. David Brooks observes, accurately, that "we have allowed our political views to be corroded with an easy pseudo-cynicism that holds that all politicians are crooks and all public endeavor is a sham."[104]

Journalist Max Frankel has noted television's "pivotal influence in our democracy."[105] And true, everybody complains (somewhat half-heartedly) about the 24/7 news cycle and the way it pressures writers, commentators, and bloggers to "ready, fire, aim." But I am convinced there's a bigger problem. Continuous cable news banter and relentless online blogging, both nourished by the entire information establishment, have set a reckless pace for consuming news. New laws and informal political pressure force unnecessary disclosure and transparency upon government. And opinion research provides partisan interpreters with only thin sets of numbers feigning facts. We can't stop the on-air and online jesting and jeering. We don't trust our government. And we are wealthy only in worthless data. These three realities have begun to subvert representative democracy.

Today, especially in an election year, there's no lack of political talk. But is the current frame of news, knowledge, and commentary helpful to a progressive effort to debate and advance our vision for a handmade democracy? Does our poll-driven, adversarial political process provide liberals with an opening to put forward an alternative vision to the discredited right-wing presumptions that we are somehow better off if government does nothing while Americans are left to their own devices? What constellation of forces in and out of government has so hobbled the process that even routine activities—confirming agency appointments, approving trade agreements, formulating and advancing appropriations bills—have just about ground to a halt? What has gone wrong? What must we undo? What new measures must we put in place?

The Marketplace Swallowed News—Gradually, Then All at Once

Of course, the character of news—what gets reported, how reporters frame it, and how they stir the mixture of ideology, opinion, and fact—has always influenced the way leaders govern. We cannot describe the problems with the media marketplace by simply pointing to singular challenges like partisan bias, political advertising, or even the 24/7 news cycle. We do not have a singular technical problem. Rather, a host of aggravating challenges has distorted our complicated political and communication system. As news has become rapid and unreflective, the underlying influence of media has pushed in one direction—away from representative democracy toward something that more closely resembles the rough and tumble of a barroom shouting match.

During the past few decades of the twentieth century, business-friendly reregulation enabled media to reorganize in ways that reinforced our troubling drift toward loudest-voice-wins direct democracy. Early on, policy makers viewed the airwaves, first radio and then TV, as a national asset, the broadcast spectrum part of our public sphere. The Federal Communications Commission granted licenses only when owners pledged to serve community interests. License renewal was a laborious process demanding months of public comment and mountains of paperwork. Station owners had to demonstrate that management hewed to a high standard of service. Because local ownership tied broadcasters to community needs and local issues, government also strictly limited the number of stations that an individual or company could own.

Regulators shaped some news content. If a broadcaster took an on-air position in support of a piece of legislation or a political candidate, the Fairness Doctrine required that the station give both voice and equal time to opposing viewpoints.

The Reagan and Clinton administrations undid seventy-five years of regulation designed to tilt media toward public purposes. Reagan completely reconfigured the media sector, relieving owners of most government oversight. Changes were dramatic. In 1981 the new president lengthened the term of broadcast licenses from three years to five and simplified license renewal. A process that had necessitated community research and extensive reporting to the FCC now required only a completed form and a postage stamp. By 1985 the number of TV stations that could be owned by one company had expanded from seven to twelve. The requirement that stations air blocks of nonentertainment (public interest) programming was removed the same year, as were limits on the quantity of advertising permitted in a given half hour. In 1987 Reagan eliminated the Fairness Doctrine (opposing voices; equal time), laying the light-touch regulatory groundwork for today's nonstop, ideologically driven cable channels.

During the Clinton administration, the 1996 Telecommunications Act topped off two decades of deregulatory change by basically lifting all restrictions on corporate ownership of broadcast licenses. (It was in the wake of this law that Clear Channel Communications scooped up twelve hundred stations, more than 10 percent of all U.S. radio stations.)

It should be no surprise that within a regulatory environment newly subservient to the marketplace, even those rules that remained were easily ignored or laxly enforced. It was the FCC's inability or unwillingness to implement a 1934 act prohibiting foreign ownership of broadcast licenses that opened U.S. television to the domineering ideological presence of Australian billionaire Rupert Murdoch. The one-two punch of deregulation and lax enforcement transformed American media. As sociologist Eric Klinenberg put it, in the 1980s and 1990s, "the federal government's blind faith in the power of markets and technology"[106] translated into critical concessions in law and regulation that changed the media landscape.

Foxed, but That's Not All

Of course, Fox News is the easy target, the poster child for the kind of media we get when government stops tilting the broadcast playing field toward public purposes. Launched in the mid-1980s to eighteen million subscribers after Rupert Murdoch managed to acquire the handful of stations constituting Metromedia, the network quickly exhibited an unsurprising enthusiasm for programming that was long on conservative opinion and short on actual reporting. Fox succeeded in responding to "credible accusations of longtime liberal bias inside institutions like CBS News and *The New York Times*." As John Avlon puts it in *Wingnuts*, "The idea was sinisterly simple: Only explicit bias could balance the implicit bias of the establishment press."[107]

First ignoring and then circumventing the 1934 law, Murdoch's Fox placed itself in a position to reshape TV news. Cable had altered the information available on television. Trusted voices aged out of their prime and off the air. And the audience had more options on the menu of news sources. Fox, in part, was at the right place at just the right time. As Marvin Kitman put it in *Harper's*, "We were on the cusp of going from Cronkite and Brokaw to O'Reilly and Hannity."[108] And, of course, the later rise of Glenn Beck made those early stars of Fox look constrained if not downright timid.

Kitman continued, "With the founding of the Fox network in 1985, Murdoch began a cultural revolution in television that overstimulates us with reality shows and undernourishes us with news-lite celebrity journalism and less-than-meets-the-eye reporting."[109] The Tea Party, with its bumper sticker slogans, outdoor events, angry placards, and wacky characters in telegenic colonial costuming, was the perfect real-life metaphor for the Fox approach to news. Analyzed as a backlash political movement, the Tea Party is better understood as a reality show. Like *Jersey Shore* or *The Biggest Loser*, the Tea Party had a hot first season, survived into a second, but never quite made it into syndication. Lacking the roller-coaster drama of a Britney Spears or Kim Kardashian, the Tea Party's half-life on center stage was predictably short.

Technology has played a big role, enabling Fox, MSNBC, and others to create a new, narrow style of broadcasting that continues to reshape U.S. politics and government. In the same way technology allowed postindustrial capitalism to expand corporate control into a slew of modern workplaces, postbroadcast television changed the way news and political knowledge interact with government. In the closing decades of the last century, at the same time that know-nothing populism gave us term limits, referenda, and Prop 13, and as the government abdicated its public interest authority by abandoning media to the marketplace, cable and satellite transmission and ultimately the Internet powered a qualitative shift in the way Americans connect with news, knowledge, and entertainment. Murdoch's Fox empire was the first but by no means the only beneficiary of the proliferation of unregulated media technologies.

Our Damaged Political Commons

The transition from *broadcast* media to narrowly aimed cable channels, radio talk shows, and Internet blogs has profoundly altered the quantity and character of political knowledge. It is a change that has only exacerbated the effects of populist suspicion of expert-directed government and the related inclination to replace deliberative legislative process with thumbs-up/thumbs-down votes of the public. Television (again, meaning information, entertainment, and advertising on screens) has been fragmented, and media has become a less dependable vehicle for educating the public on political issues.

This notion is counterintuitive, for just as Americans are instinctively attracted by change and new technology, we are equally convinced that choice is good and that more choice is always better. Aren't we happier, and somehow better off, now that cable or satellite TV brings us five, six, or seven news channels twenty-four hours a day and that *The New York Times* and *The Washington Post* are available online, to say nothing of multiple blogs and Internet exclusives like the *Daily Beast, Huffington Post,* and *Drudge Report*?

Perhaps not. Markus Prior, in *Post-Broadcast Democracy*, makes a compelling argument that while technological progress *has* increased choice, fewer choose news. Most TV viewers are drawn to entertainment.

The era when broadcast television offered programs like *The Tonight Show* with Johnny Carson, *The Ed Sullivan Show,* and the *CBS Evening News* actually nurtured an electronic cultural and political commons. News seemed popular back then; ratings for the three network news programs peaked in the 1970s, but interest in politics and current events never actually matched TV news ratings. "A combined three-quarter market share for the three network newscasts takes on a different meaning if one considers that people had hardly any alternatives,"[110] Prior says. The absence of choice in the precable era constituted a public interest plus. While some viewers tuned into news programs because they cared, many simply watched because there was nothing else available at the time or because news preceded or followed popular entertainment programming.

Two things are required if TV viewers are to encounter news: Individuals must be interested, and they must have a chance to see newscasts. The pre-cable broadcast era maximized the chance that viewers would bump into news. But as the media environment shifts toward choice, the fan of entertainment—the accidental news viewer—is removed from the political knowledge loop. Today, as Prior puts it, "News junkies get more news and entertainment fans . . . get less news than before."[111]

Further, Prior notes that voting turnout has especially declined among fans of TV entertainment, viewer/voters who tend to be more moderate than the rest of the electorate. "Their abstention makes the voting public more partisan," and as entertainment fans have become less politically active, "political news junkies" have become America's more reliable voters. But revved up by the content provided by Fox News and its near equivalents, they participate by "casting ideologically motivated votes."[112] Thus what might be termed "America's political knowledge commons" is diminished. Television viewers now wander in a sea of choice; "Although it is comforting to know that they finally get to watch what they always wanted to watch, their newfound freedom may hurt both their own interests and the collective good."[113]

And for those voters who are drawn to political information, the same variety of options that make accidental encounters with news less likely almost guarantee that a TV viewer, talk radio fan, or online blogger will be linked up with like-minded partisans whose rhetoric tilts toward the extreme. Again, there's more than anecdote here. Cass Sunstein, in *Going to Extremes*, his comprehensive review of research on the perils of group-think, notes that when like-minded individuals gather in groups, a number of negative consequences emerge. Groups encourage risk taking and polarization. And they tend to nudge outlying members toward a shared, single vision. Extremism is exacerbated in groups, and information from the outside that contradicts group positions—even information based on solid fact—doesn't cause members to revise their opinions. In fact, when challenged by a competing vision, group sentiments become more fixed and more extreme. As Jaron Lanier puts it, "If you look at an online chat about anything . . . a pack emerges, and either you are with it or against it. If you join the pack, then you join the collective ritual hatred."[114]

The role of the marketplace in political media is obvious and growing. Prior observes that in a fragmented, high-choice media environment, political advertising is more likely than news to connect with viewers; political advertising is where corporations play. In the mid-1970s, a flurry of post-Watergate reforms restricted campaign contributions, but issue-directed political action committees gradually put big money back in the game. Tightly regulated PACs entered the political scene in 1976. Since then—in a process that tracks the march of promarket reregulation—constraints on PACs have been lifted. The 2010 *Citizens United* decision, as Marvin Kitman has written, "gave the notion that money equals speech and corporations equal individuals the imprimatur of the Supreme Court."[115] *New York Review* political writer Elizabeth Drew saw the effects clearly: *Citizens United* "stripped away virtually all the constraints on the activities of corporations, unions, and wealthy individuals with respect to federal elections."[116] During Republican primaries in 2012, the campaigns of both Newt Gingrich and Rick Santorum were kept alive by multimillion-dollar donations made by individuals to super-PACs enabled by *Citizens United*.

Throughout 2012, super-PACs have been an ad revenue bonanza for media of all kinds and an open door for the intrusion of private agendas and corporate interests into the political process through partisan messaging. Former Louisiana governor Buddy Roemer puts it this way: If it takes $100 million to run for president, you can either get a million people to give you $100 or twenty people to give $5 million each. A million $100 donations is Obama 2008; twenty donors is *Citizens United*. Roemer's prescription is bleak: "We've got to buy back the country."[117]

More on the Curse of Polls

Here's a true and unappreciated observation from Mark Salter, former chief of staff to Senator John McCain: "I've been in Washington about thirty years, and here's the surprising reality: On any given day, not much happens."[118] Even a cursory understanding of how Congress, federal agencies, and administrations go about their work confirms Salter's point, but of course this reality doesn't fit with the needs of 24/7 news channels or Internet publications like the *Huffington Post,* the *Daily Beast,* or *Politico.* These outlets need to report something every day—something that if not of headline value is at least substantial enough to give on-screen or online experts, pundits, and analysts something meaty to chew on. It's an atmosphere that elevates scandal above achievement and catastrophe above progress. Reporting starts to look like the Weather Channel: all storms, threats of storms, and warnings not to travel today if you don't have to.

Early in the presidential campaign of 2000, Senator Phil Graham observed that money is the "mother's milk" of politics. It buys campaign travel, posters, consultants, and, most of all, expensive radio and TV advertising. But if money is the mother's milk of politics, polling is the lifeblood. The public opinion poll provides a candidate with a sense of how he or she is doing. It tells governors, mayors, and presidents where they stand with voters, how the public assesses their leadership, or if they can survive with a given position on a given issue. Polls provide monthly, weekly, or even daily numbers tracking how Americans—or some subset of the population—feel about an issue or piece of legislation under consideration by Congress or a state legislature. Most important, polls provide the daily churn of political description and analysis with numbers that seem to validate what is more often than not mere opinion.

This new reality plays straight into the hands of those forces pushing our system away from constitutional process toward a crude town-hall-meeting style of direct democracy.

Reconsider the NPR *Morning Edition* excerpt at the top of this chapter. The segment lasts about ninety seconds, and in that minute and a half, correspondent Andrea Seabrook quotes six polls. Senator McCain references an unnamed poll, describing the American people as "smart" because "two thirds of them want to either stop or start over." Senators McConnell and Reid, in their recorded comments, cite two more polls. Although the whole conversation is about health care reform, Seabrook wraps up by referencing a poll that poxes both houses by assessing the performance of Congress itself. She concludes, "The Kaiser Family

Foundation poll shows 59 percent of Americans think the process is stalled right now because both sides are playing politics."[119]

What was the meaning of this report? On its face, the segment exudes relevance and reality; it features comments by involved legislators, and their bite-size assertions are linked to numbers. But even as a historical snapshot, what does this piece tell us? After all, we now know that the health care bill, in compromised form, was ultimately approved by Congress and signed by the president. What is the meaning of polling that has no role in the legislative process? Why do reporters expect officials to run off and *do* something once informed that Pew, Kaiser, or ABC has determined this or that? Columnist Tom Friedman, master of the pithy quip, says that today "leadership is about *reading* polls, not *changing* polls."[120] Welcome to our new political reality, where leaders do not lead. They just read polls.

Polls eliminate nuance, dividing issues into two or three chunks of respondents—most often for or against; sometimes including "undecided." Or a poll is a straightforward popularity contest: X percent of "the population," or "women," or "likely voters" give the president or Congress or Republicans a percentage of approval or its opposite. In my experience, approval ratings above 50 percent are consistently described—or "interpreted" or "analyzed"—as good; those below 50 percent are, well, less good. Polls have very little explanatory power, they are subject to change as arbitrarily as the wind, and they very rarely get interpreted with any sophistication.

During the primary season of 2012, *The New York Times* studied the accuracy of preelection polls and found that they "have been reasonably good in the last few days before the election." But reporter Nate Silver continued, "On the other hand, polls have been pretty awful at most points prior to about three days before the election, seeing surges and momentum shifts that often dissipated."[121] So most poll results mean basically nothing, yet our media system promotes them with the intensity of a real election. On television and the computer screen, every poll seems to carry the same weight and decisiveness as a popular vote.

Poll numbers lure reporters into predictive speculation. Headlines such as "Americans Disapproving Obama May Enable Republicans," which ran in *The Washington Post* in July 2010, are commonplace. In May 2010, when asked about the mood of the administration in response to right-wing, Tea Party advances in polls and political primaries, writer Howard Fineman observed, "The White House is in a defensive crouch against the tsunami to come."[122] After the first Republican presidential primary debates in June 2011, commentators were again empowered to begin endless, daily speculation on the likelihood of a second term for Barack Obama based on (of course) his standing in the polls. What can this possibly mean?

At first glance, polls seem reasonable—they obviously draw on some kind of research and thus exhibit a facade of authenticity. But they more accurately exhibit "truthiness," as brilliantly defined by comic Stephen Colbert. And while disapproval of the president's health care initiative made Republicans feel empowered, any actual voting booth impact was more than two years away. And even if there was to be a "tsunami" (as opposed to normal off-year losses for in-power Democrats), six months out seems a little early for an administration descent into a "defensive crouch." What such commentaries share is not real consequence but a willingness to confidently forecast outcomes by relying on thin evidence that is nothing more than a murky snapshot of present-day opinion.

But unfortunately such predictions, endlessly repeated for months in advance of a defining event—such as an election—begin to define a narrative. And that narrative too easily morphs into a consensus explanation once something actually occurs. Think about this truth: In the midterm elections of 2010, Republicans chalked up victories exactly in line with typical opposition party gains in off-year elections. Let me say that again: November 2010 handed America a typical out-year election.

But the insistent poll-enabled predictions of a "tsunami," blended with images of outraged Tea Partiers, opened the door to another story-line. This election was not *typical* but *exceptional*, and Republican gains were highly ideological and tied to widespread outrage over President Obama's health care reform package and to a related fervent desire to "fix Washington" by taking on such tasks as reducing the federal deficit while shrinking government. In November 2010, a number of observers tried to remind us that Democratic losses were comparable to other majority party losses in off years, but the preelection narrative of an unprecedented Weather Channel–style disaster was strong enough to drown out cool-headed analysis; premature polling-based speculation was handed to newly elected members of Congress as the Republican action frame. As the new Republican House of Representatives organized its agenda, the preelection narrative predictably resurfaced as a "mandate" justifying a focus on a health bill rollback and spending reductions—a more extreme makeover of government than the November vote really justified.

Poll data inspired by blogs and intensified by television pundits feeds back into both the style and substance of government. In the Seabrook *Morning Edition* piece, Republican congressman Eric Cantor states, "What we are trying to do is find out why the president wants to ignore the American people."[123] But is this a real question? It asserts that the administration's job is to respond reactively to polls that claim to track the popularity of alternative policies or courses of action. This is not the way a representative democracy should work.

Our dominant present-day political given—the assumption that issues big and small are best decided by momentary popular opinion—favors anecdote at the expense of expert knowledge. While we shouldn't, according to Judge Walker, put basic rights to a vote, we've come pretty close to doing just that. Americans have certainly been willing to put transformational policy changes to the show-of-hands process that defines a referendum. When a crack team of medical experts recommended cutting back on the application of mammograms as a breast cancer preventative, the public (through polling) quickly balked. The FDA was forced to retreat. Everybody seemed to have an Aunt Sue whose tumor had been caught by a mammogram. As with much of U.S. policy making today, anecdote managed to trump science and evidence.

The Initiative and Direct Democracy

The initiative, referendum, or "proposition" movement is an example of the unintended consequences of policies designed to ensure against unresponsive government. But at its core, the initiative movement represents more than an obvious pathway enabling the popular to drive out the good; it is, in fact, a destructive attack on one of the most basic principles of American government—representative democracy. Elected officials are there to work on our behalf; it's a sometimes painful task. When New Jersey governor Chris Christie deflected action on gay marriage by promising a fall ballot initiative on the issue, he was sidestepping a basic responsibility.

The initiative sidesteps representation and replaces it with direct democracy. Not trusting officials to behave in the public interest, we simply do it ourselves. Direct democracy has an appealing ring—but it ends up empowering a government of men, not laws. Whoever projects the loudest argument, or retains the most skillful publicity machine, has the ability to overwhelm a seemingly healthy majority.

Given the strident character of messaging for or against specific initiatives—to say nothing of the truth that once a proposal makes its way to the ballot, the chances of passage are better than 50/50—it should be no surprise that an entire industry has grown up around the process of securing the signatures required to place an initiative before voters. As *The New York Times* reported in late October 2010, the initiative game is now sufficiently robust to employ hundreds of "professional petitioners," who travel from state to state, "willing to work for whatever group wants its issue on the ballot—as long as the money is right." Issue advocates have learned that representative democracy is slow and hard; special interests can more easily advance an agenda by engaging marketing professionals and "an itinerant crew of ex-salespeople, part-time students and the occasional downtrodden hustler"[124] to push an initiative than cast their fate with a tedious and messy legislative process. What results may be a form of democracy, but it's not *representative* democracy.

Americans are the victims of the proverbial "slow frog boil" made famous by Al Gore in his *Inconvenient Truth* speech. (A frog tossed into boiling water will immediately scramble out; placed in cool water that is heated to a boil a little at a time, the same frog—ignorant of incremental change—allows itself to cook.) Like our frog, over the past three decades, U.S. politics have been slowly corrupted through a confluence of forces—by no means limited to the enthusiasms of a single end of the ideological spectrum. An aggregation of partisan TV news, anger in online chat rooms and blogs, and pressure from daily public opinion polls have linked up with long-standing and well-intended progressive reforms such as sunshine laws and referenda to recalibrate democracy.

In some ways, media affronts are more symptom than cause. Despite continual attempts to blame it all on Fox News, even Rupert Murdoch lacks the clout necessary to have single-handedly shaped our current dysfunctional apparatus of politics and governance. No, the media environment and the growing domination of 24/7 partisan storytellers on respectable-sounding news outlets is part of a multifaceted transformation in the way we learn, consider, and decide on candidates and issues. The change has produced (so gradually that we've not really noticed) a democracy that would have startled, and perhaps outraged, America's founding fathers.

Progressives have never resolved the conflict between confidence in populist participation and faith in expert knowledge. Should policy be shaped by intelligent, thoughtful leaders, or should decisions be left to the people? Over the years, liberals have enthusiastically embraced term limits, sunshine laws, and the referendum and initiative, all in the name of improving democracy by advancing citizen participation, increasing transparency, and ensuring accountability. At the same time, social democrats have been equally committed to the idea that scientists—social and otherwise—represent reservoirs of insight that can be tapped to produce good public policy. The conflict is quite obvious: Populist participation and day-to-day citizen oversight clamp down on the elbow room, experimental spirit, and fact-based decision making that are the lifeblood of expert leadership. But social democrats hold both ideas simultaneously. In the Obama presidential transition, our dual mantra was "We believe in science" and "We are all about transparency in government." In the everyday practice of government, these ideas do not work well together.

As Bob Dylan pointed out, "You don't need a weatherman to know which way the wind blows," and for the past several decades, the breeze has notably favored both increased public oversight and additional constraints on the freedom of action of elected and appointed officials. Ironically, though the public expects politicians to meet and make deals, in practice the media makes us suspicious of any conversation held away from the ears of the public. We can't expect our leaders to do their work and then vilify them as "insiders" or otherwise distant from public opinion. No American politician would today dare to mount a serious challenge to the efficacy of term limits, to the reasonableness of televised courtrooms or legislative assemblies, or to the notion that issues of major import should be wrenched from the hands of elected officials and instead put to a popular vote.

All this "sunshine"—the notion that every citizen should know about every action of government as it happens and be somehow empowered to give thumbs-up or thumbs-down in the moment—has embedded a conventional wisdom that this is the way democracy should work. As a reader put it in a letter to the *Financial Times*:

> Western representative democracies have admirable free-speech, but the people (the "demos") are able only intermittently to intervene directly in the political process. . . . Why is it that today we can vote to help determine the outcome of meaningless game-shows such as *X Factor* and *Dancing with the Stars*, but we are not trusted to exercise our judgment on key issues that actually affect us?[125]

The answer, of course, is right there in the question. We are, in fact, part of a representative democracy. But to the extent that media and pollsters claim we should weigh in every day, it should be no surprise that government and politics look increasingly like *American Idol*. While the draconian antilabor policies enacted by Wisconsin governor Scott Walker legitimated public outrage, the million-signature recall petition generated by his opponents also smacks of crude direct democracy. He betrayed us; let's try to vote him off the show.

The modern rendition of "sunshine" is, of course, "transparency." We must be able to see through government, the gears and levers and the no-longer-smoke-filled rooms, to possess real-time information that will help us participate smartly in, I suppose, some poll. But does transparency really help? In the 1950s, four out of five Americans trusted government; today it's one in five. As University of Pennsylvania economist Justin Wolfers put it in an *All Things Considered* interview,

> It may be that transparency is the problem. We actually get to see there's a window into that smoke-filled backroom where we're seeing the deal is being cut. And the more we learn about it,

the more . . . you see how sausage is made; you don't like eating sausage as much anymore.[126]

Term limits likewise corrode the character of representative democracy, but in a different way. While the initiative empowers loud voices, ad agencies, and slick professional signature getters, term limits ensure that an elected deliberative body will never benefit from the presence of "wise old heads"—the state or city version of senators such as Ted Kennedy, Orrin Hatch, or Robert Byrd. To the extent that good government requires deep understanding of issues and procedures that can be gained only over time, term limits promise that elected officials will never acquire the connections and skills necessary to completely locate and grasp the handles of power.

Just as the initiative hands legislative authority to ad agencies and signature getters, term limits transfer power from elected officials to career civil service support staff. In my town, Nashville, Tennessee, our forty-member (!) city council has been term-limited for more than a decade. Unlike the old council, which featured members with real expertise in city planning, the workings of unified city/county government, and the arts, the council today must depend on advice from its staff legal advisers or from the various special pleaders who show up to influence the outcome of committee hearings.

Quite properly, the Nashville Metro Council's legal team issues an opinion on every piece of legislation that comes before the body. The intent is to have the work of the city's elected officials proceed accompanied by solid legal advice. But with a perpetually inexperienced council in the years since term limits were instituted, positions taken by unelected city attorneys have become more and more influential in the legislative process.

Cloaked in the mantle of "we the people" patriotism, reforms such as term limits and initiatives—obviously democratic in intent—bask in the sheen of motherhood and apple pie. But, as David Broder put it, they "reflect a culture that increasingly insists the criterion by which any legislature—or any individual legislator—should be judged is the readiness to carry out whatever is currently favored by their constituents."[127]

Writing about the Wisconsin gubernatorial recall, *USA Today* opined, "Costly do-overs, permanent campaigns and endless elections are more than the state, or voters anywhere, should have to bear," adding, "If there's such a thing as too much democracy, this might be it."[128]

Collateral Damage

Just as the 2012 presidential campaign was kicking off, when former Alaska governor Sarah Palin was still a potential candidate, pundit Chris Matthews riffed on Palin's conviction that everyday people had the knowledge and understanding required to govern. He wondered aloud what kind of knowledge this might be: widespread, rural, intuitive, and unschooled, but still somehow sufficient? In today's environment, this kind of neo-Jacksonian thinking, laced with populist, antigovernment, anti-intellectual positions, is inevitable and increasingly commonplace. Even if Mr. Smith doesn't actually go to Washington, our polls, pundits, initiatives, sunshine laws, and right to recall will enable everyday people to manipulate government from a distance every day.

It's no surprise that America has even abandoned the founding fathers' assumption that our elected leaders would inevitably be drawn from a pool of learned, accomplished citizens. Americans support education, and we insist that our children be well schooled for life in our market economy. We want more college grads, better test scores, and employable kids. But in one of the many doublethink notions that pervade American society, when education shows up on the resume of a politician, it's a negative. Woe to any candidate who suggests that a Harvard MBA or Yale law degree qualifies her for office. Elizabeth Warren was treated viciously by congressional Republicans in part because she was a licensed academic. It remains to be seen how university credentials will play in her Senate race. Barack Obama keeps his law degree in the background, Mitt Romney was mocked in a primary ad because he spoke French, and John Huntsman made the critical—perhaps fatal—error of uttering a few phrases of Chinese during a Republican primary debate.

Real educational achievement merely signifies an urbane sophistication that is un-American. Attacking President Obama in his Florida primary victory speech, Mitt Romney began by asserting, "Like his colleagues in the faculty lounge, he thinks he knows better."[129] In place of advanced degrees, we honor some vague kind of common knowledge— the presumed wisdom that attaches to blue-collar work, hunting and fishing, small-town life, and the mastery of everyday challenges like changing a flat tire or opening a clogged drain. Americans will sacrifice time, money, and emotional energy to educate our children, but when it comes to elected office in today's dismal environment, an advanced degree won't earn our vote.

Back in 2010, comedian Jon Stewart was roughed up by pundits before and after his Rally to Restore Sanity on the National Mall. Reporters sniffed that Stewart had inappropriately crossed an invisible line separating *The Daily Show* from "real" news. But the newsies protest too much. As we've seen in the Fox blur of reality TV, politics, and information, entertainment and news have been moving toward one another for decades.

Tim Russert died in 2008; Daniel Schorr in 2010. Bob Shieffer soldiers on. Bill Moyers is in semiretirement, and *Frontline* has lost its cachet. There's no doubt that over the past few years, an era rich in news punditry and gravitas has drawn to a close. I will confess a soft spot for Keith Olbermann (after all, in his MSNBC days, he was bold enough to read James Thurber short stories on air, something I dearly wish my mother had lived to see), but it's clear that the general level of political analysis on TV lacks the credibility achieved by an older generation of commentators who grounded opinion and analysis in decades-deep experience in nuts-and-bolts reporting. Glenn Beck was no Eric Sevareid, Rush Limbaugh is no Ed Morrow.

TV news remains a notch or two above the level of Suzanne Stone (the memorable Nicole Kidman character in *To Die For*). And there's a real chance that our *new* new generation of broadcasters and reporters will rescue news from uninformed carelessness by returning a measure of historical context, sociological evidence, and experience to news. Charlie Rose, Rachel Maddow, Fareed Zakaria, Steve Inskeep, Chris Hayes, and Melissa Harris-Perry offer promise, but such voices are not yet the norm. On-air personalities of limited capacity, hosting shouting matches between what Kurt Andersen describes as "brain-dead political partisans," still reduce the interpretation of policy and politics to the crudest representation of dueling ideologies.

The allure of the short term and trivial is powerful. Consider this exchange on MSNBC's *The Last Word* with Lawrence O'Donnell in the summer of 2011. O'Donnell was talking with John Heilemann, MSNBC regular and *New York* magazine columnist. The subject was the lineup of Republican presidential candidates and the increasing likelihood that Tea Party "purists"—Michele Bachmann in particular—would play a big role in upcoming primaries:

O'DONNELL: This is starting to be fun!

HEILEMANN: Yes, very fun!

O'DONNELL: I'm rootin' for the purists here!

HEILEMANN: I know you are![130]

Elections bring on only more of this kind of thing. Early in 2012, commentators on all networks expressed delight when Newt Gingrich scored in the South Carolina Republican primary. Karl Rove, working Fox News on election night, praised Gingrich for "keeping the process going." Chris Matthews, on MSNBC, said about the same thing a few minutes later, noting that by sustaining an "ongoing kind of barroom brawl," Gingrich was "very good news for media."[131]

Of course, it's not unreasonable to view Michele Bachman, Herman Cain, Donald Trump, Ron Paul, and the Tea Party in general as little more than an entertaining ("very fun") distraction in a political process that should exhibit a higher level of sobriety. No doubt the fights are more enjoyable for TV's political personalities if lively clowns are in the room, but what does it mean that these clowns are also real public figures running for elected office?

There exists a serious, little-acknowledged underlying point here: In the presence of irresponsible, undisciplined Internet voices, traditional media—including cable outlets—will be increasingly pushed to serve as the adults in the room. Executives, producers, and on-air personalities know this. The understanding shows up when they decry the fact that TV covers Congressman Weiner, Whitney Houston (CNN featured her funeral for four hours), Paris Hilton, or even the pronouncements of Donald Trump—just before of course they proceed to talk about them. *The Daily Show* made fun of a disclaimer offered by CNN anchor Wolf Blitzer just before he launched into yet another report about Anthony Weiner's sex/no sex scandal:

BLITZER: As you and I know Suzanne, uh, we've covered these kinds of stories—it's not a pleasure for us. It's not something we look forward to. Uh, I'd much rather be discussing economic issues, jobs, the future of Medicare, national security issues, than talking—than talking about this.

JON STEWART: Wait; what's stopping you? There's nothing stopping you![132]

Stewart is right; news producers can do things differently. It might feel risky, but viewers will still tune in to favored outlets even if prominent voices twelve-step themselves away from trivial pursuits. My advice: Withdraw slowly; cite polls only once a week; promise not to make any poll-based prediction more than a few days in advance of a vote or election; ignore any scandal that doesn't have an authentic policy dimension (think Abu Ghraib, not Michael Jackson). As the Internet political discourse spirals to the bottom, traditional media has both a real opportunity and a responsibility to regain its footing and lead a new national conversation.

It is no doubt wishful thinking on my part to anticipate, or even hope for, some conversion in the ranks of media pundits who interpret politics to us. But journalism has always relied on moral and ethical claims, and public policy can support those outlets—C-SPAN, NPR, PBS—that hew to a high standard. In fact, as most cable channels compete in a race to the bottom, collapsing what looked like a promising arena of choice into a scramble of sensationalized, cheap-to-produce reality, crime, and celebrity shows, programs like *NewsHour* become more and more significant.

Certainly it's possible to reregulate radio, television, and online information without crushing the sector's enterprising spirit. The FCC can revisit the Fairness Doctrine and Equal Time Rule of old broadcast regulation, seeking some way to seriously present alternative views outside the echo chamber shouting matches favored by talk radio and TV. In a democracy it might be reasonable for the public to simply demand, through legislation, that media makes political advertising free. Although this will be hard to achieve given the clout of broadcasters on Capitol Hill.

Harvard law professor Lawrence Lessig sees money in politics as the heart of the problem. His solution: a third party and a constitutional convention. But surely there's a simpler solution. For example, Max

Frankel, writing in the *New York Review of Books*, offered an imaginative approach to balancing election advertising on TV: "Double the price of political commercials so that every candidate's purchase of TV time automatically pays for a comparable slot awarded to an opponent."[133]

A bit hard to implement, perhaps, but easier than revising America's founding documents. Frankel's "double fee scheme" would constitute "an economic revival of the Fairness Doctrine and Equal Time Rule that once governed political expression on the air."[134] It also promises to preserve the massive profitability of election-year ad buys, a dismaying but inevitable predicate to campaign spending reform. Congress can help by eliminating tax deductions for lobbying expenses. After all, there's no reason that tax relief should apply to expenditures that have no purpose other than to provide a company, candidate, or issue with a government-enabled competitive advantage.

We also must reregulate media to generate a larger measure of local ownership of broadcast outlets and to make sure control of diverse voices—newspapers, broadcasting, Internet—is not too concentrated.

Congress can be lobbied to enact legislation stripping corporations of rights that should be reserved exclusively for citizens, and our Federal Trade Commission and Department of Justice can take a critical look at the way big media mergers and acquisitions affect not only price and the marketplace but also politics and democratic society.

Education is critical. But in the era of No Child Left Behind and our race to the top, it's all too easy to end up standardized-tested into the kind of learning that leaves young people educated but ignorant. Just as we must reconfigure the relationship between schools and the marketplace, we must strengthen the connection between education and citizenship. We desperately need citizens who understand America's place in the world, know something of the character and desires of other cultures and governments, and believe that it is acceptable, even good, to deflect the market-driven siren song that tells us that more and more is the pathway to happiness. If Americans are to engage meaningless polls; deflect calculated efforts to promote hate and fear by invoking terrorism, crime, or mushroom clouds; or cope with persistent efforts to convince us that happiness comes from borrowing and buying, we must teach and learn a new set of skills. And if math, science, and reading tests must be scaled back to provide classroom space for democratic citizenship, so be it.

3

CONSUMING

I was reminded of René Magritte and his famous "This is not a pipe" painting over the Christmas holiday at the close of 2010. The must-have gift of the season (if quantity of advertising is any indication) was the Tassimo Brewbot, "an advanced brewing machine programmed to make seven different varieties of beverages." This sleek countertop kitchen device dispenses single-cup servings by infusing hot water through ground coffee or tea leaves premeasured in "T DISCs"—"single-serve discs packed with a variety of coffees, teas, and hot chocolates." The distinguishing feature of the Brewbot—in addition to its manufacturer's claim that it offers a greater variety of beverage choices than competitors—is the technology that made it possible. It is a "programmed" device developed "by engineers" that "reads the barcode found on each T DISC to know exactly what to make and how to brew it."

This high-tech machine is many things—handsome, efficient, and modern—but there is one thing it is not: a coffee pot.

Magritte's painting *The Treachery of Images* was completed just before the stock market crash of 1929. It was both a challenge to artistic convention and a perfect representation of its time. The famous image of a pipe, depicted side view in a literal, one-dimensional, sign-painterly style, raised questions about the nature of art and its relationship to reality that would challenge critics and intellectuals and inspire Duchamp, Dalí, and other masters of modernism. The inscribed phrase with which Magritte boldly captioned his work—"Ceci n'est pas une pipe"—drives home the message implied in the title. Upon the slightest reflection, it is clear that Magritte's "This" is a *painting* of a pipe and not the pipe itself. Magritte's pipe—or its image—first exhibited just as the boom of the 1920s was about to deflate, looks like an object you might want to buy.[135]

Magritte's work is rendered in a one-dimensional flatness that is familiar today; it could be a poster, or an outdoor sign, or perhaps a primitive advertisement for a manufacturer or smoke shop. In a sense, the painting "works" because it memorializes the 1920s emergence of marketing, advertising, and the growth of consumption as an essential vehicle for extending the reach of nineteenth-century industrial capitalism. While *The Treachery of Images* raises questions about art and the real world, it also objectifies a familiar product in a fashion that inevitably encourages the viewer to wonder, "Where might I purchase one of these?" The use of a commoditized smoking device as a symbol of artistic ambiguity no doubt suited the times. Nothing in the image itself would have unsettled high-society art patrons encountering a clever comment on the place of art in society.

But if we transported Ruskin, Morris, and Marx into a late-1920s art gallery, the trio would have been startled not only by the modernist question posed by Magritte's painting but also by the pre-Depression atmosphere of excessive consumption that provided the work's context. And if income disparity, excessive display of wealth, and the overall mood of consumerism that characterized the late 1920s would have set nineteenth-century critics of capitalism rotating in their graves, today's equivalent extravagance would have had them positively spinning.

The Brewbot by Tassimo is the perfect twenty-first-century product. Smartly engineered and technologically current, the product sports a trendy design and a globalized Italianesque name. It is also completely useless unless its owner purchases the single-service modules that allow the device to emit hot beverages. From iPads to cable TV boxes, hundreds of products share this characteristic—they work only if we rent or buy something else. The Brewbot's modern perfection is qualitatively different from the chromed-steel stove-top percolator your mother used for years and different from the Sunbeam electric coffeemaker that graced the countertop when you were in college. The Brewbot is perfect because it perfectly serves the needs of its manufacturer; because, as Tom Scocca put it in the *Boston Globe,* "The goal of the market is not to have sold you things but to be selling you more things, tomorrow."[136] Although various models of the Brewbot retail for between $129 and $200, the company could actually give them away. Unless you want the device to serve only as countertop sculpture, ownership commits you to purchasing T DISC single-serve capsules of ground coffee at 50¢ to more than $1 per cup. *The New York Times* calculated that by weight, and these prepackaged, one-cup modules of ground coffee cost about $50 per pound.

Our American economy relies on consumption; "consumerism" is something different. Consumerism honors spending and buying as the surest indicators of achievement and happiness. Commoditization and advertising encourage this comingling of spending and quality of life; it should be no surprise that the process has reshaped values. In "Spent: America after Consumerism," published in *The New Republic* in 2009, Amitai Etzioni defines consumerism simply as an "obsession with acquisition." He's on target: Obsessed Americans will do anything to acquire houses that are too big, credit cards that are too full, holidays and fashion that cost too much. To Etzioni, it "seems safe to say that consumerism is, as much as anything, responsible for the current economic mess."[137]

He's put his finger on a critical challenge: How can we advance our progressive vision for democracy if quality of life is defined only by the accumulation of the things that money, or credit in lieu of money, can buy? How can we care for one another if we are driven by envy to acquire symbols of wealth? How can we craft a life of purpose if the purpose of life seems to be nothing more than having and spending more? As mere consumption has morphed into the pathology of consumerism, our values and well-being have been undermined. As neuropsychiatrist Peter Whybrow puts it, "The strain of unbridled manic pursuit, whether we enjoy it or not, is damaging to both health and happiness." How do we push back against market forces to advance the common good in a rootless society in which "consumerism has become the primary exercise of individual freedom?"[138]

Daniel Bell tracked the century-long advance of both mass consumption and its corrupting influence on democratic values. Bell's account begins with assembly line mass production—an innovation that transformed the character of work by dismantling centuries-old craft practices. But once assembly line techniques made it possible to efficiently manufacture large quantities of identical products, customers had to be found to purchase the fruits of increased capacity. Three innovations helped expand what Braverman described as early capitalism's "limited range of commodities in common circulation."[139] First the United States witnessed the creation of entirely new products, primarily developed by applying technology to household work. Activities like washing clothes and sweeping, which in the past had not required the use of electrical devices, suddenly could be accomplished by labor-saving machines.[140]

Of course, it was not enough that washing machines, phonographs, and vacuum cleaners were suddenly available; such devices had to appear both necessary and affordable. For Bell it was marketing—the

targeting of specific groups with advertising crafted to stimulate consumer desires—that made new products seem essential. Just as important was the introduction of installment purchasing and the resultant
gradual disappearance of the stigma of debt that allowed consumers
to acquire big-ticket items. These two transforming innovations of the
twentieth century enabled consumers to service desires instantaneously.
Advertising was especially important given its growing capacity to overpower knowledge or sentiments that might encourage cautious buying.
These two "social inventions"—advertising-empowered marketing and
buying on credit—worked hand in glove with the increased capacity of
American industry, providing technology-enabled products with the
ability to penetrate every home in the nation.

Thorstein Veblen first used the phrase *conspicuous consumption* in
his *Theory of the Leisure Class* in 1899.[141] In Veblen's day, American
industry offered just a few products. Today it has "transformed all of
society into a gigantic marketplace."[142] It is within this massive modern
marketplace that a Brewbot—a machine purpose-built to require the
purchase of additional products—can masquerade as a device for making coffee.

Looking back from the twenty-first century, it's obvious that absent
growth in consumption, industrial production would have topped out
many decades ago. It's a Marxian truism that manufacturers of products
must continually increase distribution and the effectiveness of messages
if markets are to satisfy their collective need for growth. If the challenge brought about by nineteenth-century industrial capitalism was
corruption of labor, the challenge of the past thirty years has been the
corruption of consumption as it morphed into an unwritten and little-
understood ideology, consumerism.

As we have seen in the entangled dance of media and government,
the cumulative impact of many individual actions by smart professionals trying to maximize profit or power can take on the appearance
of a conspiracy. It is far too easy to observe the growing interplay of

production, advertising, and debt and imagine a sinister cabal of craggy capitalists rubbing their paws together as Americans increasingly dance to their tune. But it wasn't three, six, or even a dozen business leaders plotting to trap us on the treadmill of consumerism; instead, we have witnessed the impact of thousands of artists, copywriters, and executives skilled in the creative application of motivating images and language to the purchase of new products.

Today, old-timey advertising appears quaint because its argument is so simple and direct. The 1882 Procter & Gamble national ad campaign on behalf of Ivory soap was strikingly straightforward. The company knew that everyone purchased soap; the task was to explain why Ivory was better. But by the 1960s, marketers had begun to apply strategies grounded in the insights of psychology and the social sciences. Market segmentation, the nurturing of brand image, and research into consumer identity had begun to shape the character of advertising. Experts had learned that demand was not something that was either present or not; it could actually be induced. (Think Steve Jobs and his iPad.)

The notion of fashion, a minor feature of nineteenth-century capitalism, loomed ever larger as culture was commoditized over the twentieth century. Fashion provides a reason to consume beyond need. It flatters us with the illusion that we are discerning and intelligent and provides us with tools that let us feel superior to others. The "right" wine, car, home, or suit of clothes can identify us as wise, sophisticated, and in the know. Fashion provides the empowering illusion that we are expressing ourselves through the consumption of commodities.

And it is not just about buying things that are more expensive, more ostentatious, more conventionally fashionable. No, fashion can cut hard across conventional notions of taste and popularity; a product that appears to undercut the establishment can actually employ a kind of antifashion message to impart the status of fashion icon. Alienated by the conformity and hypocrisy of mass society? Have we got a car for you! Of course, it was the Volkswagen Beetle. That famous against-the-grain Volkswagen pitch represents a triumph of advertising insight achieved in the 1960s—a triumph that was, at the time, seriously counterintuitive. Back then, bohemian culture had thrown down a gauntlet, challenging the values of bourgeois capitalism, but the marketplace neither succumbed nor fought back. Rather, managers applied new concepts—market segmentation, brand imaging, and a new understanding of consumer identity—to co-opt the very values that drove sixties youth culture. As author Thomas Frank puts it: Capitalism did not overpower the revolutionary instincts of bohemian youth. Rather, modern business offered up a new version of itself—one that equated debt-driven consumption with freedom and resistance to authority or control.[143]

Today, this kind of co-option of counterculture politics and values is old hat, scarcely worthy of mention and rarely cause for concern. Even movements that at first glance seem to fly directly in the face of consumerist values can be efficiently scooped up by the marketplace and adorned with commoditized services and new features that promise to fulfill some back-to-basics dream. In the summer of 2010, *The New York Times* reported, "At 40, Earth Day Is Now Big Business," noting that the signature environmental celebration, launched in 1970, has "turned into a premier marketing platform for selling a variety of goods and services." The article stressed without a sense of irony that "green consumerism" has today replaced a desire to produce "systemic change."[144] But of course this transformation is quite profound. For decades, environmentalism basically meant *not* doing something—not polluting, not discarding, not cleaning with toxic chemicals. Now it's about buying our way to a well-scrubbed conscience. We take the commoditization of movements, practices, and the great outdoors for granted, but it's clear that Americans have seriously underestimated the ability of postindustrial capitalism to overwhelm social innovation not by digging in and opposing reform but by converting social criticism into products and services we simply must buy.

The conversion of informal and ephemeral activities into products has accompanied the increasing sophistication of advertising. As Braverman points out, the process of commoditization is straightforward. In postindustrial capitalism, all goods are configured as products. Intangible services such as health care and legal work are then converted into commodities. Finally, new products and services are invented, clustered around newly commoditized activities, and advertised as indispensable to perceived conditions of modern life. Entire categories of human behavior are recast in this way. A concept like hospitality—once seen as a basic human instinct—is reorganized (and the term redefined) as a marketable product: the hospitality *industry.*

Our modern brand of consumerism requires an especially nuanced rendering of doublethink—the notion of simultaneously believing two contradictory ideas advanced more than a half century ago in George Orwell's famous novel *1984.* The doublethink required by the intrusion of the marketplace into every nook of life can be extraordinary. We must believe that buying a certain car or specific kind of lightbulb constitutes environmental activism; we must believe that car payments are a pathway to freedom and that a MasterCarded flat-screen TV will make us happy.

One of the most troubling symptoms of the reach of commoditization has been the loss of both public goods and those services or products that were forced, by regulation, to tilt toward public purposes. Services and opportunities big and little that were either free or regulated to serve the public—garbage collection, national parks, schools, police, water systems—have been encroached upon by the marketplace or have simply been outsourced by government. The concept of a government-run postal service is an embedded marker of our American democracy; a first-class stamp buys your letter, invoice, or invitation a trip to any home or office anywhere in the United States. The commitment to mail service is laid out in the U.S. Constitution. But today the U.S. Postal Service is being competed to death by private companies like UPS and

FedEx, which price by the mile and cherry-pick those markets flush with money and action. There's talk of closing nearly four thousand post offices. Without an eye blink and without any significant push-back from critics, the Obama administration eliminated Saturday mail delivery in its budget proposal for fiscal 2013.

Our sense of the realm of public goods, a place where planning and policy could position a range of services and opportunities available to all, developed in the late nineteenth century as a necessary response to arts and crafts concerns about the dehumanizing effects of industrial production. The public goods that came to characterize this space—street lighting, expansive urban parks, emergency health services, a social service safety net—evolved and grew during most of the twentieth century. It can be argued that despite the interruptions of war, famine, and natural disaster, in the United States and much of the rest of the world, there existed a trajectory toward egalitarianism made possible by an expansion of the services provided by government.

But over the past three decades, as the ideology of capitalism has advanced the idea of the marketplace as a mechanism of problem solving even as the capability of government has been demeaned, the public sphere has shrunk. Consider water. A system that can deliver clean water to all at little or no cost constitutes a mark of achievement for any society and its government. America not only developed community-sponsored, taxpayer-subsidized clean water systems but, by adding fluoride, significantly reduced tooth decay in the entire U.S. population. But today, we don't drink from the tap as we did when I was a kid. Instead, we visit the supermarket to purchase what used to be free from divisions of Coke and Pepsi. Our willingness to substitute a purchase for what was once a free good delivered right into our homes by an expansive public system could be just an amusing example of the power of advertising, abetted by a low hum of antigovernment prejudice, to encourage irrational behaviors. But there's a real public interest downside. It's been studied and widely reported that children reared on bottled water exhibit more tooth decay than do young people who drink the fluoride-treated stuff right out of the tap. But despite scientific evidence and common sense, Americans have with lemminglike commitment abandoned perfectly fine tap water in favor of liquids of indeterminate origin and unknown chemical composition, packaged in toxic plastic bottles and purchased at (compared to the tap) outrageous prices.

Other abdications of public responsibility are more troubling. Consider prisons. No society wants more prisons than it needs, but once incarceration enters the marketplace, corporations want as much jail time as they can get. As Adam Gopnik put it in a smart *New Yorker* piece, "The interest of private prisons lies not in the obvious social good of having the minimum necessary number of inmates but in having as many as possible, housed as cheaply as possible."[145] Gopnik quotes a revealing passage from the 2005 annual report of the Corrections Corporation of America, one of the biggest private prison firms in the United States. The report warns shareholders, "The demand for our services could be adversely affected by the relaxation of enforcement efforts" or by legal reform. "For example," the report states, "any changes with respect to drugs and controlled substances or illegal immigration could affect the number of persons arrested, convicted, or sentenced, thereby potentially reducing demand for correctional facilities to house them."[146] By privatizing prisons, our society has created a sector of business in which lobbyist-enabled corporations are encouraged by potential profit to pursue their vested interest in a criminal justice system defined by harsh enforcement and long sentences. How can this shift of prisons out of the public sphere into the marketplace possibly serve public purposes?

Braverman didn't foresee the commoditization of the public sphere; nor did he recognize the ability of empowered capitalism to transform a *way of life* into a commoditized *lifestyle product*. Consider the great outdoors. Forests, woods, and waters constitute a literal frontier on which scientific, psychology-empowered advertising could do its most sophisticated work, enabling the twenty-first century to achieve that eternal human desire, control of nature. But the marketplace didn't assert itself by chopping forests or trapping wildlife. Instead, capitalism hung a price tag on the sense of adventure, feeling of freedom, and expansion of spirit that our love of the outdoors seems to allow.

I like *Outside* magazine—its take on environmental issues, its celebration of nature and outdoor activities, and its steady supply of high adventure narratives chronicling risks I'd be too timid to take on myself. But we shouldn't be misled. *Outside* offers the freedom and adventure of the outdoors in a specific way, through the consumption of products and services touted in advertising and advanced tantalizingly in endlessly repeated "best of" lists. The freedom of the outdoors is available only if one purchases a $4,000 mountain bike, $1,000 ice ax, or $1,800 sleeping bag.

If the spiritual practice of yoga is reduced to the purchase of high-end exercise mats and special outfits, and if environmental activism means buying "green" cleaning products, then outdoor life demands exactly the right gear deployed in just the right place. Anybody who has hiked a popular trail or descended a mountain stream has witnessed the defining scene of modern nature: well-equipped adventurers enjoying fresh air, water, and greenery while casting an envious eye on one another's pricy kayaks, hiking boots, and puffy down jackets. Today you can confidently stand in the great outdoors only if you you're traveling with the right stuff.

Consider this signed message from "J.L. Powell" on the back cover of "The Sporting Life" catalog:

> As I sit in a room filled with cigar smoke and the sweet smell of scotch, planning the next trip I'll take to the Okavango Delta, I relish the debates over which rifles, what clothes I'll need in my pack, which pair of boots I'll take and I realize that it all comes down to the chase. The pursuit. The overwhelming emotions that come when you're standing on lands not known by most

and traveled by few. That chase, that connection to the outdoors is what drives me from year to year. It's the pursuit, the dreams, that will fill my head for many nights to come and fuel my passion for the outdoors.

Now this is pretty silly, and it would be fun trying to figure out just how "the chase" and "the pursuit" figure in J.L.'s "dreams" and "emotions." But what's important is that his quest is about stuff, and apparently lots of it, because he needs a smoke and a stiff drink to figure out what he actually needs to take with him. Of course, if the incipient explorer ventures first into the catalog to purchase bison leather boots ($470) and a lightweight wool shirt ($235), there's not likely to be much room left on the MasterCard for a ticket to the Okavango Delta.

Critics have reflexively characterized advertising as the marketplace's "mechanism of control" that tricks us into purchasing. But nothing could be further from the truth. J.L. Powell is not trying to control us; he is striving to get into our heads. Advertising has simply been reconfigured to enable us to experience consumption as a vehicle for dream fulfillment, or even as a means to pursue liberation and social revolt. Thomas Frank again:

> What changed during the sixties . . . were the strategies of consumerism, the ideology by which business explained its domination of the national life. Now products existed to facilitate our rebellion against the soul-deadening world of products, to put us in touch with our authentic selves to distinguish us from the mass-produced herd, to express our outrage at the stifling world of economic necessity.[147]

For J.L. Powell, a collection of break-the-bank men's clothing isn't about excess or debt or priorities. No, a high-end wardrobe is just "what a guy needs and deserves to wear when he lets those dreams of exploration and travel take him to all corners of the earth."[148]

And here's where the doublethink comes in again. We know what it takes to truly pursue a life of outdoor adventure: time, proximity, and a certain level of expertise in skiing, boating, wilderness survival, biking, and the other appealing activities that draw us toward nature. The men and women I know who have lives like this work as waiters, cooks, maids, and babysitters in towns like Boulder, Colorado, or Jackson Hole, Wyoming. They drive 1978 Ford pickup trucks, wear beat-up running shoes and twenty-year-old hiking boots, and work nights to be free—really free in the sense of being left alone to think, plan, choose, and act as they wish in the outdoors.

It doesn't take much of a thought experiment to uncover the truth: The new SUV generates a hefty car payment; the high-end bike a substantial Visa bill. Debt is debt. It keeps us tethered, forces us to take on the grind of a steady job. In truth, consuming constitutes a choice—we give up the opportunity to actually live outdoors to honor the false promise of a commoditized version of the reality we claim to desire. This is Matt Crawford's "freedomism." Freedomism is a "marketing hook" that promises liberation but always entails "buying something new, never conserving something old."[149] As in the classic definition of insanity, we fall for this again and again, each time believing that a purchase will secure happiness while at the same time knowing full well that buying things is about spending and most likely owing money. Deep down we understand that real opportunity and access to the life we want requires consuming not more but less. When Teddy Roosevelt advanced his progressive vision of a life made vigorous and meaningful through engagement with the outdoors, this is not what he had in mind.

Over the past half-century, installment buying, credit cards of all sorts, easy auto and home loans were progressively extended to every level of income and applied to the smallest purchase. Truly new technologies—cell phones, smartphones, netbook computers, satellite radios, iPods, iPads, and Kindles—now give consumers multiple new opportunities to buy into brave new products—products that were themselves open-ended pathways to additional expenditures on equipment and services that promised instant communication, entertainment, popularity, satisfaction, and freedom.

Companies such as Microsoft and especially Apple have mastered the sleight of hand required to make products and services that we would not automatically desire appear somehow essential. After all, high-tech products are almost always versions of business machines or devices, such as telephones, that were once seen as useful but never glamorous or exciting. Companies have found ways to stir ego, stimulate envy and anxiety, all in the pursuit of sales. It's a trick executed at the level of belief and deep emotion. Just as a new SUV seems to offer the freedom of the outdoors, the latest cell phone or netbook promises another kind of freedom: efficiency, convenience, and mobility. But as author Walter Kirn points out, to think of freedom this way requires both that tech companies reimage products and that customers think about being free in a new way: "Human freedom, as classically defined (to think and act and choose with minimal interference by outside powers), was not a product that firms like Microsoft [or Apple] could offer, but they recast it as something they *could* provide."[150]

A $1,200 bronze sink is not natural. An SUV is not a freedom machine. A Brewbot is not a coffee pot. I'm still not certain what an iPad is for.

I know some of this probably feels like reheated conventional wisdom. The trends that have taken America to our current dismal state have been with us in one way or another for the past one hundred years. And dozens of experts writing across many decades have decried the power of television, the impact of technology, and the manipulative sophistication of marketing. It is not their mere existence but the exaggerated power that media, technology, and advertising have acquired over the last three decades that have dismantled core values of America's social democracy.

The ideology of consumerism did not overwhelm Americans through marketing alone. After all, TV does more than rent screen time to advertisers. Most of the time, television drama, game shows, and gossip-laden entertainment and celebrity news programs bombard audiences with endless representations of lives filled with wealth and glamour. At the same time that television advertising sells us commoditized products, services, and lifestyle opportunities, the programming stuffed between commercials offers a worldview that, though skewed, is close enough to reality to influence attitude and action.

Television exaggerates and dramatizes everyday life. It tilts toward the sensational and the immediate, and it has difficulty taking on complex, slow-to-evolve, gray-area issues of life, politics, and society. And because television is a commercial medium, the relative cost of different kinds of programming shapes what we see. Prime-time drama and global news coverage are expensive, but games, home improvement strategies, kitchen adventures, dangerous occupations, people in jail, and the lifestyles of wives, teens, and drinking buddies are cheap. Cost has encouraged cable television's striking race to the bottom.

Television has played an extraordinary role in reshaping how Americans think, what Americans want, and how Americans perceive happiness, power, and quality of life. Again, this is not entirely new. Television has been viewed with caution—sometimes with alarm—since FCC chairman Newton Minow famously labeled it a "vast wasteland." Historical criticism has focused on three interconnected observations: television is vapid; violent and sexually explicit content is a bad influence on behavior (especially of young people); and viewing embeds slothful passivity.

Each of these observations is true in its own way, but the modern era of television narrowcasting through cable and satellite transmission has greatly empowered the medium—traditional critiques of TV highlight the least of it. Further, telephones and Internet-enabled computing and reading devices—early on advanced as gateways to privacy, choice, and creative freedom—have taken up and expanded on the basic character of old-time TV. They are engaged in selling us goods and services, but they also tell us stories. Much if not most of what we think about the world comes to us through moving images on screens. And it goes without saying that present-day screen media is qualitatively unlike that of the 1950s and 1960s; old-timey TV ads for aspirin or new cars have today been superseded by a ramped-up, sophisticated, multiplatform jugger-naut of anxiety and envy that can be assuaged only by buying some-thing. And, as Peter Whybrow points out, today's media is especially obtrusive, because "technology is now mobile and targets the person rather than a place."[151]

Television has matured into a medium that distorts daily life like a low-grade infection. The distortions are found at the heart of crime-and-punishment dramas, in hospital shows, in documentary programs about celebrities or working-class Americans engaged in dangerous occupations. TV's exaggerations elevate the rich, the athletic, the beau-tiful, and the powerful while simultaneously portraying the world as more menacing, more populated by violent or duplicitous criminals than it really is. In advancing these distortions, fiction and news blend seamlessly. Columnist, actor, and economist Ben Stein says, "News media will catastrophize anything they can."[152] Even the Weather Channel—once a sleepy purveyor of forecasts and wind chills—has learned that audiences are attracted to disaster. Today every cold front is mined for images of iced-over interstates, flood-borne flotsam, or tornado-flattened farms.

This persistent subtext of a damaged and dangerous world—the message that we are not handsome or beautiful enough, that the neigh-borhood is probably infested with gangs, that the other guy has a better sex life, that dangerous weather is everywhere on the upswing, and that we don't quite have enough money to live the way we should—stirs up and sustains a disquieting atmosphere of uncertainty and anxiety. The fact that Americans *are* more anxious today than ever before should be no surprise, given the feelings of envy and insecurity that television reinforces at every turn.

Not only does television drive home a relentless series of lies about life and society, it has also become the purveyor of a range of products, services, and ideas that purport to resolve the very anxieties and insecurities induced by its warped on-screen storylines. Accompanying fear-inducing drama, wealth-and celebrity-worshiping entertainment shows, and "catastrophized" news and weather reports are countless advertisements for the diet programs, exercise gear, cosmetics, drugs, home security systems, and investment opportunities guaranteed to solve the very problems television parades before us day after day.

Entire cable networks are devoted to investing or to buying, selling, and remodeling apartments and houses. Half-hour sales events complete with hosts and enthusiastic studio audiences are interspersed among regular shows, scarcely distinguishable from standard programming. Once-routine human activities like cooking and sleeping are reconfigured and commoditized in every possible way. Chefs become TV stars, hawking exclusive lines of pots and pans. Beds and mattresses that rise, twirl, and tilt guarantee a good night's rest. Just as sports were long ago transformed from an activity into an entertainment, cooking has shifted from something you do into something you watch, reconfigured into "yet another competition of spectacle and celebrity that keeps us pinned to the couch."[153] In the same way an expensive off-road vehicle can masquerade as a "freedom machine," "convenience foods have been sold to women as tools of liberation."[154]

In the run-up to Christmas 2010, *The New York Times* reported, "Shopping on cellphones and portable tablet computers like iPads accounted for about 5 percent of online sales in November." A young New Jersey resident bought her mother's holiday gift "when the eBay mobile app alerted her that the auction was about to end while she was out in Greenwich Village." She then used eBay's RedLaser app to complete a quick comparison to ensure that the gift intended for her brother (also online, also using her cell phone) was purchased at the lowest possible price. The mobile shopper loved the transaction: "It's saving me time and saving me money."[155]

In the digital era, the interactive character of the Internet and the reach of portable Internet devices have allowed the television model of consumption to be fully realized. As effective as TV advertising could be—its messaging cleverly crafted and psychologically empowered—the couch-bound viewer at least had to rise, fire up the family car, and drive to the mall. Viewed from the perspective of one-click shopping, old-model consuming seems balky and prone to false starts and unrealized intent.

To again paraphrase my friend, media journalist Lon Helton, television is in the business of renting eyes to advertisers. With the advent of the Internet, advertisers are not only buying access to eyes but to millions of mouse-clicking, app-launching, touch-screen-tapping fingers.

TV on Steroids

In politics and government, technology—small-screen; smart phone; tweeting and texting—mostly enables thoughtless shout and response. Technology is just as firmly at the heart of American consumerism. As Jaron Lanier puts it, "Advertising is elevated by open culture from its previous role as an accelerant and placed at the center of the universe."[156] The ability of Yahoo, Google, and Facebook—companies that employ few people and don't really deliver what we usually think of as products—to secure astronomical market valuations testifies to the role of advertising in shaping the character of contemporary America. Jaron Lanier again: "If you want to know what's really going on in a society or ideology, follow the money. If money is flowing to advertising instead of musicians, journalists, and artists, then a society is more concerned with manipulation than truth or beauty."[157]

And it *is* all about advertising today. Readers who watched old-style television can remember a kind of "gentlemen's agreement" between viewers and advertisers: We would enjoy an evening television program and in return allow advertisers to have at our eyeballs for a fixed time. Today no such bargain exists. Instead, advertising is inserted into workplace communication, any consumption of music, TV, or movies, and back-and-forth chatter with friends. And this advertising is targeted just at you, effective because we are willing to yield huge chunks of privacy.

A few years ago my friend Mary moved into an industrial loft space. As a housewarming gift, I hopped on Amazon.com and purchased a half dozen books on "loft living." You can guess the result: Amazon's crude (at the time) algorithm decided that I wanted nothing more in life than to acquire a massive library of books about lofts. Every time I logged on, I was teased with publications that I might like because I had liked that other thing. It felt nosy and presumptuous, and of course it was wrong. I'd purchased all the loft books I would ever need, thank you. But Amazon had revealed the tip of a massive private information iceberg. As author James Gleick writes about Google, "Seeing ads next to your email . . . can provide reminders, sometimes startling, of how much the company knows about your inner self."[158]

When viewed in the shadow of the market-driven Internet's great transformer, Facebook, ads planted beside e-mail are nothing and Amazon's attempts to sell me new, glossy "loft living" volumes seem quaint. For technology writer Evgeny Morozov, everything that once defined life online—"solitude and individuality, anonymity and opacity, mystery and ambivalence, curiosity and risk-taking"[159]—is under assault by that company. Facebook—by the spring of 2012 one of the most valuable companies in the world—is worth billions for just one reason: It has commoditized a level of information that children reared in the twentieth century would have almost certainly considered off-limits. As *New York Times* reporter Somini Sengupta put it:

> Personal data is the oil that greases the Internet. Each one sits on our own vast reserves. The data that we share every day—names, addresses, pictures, even our precise locations as measured by the geo-location sensor embedded in Internet-enabled smartphones—helps companies target advertising based not only on demographics but also on the personal opinions and desires we post online.[160]

As Morozov observes, "Facebook wants to build an Internet where watching films, listening to music, reading books and even browsing is done not just openly but socially and collaboratively."[161] This Internet, when tracked and mined for data, constitutes an invaluable resource for a marketplace committed to continually teasing out new nooks and crannies of perceived desire and need into which products can be sold. Its ultimate goal is just like television of old, but with the added capacity to harvest private thoughts and actions, aggregating them to produce knowledge meaningful to the *real* Facebook customers—the company's advertisers.

Early in 2012, the revelation that Apple-approved apps for the iPhone had been routinely invading digital address books, extracting all sorts of data, created a dustup on the Internet and in old media. As Jennifer Van Grove reported in the online news service VentureBeat, "Facebook, Twitter, Instagram, Foursquare, Foodspotting, Yelp, and Gowalla are among a smattering of iOS applications that have been sending actual names, email addresses and/or phone numbers from your device's internal address book to their servers." This violation of "the digital repository of personal and professional relationships you've amassed in your life"[162] constitutes an enormous invasion of privacy. Although the perpetrators claimed otherwise, such data is part of the essential currency of the "eyeball to advertisers" character of our new Internet.

Of course, this software overreach is not necessarily only about selling you things. If you've been e-mailing your lawyer, consulting a financial adviser, or calling a friend who's been caught cheating on a college entrance exam, both your reputation and your résumé could be compromised. Chicago law professor Lori Andrews has written about the way accumulated data—where you've shopped, how much money you earn or stow in an account—can be used to edit the trajectory of your life. Do you get that loan or that job? Is the IRS trolling for evidence that you've held back on taxes? She's dead right about the great leap Facebook represents: "It's not just about whether my dinner will be interrupted by a telemarketer. It's about whether my dreams will be dashed by the collection of bits and bytes over which I have no control and for which companies are currently unaccountable."[163]

Privacy is a huge part of the American democratic bargain. Our constitution devotes hundreds of words to guarantees that protect us from unwanted intrusion into our private lives. But we have given away this and other essential, basic freedoms in return for the shallow allure of shopping, fun, and instant communication online.

Technology

The Internet, iPhones, Kindles, BlackBerrys, and netbooks not only taunt us with advertising at every turn, but technologies are themselves a product—one that is uniquely suited to the expansive instincts of the twenty-first-century marketplace. Think of our Brewbot—the non–coffee pot that has meaning only if we, the consumer, continually purchase a stream of interchangeable parts: little premeasured packets of espresso, latte, and decaf.

This is what Apple does to us with iPhone 4, 5, and 6. This is what new versions of Windows and Word are all about, and this is what faster, more powerful, more efficient notebooks and netbooks and tablets are for. In fact, the marketplace has effectively switched the function of high-end technology. Think about it. A half century ago, if you invested in a Leica camera or a Bose stereo system, you were purchasing cutting-edge technology with the understanding that you were in part insulating yourself from insubstantial fads. My grad school housemate Elliott showed up at Indiana, in the fall of 1966, packing an AR stereo system. His gear was far better than anything owned by his fellow students; we spent many nights in his cramped apartment, drinking beer and smoking cigarettes while auditioning the newest Beatles or Rolling Stones release. Elliott moved to L.A. but was still listening to the same system twenty years later. Nothing unusual here; a consumer of high-end 1960s technology could fully expect a device to be working just fine in ten, fifteen, or even twenty years.

Today we're lucky to get even three years from a new camera or phone. My beloved Motorola RAZR was drawered two years ago, and a still-in-use five-year-old PalmPilot (to which I am inordinately attached) elicits chuckles whenever I tap its museum-piece black-and-gray screen for an address or phone number. We simply take it for granted that the three-year cycle of purchase, consume, dispose is acceptable or even a good thing. We're repeatedly told that the GPS, smart phone, or ThinkPad is opening opportunity, expanding our horizons, providing access to new ways to buy, new places to eat, new friends with whom to share a vast horizon of choice and adventure. But scroll back to the SUV as a pathway to the outdoor life. Like the car that chains us to a monthly payment, and perhaps to a dead-end job, the latest electronic device positions us firmly on a treadmill of endless obsolescence and replacement. As Jaron Lanier put it, "Our willingness to suffer for the sake of the perception of freedom is remarkable."[164]

Technology has also enabled the marketplace by converting a long-standing ownership model that placed art, information, and knowledge on our bookshelves into a frame in which culture is always elsewhere, available under special conditions for a limited time for a fee. Yes, Rhapsody, iTunes, and Netflix give us access, for a price, to thousands, if not millions, of titles, but music and movies are streamed or fenced by tethering software that prohibits consumers from exercising anything close to what a citizen of the last century would think of as ownership rights. Yes, I can rent anything, but in America's brave new economy, we just don't own as much as we used to.

Think back to the Scocca line about "selling you things tomorrow."[165] He's right; and from the point of view of the marketplace, rental represents a modern ideal. In fact, rent is a step beyond the forced consecutive purchases imposed by my Brewbot; rent means replacing a one-time sale with a steady, often entirely predictable sequence of payments. About three months ago my monthly Comcast cable bill quietly wandered past $200. It's my job to keep up with popular culture, so my subscription includes premium networks like HBO and Showtime; I also rely on Comcast for my in-home wireless Internet service. But, still, $200? That's $2,400 per year and does not include my cell phone and landline services in Nashville or at my summer place in Michigan. I've also got satellite radio in two cars and a separate unit linked to my stereo system at home—you get my point. All in all, I spend about $7,300 per year in monthly fees to communicate and consume information and entertainment. This total is astounding and not unusual.

And even when we pay the bills, rent the movies, pay the subscription fees, replace old hardware and software with new, we don't end up really owning much of anything. I personally know a half dozen people who have lost big collections of music or photos to the random quirks that haunt the digital world. Writer Carina Chocano's experience feels uncomfortably familiar. Her "glitchy" phone died, taking with it every photograph of her daughter since birth:

> I hadn't backed up my phone because I couldn't connect my new
> laptop to my old external hard drive and had been planning to

switch from Mobilite (to which I'd forgotten the password) to iCloud (I was holding off until I could back up everything on a hard drive, not yet purchased).[166]

We've all heard stories just like this, and it's really quite striking that we live this way, accepting the loss of beloved photos, songs, and novels as a "new normal" imposed on us by the conversion of knowledge and entertainment into data and the transformation of sturdy implements like cameras, photo albums, and record players into glitchy devices that not only let us down with startling regularity but absolutely demand that we upgrade or replace them every few years. Everyday common sense suggests that spending big bucks on this model—even claiming to love it—requires an inexplicable suspension of disbelief.

I say I consume "some" online information and entertainment because I'm not a real convert. I still get my print the old-fashioned way, through books and magazines, and I still buy music on compact disc. I purchase old media partly out of loyalty—I think music and writing are best served when the recording and publishing industries are in decent shape. But I also believe in permanence. My CD collection sits in a cabinet and is available, barring fire, flood, or theft, pretty much anytime I want to hear music; likewise my print library. And my collection of old-fashioned "hard goods" will be there for me regardless of my monthly paycheck. Tough financial times might push my listening away from Lady Gaga toward the hard luck songs of Hank Williams, but through thick and thin, a real music collection, like a print library, will simply be there waiting for me to drop a CD in the player tray. Music and books that reside in "the cloud" just aren't present in the same way.

Americans have faced the commercial effects of new technologies before—consider the introduction of color TV back in the 1960s. But this is something new: slick advertisement seamlessly inserted into the mechanism of everyday shared experience; brilliantly designed gadgets armed with preset obsolescence; knowledge and entertainment rich in variety but available only if we rent again and again and again. Technology and the power of sophisticated advertising have allowed the marketplace to expand desire. To again quote Etzioni, it "seems safe to say that consumerism is, as much as anything, responsible for the current economic mess."[167] If America's "obsession with acquisition" is a weakness in our value space, how can we push back just hard enough to regain a degree of citizen authority in a market-driven, advertising-enabled, Internet-commerce regime?

Pushing Back

The pursuit of happiness through debt-enabled consuming is a national pathology. It may be immoral, dysfunctional, and not especially effective, but it's not illegal. A revitalized civics regime in school, perhaps combined with a fresh approach to home economics, could begin to arm citizens with the critical insight necessary to resist the allure of advertising and careless spending. We can teach young people to read the fine print, to understand what they might be giving up when they click "agree," but America won't pass laws to limit advertising, scale back access to credit cards, or stop consumers from buying bigger houses than they could ever afford. However, if Americans recommit to a revitalized American idea—to a strong value space—we can minimize the worst excesses of consumerism.

Legislation can address the threats to privacy that grow as the Internet is fully commoditized. After all, personal information is the only real product of companies like Google, Facebook, and Twitter. And to the extent that Facebook ever comes close to justifying its astronomical potential market value (think $80 billion or more), it must assure investors that the online service has an unrestricted ability to reconfigure and sell endless lists of names, addresses, faces, and preferences. Increasingly, Internet users strike a lopsided Faustian bargain. We accept "the short-term value of a cloud-based information service subsidized by the long-term monetization of user data."[168] The texting, tweeting, and shopping are all on the front end; our loss of essential privacy pushed off into the future. The perceived short-term benefits are clear; the potential costs vague and remote. Services that appear to be free are really purchased with a new kind of virtual dollar—our private information.

European policy leaders have taken up Internet privacy issues; the United States for the most part has not. The European Commission has proposed incorporating a "right to be forgotten" into existing privacy law. Such a right would simply enable Internet users to demand that personal information be deleted, including elimination of the metadata that tells aggregators where, when, and by whom a text or photo was created. Since personal data is the only thing that gives Google and Facebook any value, these and similar companies will fight any consumer protections tooth and nail. Informed citizens must demand that political leadership take a determined proprivacy stand.

Legislation, reregulation, and revised government practice can help push the marketplace out of what properly belongs in the realm of public goods. Three decades of low taxes, combined with the unwarranted elevation of capitalism and market values to the stature of political philosophy, have in fact diminished government. Today private contractors fight in place of soldiers, charter schools nudge public equivalents aside, state psychiatric hospitals have been shuttered. We've allowed big private foundations (Gates, Clinton) to provide disaster relief and health and lifestyle interventions in developing countries, effectively privatizing foreign aid. The Internet itself, once an obvious public good created by government, has today morphed into a landscape parceled and managed for efficient retail and for the harvest and commoditization of information. Whenever government—starved for revenue, lacking options—struggles to provide a traditional public service, business is quick to offer a privatized alternative. But it's never quite the same; attention flows to the better students, the more populous parts of town, the websites where profit can be found. As in the case of privacy protection, lobby-aided corporate interests will fight to prevent the return of key community services to the public realm.

Policy can protect privacy and rebuild public goods, but a responsible America must choose alternatives to consumerism. At a conference a few years ago, social critic Benjamin Barber described two kinds of desire: "I want a Hummer but I *want to want* a Prius."[169]

Barber has identified our twenty-first-century challenge: How do we increase our understanding and our will around what we want to want, with all the implications for self-discipline and societal good that the phrase implies, to a degree sufficient to resist, or at least edit, the allure of advertising and media? How do we replace consumerism—the restless pursuit of meaning through more—with smart consumption, the reasonable satisfaction of needs and desires essential to a meaningful life in our modern economy?

Confession: A few months ago I purchased a Brewbot. Then I bought one for my partner, Susan. Tax-deductible research, of course, but the coffee is fine, and we both like them quite a bit.

4

RESPONSIBILITY AND HAPPINESS

Our panel discussion was winding down, and Tom Friedman was talking. A few of us had been asked to discuss the "creative economy" in a session hosted by the Center for American Progress at the think tank's Washington headquarters, in the same room in which Susan Thistlethwaite had suggested, "You are not alone." Friedman had just returned from a conference in China, and he moved off point a bit, highlighting new construction, sparkling airports, and high-speed rail travel he'd experienced on the other side of the world. The United States was not engaging the challenges facing our economy with sufficient creativity, he said. Responding to a "What should we do?" question from the packed hall, the columnist tossed off this line: "Right now, of course, the U.S. is not a serious country."

He was building on what he'd observed on his China trip, arguing that we lacked the competitive drive, willingness to sacrifice, commitment to learning, and openness to collective action that had already made China the twenty-first-century's newly minted paragon of economic progress.

Friedman's point was narrow, but to me, his offhand comment signaled much more: our inability to resist the allure of consumerism, our unwillingness to sacrifice luxury to achieve income equity and social justice for all, our glorification of self-esteem as the gold standard of a fulfilled childhood, our tolerance for diminished, routine-dominated work, all this maintained by a blank-stared acceptance of a political system that uses crude bait-and-switch tactics to prod us to vote on immigration, guns, or abortion when we know that the challenge is really wars and jobs and the maintenance of a just society. The failure of marketplace ideology and the absence of a progressive vision for a united society in which mutual commitment enables individuals to define and sustain a high quality of life have eroded national character. Where can Americans find the markers of a serious society? What are the traits of character and the attributes of achievement that must be nurtured if we are to recover the soul of our "American Idea"?

Amy Chua's book *Battle Hymn of the Tiger Mother* kicked up a storm not only because of its unconventional take on parenting but because Chua's argument took to task the undisciplined softness extended to children by modern American society. As Diane Johnson put it in her review of Chua's guide to Asian-style motherhood, in the end, "Chua's point is that a delusional culture based on unearned self-esteem can't for long be a realistic player in a global competition for influence, power, and resources."[170]

Friedman's notion that we're not "serious" right now suggests that in education, job creation, and trade, we have not evolved tough-minded, effective public policy. But even if we get the policy frame right, will reconfiguring law and rules of the road be enough? If we are not alone; if we are to construct lives of purpose through work, family, and community; if our engagement with immigration, gender, and minority rights can set an example for the world, can government carry the burden? If

Americans are obligated to one another, where does the role of public policy end and personal responsibility begin? Social critic Daniel Akst puts it this way: While the financial breakdown of 2008 may be argued as a kind of systemic breakdown—a collapse of regulation and corporate practice—it was in many ways nothing more than a "colossal failure of self-control."[171]

The unshakable liberal conceit that government and the reordering of law and regulation are capable of effecting social progress is the Achilles heel of social democracy. We too often ignore the truth that human beings are intractable—determined to live the lives they want even in the face of well-intentioned instruction from do-gooders and government. We *will* shop, text wherever we want, and now and then drink and drive. Rich and poor, we are simultaneously shaped by education, experience, environment, and natural ability. Accumulated lifestyle habits in poor (or rich) communities can be passed along from generation to generation with unfortunate social consequences. Human fallibility makes conservative social critics such as Charles Murray and Daniel Moynihan—like stopped clocks—exactly right every now and then. Sometimes the poor really are to blame. Liberals need to acknowledge the truth that just as government can often be trusted to help, reality sometimes eludes the reach of public policy. And if progressive government *is* to produce responsible behavior, policy must be buoyed by public opinion. As Harold Meyerson observed in *The Washington Post,* "In America, major liberal reforms require not just liberal governments, but autonomous, vibrant mass movements."[172] If America is to reemerge as a serious nation, lots of people have to care.

We have witnessed this kind of mass transformation of public attitudes in the past. I'm thinking of Tom Brokaw's "Greatest Generation," the cohort of Americans who—steeled by the shared hardships of the Great Depression and participation in a global war—knuckled down, saved money, purchased modest homes, settled into (mostly) stable families, worked in offices and factories, and reared and educated a younger generation that would turn out to be, well, not quite so great. Today's great-grandparents stand as the "grown-ups" of the twentieth century, and their presence on the receding historical horizon is both an inspiration and a rebuke to those caught in postconsumerist malaise.

War, natural disaster, and economic collapse can inspire the kind of moral transformation the United States witnessed in the 1930s, 1940s, and 1950s, but we've buffered ourselves against equivalent threats today. Our wars are being fought by volunteers—in many cases by poor or otherwise marginalized young people whose suffering doesn't rise to the level of middle-class dinner table conversation. Gold-star mothers and military burials are on the fringe of peripheral vision. It's the same with the economy. While I was working on the Obama presidential transition, there was real fear that the American economy might collapse. But in the end, the disaster of 2008 didn't quite get our full attention, because in part those most affected were blue-collar factory families—citizens only a step or two closer to political power than our volunteer military. Widely shared losses in real estate and equity markets could have triggered an era of bipartisan problem solving, like that experienced in the Great Depression, but it was not to be. As Republican financial adviser G. William Hoagland put it, "I used to think it would take a great financial crisis to get both parties to the table, but we just had one."[173]

Two obstacles stand between America today and the promise of a revitalized democracy, and our argument on behalf of a handmade America—about work, government, politics, and consumerism—ultimately turns on two begged questions: First, can we envision the constellation of values that will define a high quality of life in a post-consumerist society? Second, absent out-and-out financial collapse, can Americans recover the resolve and commitment to self-sacrifice necessary to define and animate a progressive democracy that serves all? If times are not going to be terrible but only bad, can we find the spirit of dedication and cooperation required to put some gremlins back in their boxes, push back against self-serving power, and deliver a better life to our children?

Early in 2012, *New York Times* blogger Thomas Edsall asked a group of liberal commentators to outline "What the Right Gets Right." (He also solicited equivalent assessments of the Left from conservatives.) Responses included the following: "They [conservatives] understand people's more innate belief in hard work and individual responsibility." They place "a high value on good parenting," and "they detect threats to moral capital that liberals cannot perceive."[174] No matter how well designed and sturdy our framework of government practice, our American democracy can be revitalized only if citizens believe that they, as individuals, are responsible for the character of the American experience.

My progressive colleagues and I remain convinced that our democracy—our democratic government—must maintain a framework in which Americans can pursue meaning, happiness, and an American dream. But it is possible to expect too much of government, and here I must confess that to me there's something to the conservative assertion that liberals are far too confident in and much too dependent on the capacity of legislation and regulation to define and sustain the American experience. Although the Reagan-era conservative conceit is dead wrong—government is *not* America's problem—it is not always the solution either.

Corporations and Government

Early in the 2012 Republican presidential campaign, candidate Mitt Romney, responding to a heckler at the Iowa State Fair who loudly urged the increase of corporate taxes, famously asserted, "Corporations are people, my friend." Of course, Romney was promptly thumped by the punditry, but his offhand comment was revealing and, based on actions of lawmakers and our courts, essentially true. It was a revelation to see the ease with which a seasoned business pro like the former Massachusetts governor assumed and then asserted that a corporation was just the same as any citizen. If taking responsibility is critical to good government, a healthy society, and meaning in life through work and community, can we look to corporations as the source of leadership, values, and vision that a handmade America requires?

If Romney had considered the question a few seconds more before his on-the-stump response, the candidate might have said something quite different. As James Gleick observed in an essay about the impact of Google, "The modern corporation is an amoral creature by definition, obliged to its shareholder financiers, not to the public interest."[175] So how could such an "it" be a person? Columnist Maureen Dowd offered part of the answer: Romney "was articulating the same fundamental concept of the American right that Justice Antonin Scalia propounded in the Citizens United case."[176]

This is not news. The Supreme Court's decision in *Citizens United*—enabling unlimited, direct campaign contributions on the basis of a right to free speech—was only the latest in a string of judgments that have attached human rights to a mere legal construct. But with the exception of paying taxes (relentlessly avoided), the modern corporation attaches no public interest obligation to its expanding status as a citizen equivalent.

Can Romney's "corporate people" be responsible? Can they exhibit the compassion and concern for the public good and the character of our public sphere required of citizens in a democracy? The truth is plain: Corporations have been vehicles for amassing profit for shareholders and leveraging competitive advantage by exercising political influence, while all too often experimenting with risky, unproductive, financial instruments and schemes.

Maybe one could make a case for social benefit back in the days when corporations were owned by titans of industry and actually made things by employing American workers. In fact, "Henry Ford perhaps deserved his fortune because he created many good jobs and cheap, utilitarian cars."[177] But that was then. Today, real wages have been stagnant or in decline for a decade; most manufacturing jobs have been lost to foreign competition or consolidated and simplified by new technologies. Corporate profits are at an all-time high, and marketplace profits are extracted from packaging and trading financial instruments, not from actually making and selling things. Henry Ford can be defended because he instinctively grasped a truth that the modern marketplace has abandoned: that America's emerging consumer economy required both the efficient manufacture of products and an employment picture sufficiently robust—both in jobs and wages—to ensure that goods would actually be purchased.

Today the corporate world is content to use increased productivity and outsourcing to suppress labor costs, parking the resulting profits (as much as $1 trillion in early 2012) on the sidelines. If our corporate "citizens" cared, that money would be paid to workers. But while record corporate profits are held back, only 58 percent of Americans of working age have a job, and the average time of unemployment is at an all-time high—in excess of forty weeks.[177] "Responsibility" wants to know, "What is right?" The marketplace, stock exchange, and boardroom ask only, "Is it profitable?" Corporate America's persistent enthusiasm for marginalizing labor and holding down wages is neither responsible nor moral; the pursuit of wealth through the manipulation of financial machinations that ultimately must be paid off by taxpayers scarcely constitutes citizenship. Romney's "corporate people" have managed to have it their way, embracing the prerogatives of citizenship while dodging attached communal obligations.

Lobbying has become a critical "business of business."[179] Legislation and reregulation as instruments of competitive advantage have come to define the work of Congress, pushing public purposes to the margins. Historian Richard White traces the influence of money in Congress to the same nineteenth-century railroads that instigated "corporate citizenship." Those old-time corporate giants invented modern lobbying and in the process "made politics a realm of private competition."[180] Conventional wisdom argues that the marketplace favors deregulation. Business hates government and the rules it imposes. But corporations don't actually favor a level playing field. Instead they depend on favorable regulation, helpful legislation, and the ability to tilt Washington in the direction of laws and rules that benefit one company, one industry, or one sector over another. Corporations spend heavily to get the favorable regulation they need. The past thirty years of market-oriented public policy, touted as deregulation by corporate advocates, is better described as reregulation—the reshaping of rules to suit the objectives of business.

The recent battle over proposed legislation designed to protect the intellectual property of the film, recording, and television industries ("content providers") on the Internet illustrates the extent to which in this regard, the U.S. Congress is little more than an arena in which amoral market interests spend money to gain competitive advantage. If enacted, the SOPA and PIPA bills would have imposed severe, hard-to-enforce penalties on Internet service providers accused of copyright infringement. House and Senate versions of the bills were supported aggressively by the entertainment industry, a sector notorious for spending millions on Capitol Hill. These intellectual-property-dependent industries were confident that their investment in countless campaigns and political fund-raisers would ensure passage of SOPA and PIPA.

But the newer end of the technology sector—think Facebook, Google, and Yahoo—pushed back. Websites shut down, Wikipedia went dark for a day, and congressional offices were bombarded with millions of e-mail messages critical of the two bills. Members of Congress assumed to be in the pocket of the entertainment industry experienced sudden changes of heart. The legislation failed.

To be sure, the proposals overreached; the bills were simply not good legislation. But this is scarcely an example of the public interest winning one against the nasty entertainment industry. On the contrary, public purposes were at best a sidebar to a high-priced battle between market sectors, each determined to bend the U.S. legal system to its competitive advantage. Around issues big and small, corporate America exercises its personhood just this way every day.

Beloved technology companies are no less cutthroat than their industrial predecessors. Apple's Steve Jobs cultivated an image as a masterful imaginer of beautiful digital devices, but his company used a "ruthless intellectual property strategy" to assert "absolute control over the computing ecosystem."[181] So it has always been, and it's not unfettered capitalism—far from it. Like IBM, RCA, and Bell Labs generations ago, Apple and Microsoft are completely dependent upon government regulation that allows them to police patents and copyrights. To the extent that tech companies offer exciting products at low prices, they also need light-touch regulation in other countries, which produces a classic and frankly inhumane business strategy: "cheap Chinese labor in massively dehumanizing monster manufacturing complexes."[182]

As Facebook prepared to go public, with its ultimately flaccid IPO, an alarming set of privacy concerns cropped up around the commercial efforts of the social networking giant and its codependents in the technology sector, Google and Apple. As we've seen, iPhone apps were secretly harvesting personal data from smartphone address books, and Google had developed a way to work around cookie blockers installed in Apple's Safari Internet search engine. This news, combined with the impending public offering of Facebook shares, generated a wakeup-call awareness of the extent to which online social media is dependent, *totally* dependent, on its ability to deliver detailed personal data to advertisers. We've seen that advertising directed by personal data mined online helps drive excessive consuming. In fact, the social media enterprise can sell you things only if it knows more about you than you think appropriate. Without access to information about friends, contacts, preferences, and interests once assumed to be private, companies like Facebook wouldn't have a business model at all. Advertising now maps our inner lives, manipulating hidden impulses and inchoate needs, extracting value from the part of our being that we once would have defined as the soul. As we've seen, this is TV on steroids, renting not just eyeballs to advertisers but hearts and minds as well.

It should be no surprise that lobbying has placed government in the service of the marketplace. Americans have a right to expect policy leaders to craft rules to protect the public interest—especially in areas like free speech and privacy—but government response to the personal data dustup has been predictably tepid. In late February, the White House issued a set of "online privacy principles" designed to help consumers protect personal information. But the proposed self-regulation does not affect search-related advertising (the heart of the Google model), and it is unclear if a one-click opt-out icon would really stop the flow of all personal data to advertisers from private online activities. And as *The New York Times* reported, these are recommendations only: "Much remains to be done before consumers can click on a button in their Web browser to set their privacy standards."[183]

As in online media, reregulation and confidence in markets have allowed corporations in defense and other policy arenas to make decisions that should be reserved for elected officials and government regulators. The role of the marketplace as a policy actor has expanded for two reasons. First, the march toward promarket regulation, begun in the 1970s but greatly accelerated over the past thirty years, has transferred authority in defense, transportation, media, and international affairs from Congress and the offices of federal agencies into corporate boardrooms. Much of this outsourcing has been argued in the language of efficiency. Second, as we have seen in *Citizens United* and related cases, American courts have increasingly seen fit to bestow on corporations constitutional rights that once were reserved for individuals. Investing an inanimate legal entity with individual human rights has created a "pseudocitizenry" capable of exerting extraordinary power in aspects of society critical to quality of life.

Government has traditionally provided a wealth of what economists call public goods—street lighting, a standing army, trash collection, highways, daily mail service—but Republicans hate government and over the past thirty years have privatized many public services. Outsourcing of responsibility for the kind of collective activities usually reserved for government has profoundly reshaped many arenas of public policy. World War II–era military leaders would today be surprised that the army contracts with private air carriers for transportation to and from zones of conflict and would be equally surprised to learn that mess hall operations and the construction of barracks, roads, and runways—once staples of military lore and legend—are today the responsibility of profiteering contractors. These same military old-timers would be positively shocked to learn that the very term *contractor*—suggestive of "back-of-house" duties like building highways, runways, and barracks—today denotes a class of mercenaries: hardened career war makers, generally armed to the teeth, pursuing an undisciplined rendition of American war zone interests, functioning without the constraints of military rules of engagement.

Even at the community level, city services like garbage collection and street cleaning are often outsourced; when New York City braced for a January snowfall in 2011, the mayor contracted for plows and dump trucks. The abandonment of public education in favor of the presumed benefits of charter schools is an especially dismal fate for a government service once cherished as a shared public responsibility. Today, students, teachers, and schools are cut loose to sink or swim in the vagaries of the nonprofit marketplace.

For true believers in market fundamentals, transfer of authority over public goods from government to the private sector is simply the successful outcome of a thirty-year Republican effort to reduce the size of government—"to get government off your back." The difficulty with Grover Norquist's infamous prescription—to "shrink government until it can be drowned in the bathtub"—is that it comes with an important caveat: You can shrink government, but you can't shrink society. Even if you're paying an independent contractor rather than a civil servant, garbage must still be collected; children will still go to school; soldiers will still stand in line for "mystery meat" and canned beans. And citizens will still, one way or another, pay the price.

This is the big lie that hides, like soldiers in the Trojan Horse, within conservative successes at downsizing government. The transformation accomplished by the Right is not in the scope of services to citizens but in the shift of responsibility out of government into the offices of private contractors. This shift may eliminate certain functions—like meal service at military bases—from the army's budget, but bad cooking soldiers on. And when power and decision making about defense, transportation, communications, and education are handed over to corporations, America loses the capacity to bend services essential to society in the direction of public purposes. Power and accountability are distorted. As Rachel Maddow put it in her well-argued critique of America's military culture, *Drift*, privatization severed "the mooring line tying our wars to our politics, the line that tied the decision to go to war to public debate about that decision."[184]

A privatized, market-dominated regime of public services is inevitably corrupted by the excesses that arise when the demand for profit and increased shareholder value influence or even control power in critical sectors. Among other things, a privatized system of core services is continually threatened by what economists call moral hazard—excessive risk taken by private purveyors because corporate leaders know that should charter schools, Amtrak, military contractors, or snow removal falter, government will always step in to save investors from disastrous mistakes. Too often, privatizing public goods moves key services off government balance sheets by transferring costs to families. State universities, once commanding symbols of our shared, tax-supported commitment to public education, have now been essentially privatized. Today, important institutions like the University of Michigan and The Ohio State University receive tiny proportions of their annual budgets from state appropriations. As public money has been withdrawn, tuition has increased, and a debt-free college degree becomes an entitlement of financial elites.

We've seen that water is easily commoditized, and today we spend millions on environmentally damaging plastic. Water purchased by the case and lugged home from the supermarket "women at the well" style is, ironically, frequently bottled straight from the tap and generally less tested than our public water supplies. And, the commoditization of water has contributed to the diminished overall standing of once thoroughly public services. Today, a public education seems second-rate, and water from the tap is, well, undrinkable.

It's a truism that markets move through cycles of boom and bust, but these cycles are often set off by greed-induced bubbles of excessive risk taking by corporate actors. Privatized risk backed by implied government guarantees is the oxygen that inflates economic bubbles. The collapse of 2008 was exactly this kind of event. Financial instruments of uncertain value, opaque bundles of debt, sharp lending practices, and greed generated a massive set of obligations that ultimately fell back on the shoulders of American taxpayers. It's been said of socialism that, sooner or later, you run out of other people's money; in 2008 the same thing was true of capitalism in the West.

So it's clear—responsibility is simply not within the DNA of corporations. Richard Bruce Anderson, writing in *Adbusters* (famous for incubating Occupy Wall Street), put it this way:

Corporations are "fictitious persons," having all the rights of individuals to own property and transact business. But corporations are not human; they don't suffer and bleed, they don't have consciences or souls, they don't go to jail. They are legal fiction. Nevertheless, they act as if they were individuals.[185]

For a century and a half, we've ceded authority to our selfish, uncaring corporate citizens. Today, educators, firefighters, police, and highway maintenance workers are slandered as deadbeat drags on the economy. It's corporations that are empowered. Elected leaders tremble when Wall Street wags its finger. This is no way to run a democracy.

Parenting and Kids

Americans believe in responsible child rearing. Amy Chua's discomfiting *Tiger Mother* stands as a critique of America's "go-easy" culture, but its proximate target is Western-style parenting. There is no project more alluring, none more prone to obsessive and excessive focus, than the job of raising children in America. Nor is there any aspect of modern life more burdened by the weird doublethink that allows us to engage in self-canceling interventions in the child-rearing process. We want our children to be resilient and capable but also want them to be comfortable and safe. We expect our children to be independent but always secure, creative but highly disciplined, wired for success but also somehow at ease. We expect kids to attempt great heights but to never fail. We, the grown-ups, are in control, responsible, and worried. As psychologist Lori Gottlieb puts it, "Underlying all this parental angst is the hopeful belief that if we just make the right choices, that if we just do things a certain way, our kids will turn out not just happy adults, but adults that make *us* happy."[186]

Chua's harsh assessment of American parenting taps into fear that we may not be doing the right things in the right way. As Diane Johnson puts it, Amy Chua uncorks "a sneaking sense that we haven't spent enough time with our kids or helped them on to the distinctions that might have been inherent in their natures."[187] As another observer put it, parents have "borrowed from family, used house equity accounts and run up their credit card accounts to pay for all the stuff they believe their children just cannot miss,"[188] yet we're afraid our investment of time and money might be falling short.

We want our kids to be resilient, but we want them to be secure: safe not only from physical harm but protected from conflict, intimidation, and psychological threat. It wasn't always this way. As a small-town kid in northern Michigan, I was expected to either go to school or otherwise occupy myself away from the house just about every day—summer or winter. We played pickup baseball games on vacant lots, built snow forts on December afternoons, walked unescorted to the movie theater for Saturday matinees, and generally made the neighborhood and surrounding hilltops and woodlands our own. Kids were expected to come home for meals, but unless broken bones or active bleeding was involved, you took care of yourself until it was time to close up shop for supper.

In this freewheeling childscape, I was bullied and in turn picked on others. I got into fights, forged friendships, played with matches, carried a pocket knife, and learned the rules governing marbles, hopscotch, and baseball. I know, I know, it was a different time and to all appearances a more benign place, but do we really need to manage every minute and to know where our children are at all times? Yes, dangers lurk in the outside world, but, as Richard Louv, author of *Last Child in the Woods* points out, we've also been pushed around by the "bogeyman syndrome"—the notion that menacing criminals lurk in every cruising automobile or behind every bush. We fear the worst despite the truth that stranger abductions are extraordinarily rare and that rates of violent crimes against children, by 2005, were well below 1975 levels and dropping.

Again, television—news, movies, blogs, crime shows—has helped put parents in this defensive place. Advertising reinforces impressions advanced by news and drama. Products and services designed to keep kids safe abound. Modern kids are fastened, backward, into high-end car chairs. High-end baby strollers float across the pavement like flagships of the Spanish armada.

When we shift from care to play, kids are sent to highly organized activities (soccer teams, Little League), to computer simulations of things like driving a car, playing football, or flying an airplane, or simply to television programs. Organized recreation and media are attractive because activities are either closely supervised or safely indoors. The continuing penetration of passivity-dependent media, especially TV, is impressive. In 2011 nearly half of all children ages five to eight had TV sets in their bedrooms. The percentage is only slightly less for the very young, ages two to four. American children spend about 3.25 hours consuming media every day, and TV occupies about half of that time.[189] We like activities on screens because they fit our work schedules and keep kids at home but not underfoot. Technology offers kids a safe alternative to random encounters with nature. However, as Louv points out, "Though many would like to believe otherwise, the world is not entirely available from a keyboard."[190]

We're ambivalent about education. We are committed to high-end schools, rigorous standards, and measurable outcomes, but, doublethink fully deployed, we get offended if little Jill doesn't get terrific grades. A teacher, quoted by Steven Brill in *The Wall Street Journal*, laments, "I get disrespectful pushback from parents all the time when I try to give their kids consequences."[191] As Lori Gottlieb argues, "Parents would prefer to believe that their child has a learning disability that explains any less-than-stellar performance, rather than have their child be perceived as simply average." Today "every child is either learning-disabled, gifted, or both—there's no *curve* left, no average."[192]

No doubt our determination to see our children as anything other than average contributes to medicalized learning. In the past thirty years, there has been an astounding twentyfold increase in the consumption of drugs for the treatment of attention deficit/hyperactivity disorder. Sales of ADHD medicines increased by more than $3 billion over the past few years. It is possible, of course, that we've witnessed the emergence of an epidemic of distraction and "acting out," but it seems more likely that American parents are using prescription medicine to suppress the exuberance and lollygagging that pervade a regular childhood. The process of redefining bad behavior as a treatable condition has been going on for years and is about more than the well-being of children. Alcoholism, sexual promiscuity, drug abuse—activities that once were "sins"—are today viewed as "addictions." This represents a big change. The addict is a sympathetic creature not responsible for her behavior. The addict can be addressed by professionals, treated with intervention, counseling, and drugs (even drug addiction is treated with drugs). But treating problematic behavior as illness simply obscures larger, more fundamental problems such as disadvantaged, troubled home lives. As Alan Sroufe wrote in *The New York Times*, "The illusion that children's behavior problems can be cured with drugs prevents us as a society from seeking the more complex solutions that will be necessary."[193]

Today, parental insistence that children feel good about themselves—think self-esteem—trumps challenge, discipline, and achievement in both academics and athletics, producing a "burgeoning generational narcissism that's hurting our kids."[194] As psychologist Jean Twenge wrote in *Generation Me*, "In the early 1950s, only 12% of teens aged 14 to 16 agreed with the statement 'I am an important person.' By the late 1980s, an incredible 80%—almost seven times as many—claimed they were important." These kids clearly thought highly of themselves, but it's traits like perseverance and resilience that actually better predicts "life fulfillment." A positive self-image, "especially if the self-esteem comes from constant accommodation and praise rather than earned accomplishment,"[195] is not very helpful.

In fact, young people's success and even happiness may mostly depend on how they deal with failure. Low self-esteem doesn't cause problems; it goes the other way. After all, "being a sixteen-year-old pregnant heroin addict can make you feel less than wonderful about yourself."[196] And if a parent or friend convinces you that in that situation you're just fine, he or she has done you no favor. Real self-esteem grows from achievement, and achievement comes from the application of what author Paul Tough labels "performance character": a constellation of traits like "zest, grit, self-control, social intelligence, gratitude, optimism and curiosity."[197]

Parents accept responsibility and assert authority around the wrong things. Our streets are safer than ever; we've made certain that teachers and schools are too timid to undermine little Johnny's self-esteem with a C; preparation is under way for violin recitals, SATs, and college entrance. But what's really at risk isn't grades—it's health. Americans have been remarkably unwilling to address exercise, diet, and obesity. Columnist Jane Brody remembers that her childhood included after-school milk and cookies, "but then we went out to run around and play until dark." She continues:

> When I was growing up in the 1940s and '50s, I had to walk or bike many blocks to buy an ice cream cone. There were no vending machines dispensing candy and soda, and no fast-food emporiums or shopping malls with food courts. Nor were we constantly bombarded with televised commercials for prepared foods and drinks laden with calories of fats and sugars.[198]

To protect the health of our kids, we—and they—must resist hyped fast food, carbonated beverages, and juiced-up energy drinks. We have to turn kids loose, encourage them to get up from the computer screen to walk, run, and play. Responsibility of this sort requires instilling something more than self-esteem.

Envy

Essayist and educator Joseph Epstein smartly observed, "Of the seven deadly sins, only *envy* is no fun at all." He's onto something, adding that envy "is the one [sin] that people are least likely to own up to, for to do so is to admit that one is probably ungenerous, mean, small hearted. It may also be the most endemic."[199] And in the era of market morality, it's emerged as the most American. When candidate Mitt Romney accuses the president of engaging in "the politics of envy," we may not agree, but we know what he means. If I could wave a magic wand and strip away just one symptom of our twenty-first-century pathology, I would purge society of envy; it corrodes character without even offering the questionable benefit found in self-indulgent pleasure. Envy is the obverse of the "Why do bad things happen to me?" lament. Envy asks instead, "Why them? Why did they have the outrageous good luck to be born athletic, beautiful, talented, wealthy? What entitles them to all that money, attention, love, easy living? Why them and not me?" For Epstein, envy "stirs people to aspiration, incites them to buy goods: one way to keep up with the Joneses is, after all, to outbuy them."[200] Envy is the high-octane fuel of consumerism.

The lonely pastime of constant, unsatisfying comparison to others undermines quality of life. If I feel depressed, it is because I don't have the house, job, wealth, car, accomplished children, or hard-bodied, tanned physique that belong to my neighbor, or to the imagined neighbor seen on television or my iPad screen. And by constantly measuring ourselves against others, we incubate a persistent resentment that poisons our view of humanity and our fellow citizens.

Envy affects parenting. Susan Dominus, reviewing Amy Chua's *Battle Hymn of the Tiger Mother*, describes the book as "a hair-raising child-rearing memoir that has struck fury, envy or doubt in the hearts of tens of thousands of parents across the country."[201] Fury, some; doubt, no question. Envy? Absolutely positively. From birth, children are protected as precious, fragile assets. But they are also malleable clay, undefined lumps we can shape into personifications of masterful parenting. Our twenty-first-century sense of child rearing "holds that the right combination of genetic makeup and environmental control will produce hugely successful—happy, achieving, creative, sweet—children."[202] In the end, we envy the Tiger Mom who has employed rule enforcement and metered affection to produce kids who really perform.

Envy has us boxed in, partly because something is missing. Americans are living—perhaps for the very first time—without a vision of success or a sense of purpose and opportunity that isn't framed by the insistent need to get what somebody else has. Envy keeps us on a treadmill. You can't compete or earn your way out from under the burden of envy. Check off each goal—get the kid in the best college; move into the bigger house—and envy recalibrates, replacing one desire with another. Epstein is dead on. Of the available sins, envy is just no fun.

And envy is a true public/private partner. It's an open door welcoming the ambitions of corporate titans into our homes, our schools, our families. For every heartfelt longing to possess the clothes, the shiny teeth, the zoomish cars, or the glammed-up vacations of the wealthy and famous, an advertiser-empowered company stands ready to egg you on and reel you in, offering the array of stuff that makes everybody on television appear so happy. As Epstein puts it, "The entire advertising industry . . . can be viewed as little more than a vast and intricate envy-creating machine."[203]

And modern-day envy has taken on a particularly American cast—a way of life we've done our best to spread around the world. We no longer envy an actor's talent or acquired skill. No, that would be too reasonable. Instead, we envy celebrity for its own sake. We don't envy Donald Trump's business acumen; we are envious of his limo and hand-tailored suits. We don't envy Tom Friedman's capacity to write hypnotically readable (if too lengthy) books; we envy his ability to act smart on sound-bite television. American envy is about longing for the things we've come to believe money can buy and admiration for the thinnest trappings of fame.

Envy makes us miserable, but most fundamentally, envy undermines our self-control. We envy the neighbor's home, and we borrow too much to own one as big or bigger. We engage in all kinds of risky behavior to get what we see that somebody else already has. While subprime mortgages are symptoms of capitalist scheming, it takes two to tango. We signed for those crappy loans, making the collapse of 2008 truly "the people's crash." And envy keeps us in restless motion. We chase things; we change houses, neighborhoods, jobs, and friends to get to something we see on the horizon that seems like something we need. Envy, enabled by advertising, is the necessary handmaiden of consumerism. The marketplace stirs the disquiet of comparison, longing, and need. In the end, society is corrupted as we all give in to what we know we shouldn't do.

Envy may be no fun at all, but it remains irresistible, in part because it is the most reinforced weakness of all those that afflict American behavior. How can we forgo some in-the-moment pleasure or purchase when advertising and celebrity media continuously project "the better life" and the opportunity to buy satisfaction and happiness right now? And just as advertising taunts us with visions of things we wish we had, technology "spells trouble on the self-control front because it drives down the cost of nearly everything, stoking temptation by bombarding us with affordable novelty and enticement."[204] My Sony Reader sits in a drawer, supplanted by a Kindle; my early adopter forty-two-inch high-def TV set looks, just four years after I bought it, not quite up to snuff. I have a pile of dead cell phones, a half dozen pocket calculators that don't work, and enough orphaned battery charger cords to strangle a dragon. Everybody was buying them, and each item was irresistible in its time and cheap enough to make it all too easy to move on to the next purchase. Unlike my parents, who watched their first color TV set for twenty-five years, I'm drowning in leftover devices that I've cast aside just because they're not the latest thing.

We will never recover self-control, or put envy in its proper place, without crafting a humbler vision of the good life that sets aside the demands of material wealth. We need to be reminded that things have not always been like they are now. In *The Time of Our Lives*, Tom Brokaw describes his family home as a teenager, "a two-story, three-bedroom house on a corner lot with an attached two-car garage." Purchased for the "princely sum" of $11,500, it had three small bedrooms and a single bath for a family of five.[205] This is not mere nostalgia; the relationship among income, housing prices, and the perceived essentials of lifestyle was fundamentally different in the mid–twentieth century. Brokaw describes the start-up home he and his bride purchased in Los Angeles: It was forty years old, fourteen hundred square feet, and cost "just slightly more than my annual salary." That modest house was "California bliss" for Brokaw's young family, good enough to host "neighbors and friends, movie and television stars, presidential candidates, local politicians, famous athletes, and business moguls." Though he has "no idea what the current value might be . . . it must be at least two or three million dollars."[206]

When I was young, my parents and their friends were not especially interested in wealthy people. They seemed to want extra money only for the purpose of acquiring what might be termed "glorified necessities," not mimicking the excesses of the rich. Of course, these were the 1950s, and media and advertising had not yet totally fleshed out the manipulative process of advancing great beauty, wealth, and power as an engine of envy-driven consumption. My family's frame of reference hadn't yet been reshaped by television, and whatever envy was generated by disparities of income and influence in our little town seems laughably modest by today's standards. Yes, there existed a smattering of inherited wealth in our Michigan mining community, and local doctors and lawyers drove Cadillacs instead of Fords or Chevys and purchased (slightly) finer homes than the rest of us, but comparisons weren't stark enough to make anyone feel really deprived. Sure, I longed to drive my own car, as a handful of my wealthier high school friends did, but it didn't worry me much; envy seemed a third-tier sentiment.

We can't go back to those days. As we've seen, when information and entertainment are not themselves generating longings, anxieties, and comparisons with others, news, drama, games, and personal communication are framed by advertising that tells us again and again that this car, this hair-care product, or this pharmaceutical will ease the pain. But just as money accelerates and intensifies cracks in our political process, envy serves as fuel for consumerism and debt.

Personal Responsibility

Personal responsibility lurks in the shadows of every argument for change and progress. It's ultimately up to us to resist the corrosive, unhappy habit of envy. When early in his administration President Obama exhorted Americans to "turn off the television; put away the Xbox," he was by implication encouraging us to push back against the weight of advertiser-enabled consumption by substituting active, meaningful behavior. If we believe that our children must be strong to navigate our new economic reality, it is up to us to insist that teachers reward achievement and that versatility, resilience, and grit replace the feel-good gold stars of self-esteem as attributes of modern success. Public policy cannot force us to do this. Workers, parents, and children must on their own bring forward a commitment to community, family, and personal creativity strong enough to blunt the power of market forces and the allure of passivity. We cannot engage the dream of social democracy if citizens expect that the components of a high quality of life will simply be handed to them like some free iPhone app.

Religion can't be the answer. While it is tempting to invoke Judeo-Christian values as a reservoir of both resilience and responsible behavior, America's constellation of religious sentiments is not, in a historical sense, enough to cast us as a truly religious country. Few Catholics attend Mass every day; even observant Jews reserve worship for Saturdays. A leader in business or government who *truly* makes decisions through prayerful consultation with God is a rarity viewed with understandable suspicion. When some outlier executes a heinous crime because "God told him to do it," we never believe it's true. When ex-senator Rick Santorum argued for a closer link between church and state during the 2012 Republican primaries, his poll numbers went down.

While many Americans pay lip service to the Almighty, worship, and prayer, we actually function as if it's all up to us. As *Good Without God* author Greg Epstein puts it, "if the universe we live in does not have competent moral management, then . . . we must become the superintendents of our own lives."[208] It should be no surprise that the endless books that work to inspire good behavior and character improvement are mostly in the business of recasting religious principles to make sense in a secular context, enabling us to find our own way.

If challenged to consider a good life absent the distraction of consumption and pursuit of wealth, most Americans would identify an engagement that "affirms our ability and responsibility to lead ethical lives of personal fulfillment, aspiring to the greater good of humanity."[209] We come by this way of thinking honorably. The great achievement of the founding fathers was to rise from beneath the weight of "divinely empowered" kings to craft the outlines of a society that could provide opportunity and occasions for happiness while reducing suffering here on earth, not in an imagined afterlife.

Prescriptions for the good life abound. Economist Robert Fogel, in *The Fourth Great Awakening,* written at the end of the last century, offered fourteen "spiritual resources" essential to self-realization. These attributes included a sense of purpose, a strong family ethic, the capacity to resist hedonism, a sense of community, and a thirst for knowledge. Christian writer Karen Armstrong offers *Twelve Steps to a Compassionate Life,* beginning with the application of the ancient and ubiquitous Confucian principle: "Do unto others as you would have them do unto you." Armstrong expands her argument through chapters titled "Empathy," "Mindfulness," and "Knowledge." Astrophysicist Neil Tyson, looking to the stars, proposes a "cosmic perspective"—a view of life that is humble, open-minded (but disciplined), aware of beauty and the universe, able to "see beyond our circumstances." The cosmic perspective is "spiritual but not religious"[210] and allows us to assess our place in the universe, embracing our kinship with all life on earth.

Greed and carelessness have marginalized our historical sense of virtue while at the same time, somewhat ironically, driving our economy over a cliff. We've come to take for granted disparities in wealth that we haven't seen in America for three-quarters of a century, and observers have tracked unprecedented levels of depression and anxiety. Remember, our assessment of ourselves as a "happy" people peaked in the 1970s.

Everybody Get Happy

In his book *Happiness,* Richard Layard asserts, "The greatest happiness is the right guide to public policy." But happiness also comes from setting aside envy. "People are happier if they are able to appreciate what they have, whatever it is; if they do not always compare themselves with others; and if they can school their own moods."[211] Folksinger Pete Seeger, a self-described "professional Spartan," offers this guide to a good life in hard times:[212] "Marry a bohemian; nothing is garbage; one is enough; grow your own; indulge in the occasional rich-guy perk."

Seeger's homily inspires an uncomfortable chuckle. His formulation of a high quality of life is markedly free of consumerist dreams and not at all subservient to envy. We know he is right, and there exists growing evidence that what we say we want from life—to be happy—is more attainable if we stop buying what modern capitalism and its enabler, advertising, tell us is just the thing.

Late in 2010, UK prime minister David Cameron delivered an address on well-being. Acknowledging that "the whole thing is a bit woolly," and even though "you can't legislate for fulfillment or satisfaction," he said that "government has the power to help improve well-being."[213] Cameron's markers of a life of happiness and well-being chart no new ground. They resemble the prescriptions of Fogel, Armstrong, and others: control over our own destiny, choice in health and education, purpose in work, being part of something bigger than ourselves. Cameron's argument may gain traction in England, but Americans have long dismissed the notion of happiness or well-being as a public policy objective. "Just give me enough money and I'll be happy" is the kneejerk response.

There exist plenty of indications that Americans are not happy. Jean Twenge compared 269 studies of anxiety conducted in the United States between 1952 and 1993. They showed "a continuous upward trend."[214] Ten percent of all Americans over the age of six are now being treated for depression. We've seen that mental illness in general has been reconfigured into a pill-treatable disease, but this transformation has not produced a cure. Far from it. Modern medicine has instead shaped a social regime in which symptom-suppressed patients populate our homes and offices as a permanent class of drug-addled walking wounded. And of course money is not the answer. Think about it: Over the past two decades, Americans have tried every trick to prove that "enough money" would make us happy.

But the idea of *real* happiness—not the umbrella-drink-on-a-beach variety but something deeper—is worth exploring. Psychologist Martin Seligman has been refining his ideas about happiness for more than twenty years. He began by chiding his fellow psychologists for their excessive—if not obsessive—focus on studying the debilitating effects of mental illness. He thought professionals should do more to understand why most people, despite childhood trauma and adult disappointment, managed to construct satisfying, functional lives.

Seligman argued that true happiness was about more than mere pleasant sensation, more than the things money could buy. At a 2007 conference, he proposed three levels of happiness.[215] First was *positive emotion,* the pleasant sensation that arises on a holiday, at a party, or in the midst of an enjoyable sexual encounter. Positive emotion is what we mostly consider when questions about happiness arise. Seligman called his second level of happiness *engagement.* Playing a musical instrument, drawing, mastering a complex sport, or competing at chess—these activities require training, concentration, and involvement. This kind of happiness approaches the heart of arts and crafts thinking about the character of work: the satisfaction that arises when we apply skill to a complex task to produce something beautiful in its simplicity and usefulness. For Seligman, engagement provides the pleasure of accomplishment and connection with something outside ourselves—the integration of mind, hand, and task that psychologists have termed "*flow.*"[216]

Seligman's third tier of happiness, *deep meaning,* is important because it contradicts the easy assumption that happiness is always about pleasurable experience. In fact, Seligman argued, deep meaning can accompany activities that—at least on the surface—are no fun at all. The easiest-to-grasp example of happiness through meaning is child rearing. From birth to college graduation (and today, unfortunately, beyond), the task of participating in the emergence of an adult is no walk in the park, no beachy umbrella drink. But despite the challenges, frustrations, and pain of parenthood, it unquestionably makes people happy—at least satisfied enough to do it again, and again, and again.

Over the past decade, Seligman has continued to refine his concept of happiness. Today, like an Eskimo parsing snowfall, the psychologist has identified subsets of the things that bring us satisfaction. Under his self-invented acronym PERMA, Seligman now includes *positive* emotion, *engagement, relationships, meaning,* and *accomplishment.* Happiness, in this enlarged sense, enables human beings to *Flourish* (the title of his latest book).

Happiness as deep meaning is both an objective and an attribute of a "serious country." More than fifty years ago, political scientist James Q. Wilson analyzed the different incentives that induce citizens to join and support organizations and movements.[217] Material interests can encourage participation in a corporation or business enterprise, and the desire for connection with others—a sense of solidity—can inspire membership in sororities or social clubs. But people also join together in support of policies, vision, and objectives. Such "purposive" joining encourages individuals to subsume financial well-being and social comfort beneath objectives like abortion rights, clean water, and immigration reform. Purposeful engagement is critical to the work of democracy, essential to government's ability to tax citizens, define common goals, and enact empowering legislation. Like parenting, purposeful engagement is an arena for achieving happiness through meaning.

Advertising and consumerism offer plenty of opportunities to pump up positive emotion—the most obvious and most readily grasped rendition of happiness. Everything else in the PERMA list tilts away from pleasurable sensation, instead encouraging activities that demand restraint, self-discipline, and a willingness to connect with others. But the marketplace doesn't care if our engagement is deep and our accomplishment meaningful. No, capitalism wants us to behave like one-trick lab rats trained to punch the same pleasure button over and over. As Richard Bruce Anderson wrote in *Adbusters,* "We are constantly subject to a bedlam of manipulation, slogans and images, tales and fancies whose only objective is to stimulate desire."[218]

True enough. And, he continues, "Greed, pride, fear, sloth, lust—the deadly sins—are the openings, the doors to demand for more products." In this way advertising upsets the necessary balance between what Tyler Cowen calls the "rule-oriented self" and the "impulsive self." Marketing and advertising are all about impulse, and technology makes things worse. It "undermines constraint by making everything happen faster."[219]

One thing is clear: We must stop living inside the constraints of envy and consumerism if we are to achieve a meaningful level of real happiness.

Regulating the marketplace is critical. After all, it's obvious that, if a corporation is a person, it's a pretty unruly one. As Obama adviser Steven Rattner put it, "Capitalism is like an energetic child who needs boundaries and discipline."[220] The *Financial Times* seems to agree. As its series "Capitalism **in Crisis**" progressed through the first months of 2012, one theme surfaced again and again. "Capitalism works best," the *FT* editorial board intoned, "when people's free choices are also governed by moral values." Business school dean Kishore Mahbubani put it this way: "For all its flaws, capitalism remains the best system to improve human welfare. But it is also an imperfect one. It requires careful government supervision."[221]

So the oxymoronic phrase "corporate responsibility" can be reconciled only if government imposes rules. Mahbubani recommends four on-target changes in the landscape of postindustrial capitalism that, taken together, could bolster the moral dimension of markets. First, it is time to abandon the belief in capitalism and free markets as an "ideological good." The financial collapse of 2008 and the multiple incidents of greed, arrogance, and stupidity that brought it about should make for a reassessment of capitalism's capacity for virtuous self-correction. Markets don't know what is best; nor does the pursuit of profit default to anything close to a democratic public interest.

Second, the state must play a regulatory role. Daniel Akst puts it this way: "At the very least government needs to step in where informational asymmetries or dangerous appetites make people easy marks for amoral profit seekers."[222] The third Mahbubani prescription also requires government intervention: If capitalism is to maintain its standing as the best mechanism for achieving human potential, all classes must benefit. The disorganized and unfocused Occupy Wall Street movement managed to strike a nerve when it separated the 1 percent from the rest of America. In 2011 the U.S. economy grew by 1.7 percent while median wages fell by 2.7 percent; this at a time when Wall Street and investment bank bonuses began clawing their way toward prerecession levels. The misapprehension that the United States is an egalitarian society blessed with unmatched economic and social mobility is deeply embedded in the American psyche, and we resist the hard-time temptation to punish the rich. But even here, vast, endemic disparities in wealth and income will ultimately trigger unrest and unpleasant political outcomes. But as recovery guru Steven Ratner points out, "In 1993, the 400 wealthiest Americans paid 29.4 percent tax; in 2008, it was 18.1 percent."[223] Such a trajectory is neither moral nor politically sustainable.

Mahbubani's fourth point may be the most important. Leaders need to tell citizens and workers the truth about the sometimes destructive effects of capitalism. Throughout the first decade of the twenty-first century, globalization was advanced as an unmitigated good that would produce market efficiencies, maximizing the utility of technology and instant communication to invent a new economy blessed with low prices and exciting knowledge-based jobs. We got the first part—low prices—at the cost of nineteenth-century conditions imposed on workers in China, India, and Malaysia. Cheap iPhones and Walmart appliances and rising home prices obscured the truth that America's entry into a global economy would destroy domestic industrial production and cast an entire generation of the middle class into the uncertainty of shrinking incomes and unemployment. Political leaders and their enabling economists knew this was coming; it's not rocket science. But persistent dishonesty about the trade-offs required when technological efficiencies and third world competition combine to disrupt the U.S. economy ultimately undermines confidence in democratic capitalism.

When asked, Americans really don't long for all that much. In the midst of the big recession, mid-2009, a *New York Times*–CBS News poll about what Americans wanted turned up phrases like "a chance to succeed," "to be healthy and have a nice family," "to have a roof over your head and put food on your table," and "just financial stability."[224] We know that money by itself does not confer happiness, that work is an especially valuable source of self-esteem, and that we seek fulfillment in commitments to ideas larger and more meaningful than the envy and competition that accompany material success. In mid-2012, implementing its new emphasis on well-being, the British government began asking citizens to rank feelings of happiness, anxiety, and life satisfaction on a scale from zero to ten. It is ironic, of course, that this new emphasis on happiness in the United Kingdom is a subset of an official commitment to austerity and to the shrinkage of many public services and subsidies. But even if the results of such a quarterly happiness survey remain inconclusive, the very act of thinking about our lives—considering how we feel about satisfaction, work, and the arc of our lives—will by itself focus critical attention on wealth, family, and the meaning of things money can't buy.

It's not likely to happen here. As Alan Wolfe wrote in his review of Derek Bok's *The Politics of Happiness*, "Government has the potential to produce happiness, but Americans dislike government."[225] What the U.S. government *can* do is reregulate corporations to help ensure that markets generally serve public purposes, or at least that rules are tightened enough so that excessive risk, greed, and lack of responsibility are not institutionalized in the everyday practices of the business community. "Capitalism cannot thrive without *some* moral and cultural framework,"[226] and while imposing constraints on postindustrial capitalism may not make citizens happy, a good bit of misery can be headed off.

A decades-long promotion of the right-wing view of government has undermined the very idea that elected and appointed leaders can play a positive role in society, shaping the public realm to enable us to achieve big things in the public good. It is that kind of pre-Reagan thinking that enabled the interstate highway system and our trek to the moon. But such dreams, and such achievements, require confidence in government as an agent of collective achievement and a willingness to sacrifice—the notion that we must each give a little to accomplish something great. We pay taxes to do things together. But today Americans have come to see taxes as nothing more than an uncompensated reduction in earnings. Everybody, even my liberal friends, talks about taxes this way. The notion that tax dollars purchase services and facilities, opportunities and experiences that actually make our lives better, has been completely shoved aside.

Again, my argument circles back to education. What young people learn in class should prepare them for meaningful work. But more importantly, school must equip them for participation in our democracy and arm them with the tools necessary to resist the manipulations of advertising and the allure of consumerism. As John Ruskin put it, "Civilization is the making of civil persons,"[227] a process that demands an ethical, as well as a practical, education. The precepts advanced in Ruskin's *The Seven Lamps of Architecture*—sacrifice, embrace of resistance, tradition, and beauty—intersect Fogel's "spiritual resources."

If schools offer a "new civics," it must promote a vision of happiness grounded in engagement and meaning and provide students with practical steps to achieve a sense of well-being deeper than what is communicated by "the next email in a relentless life."[228] In this sense, our new civics must teach a kind of "secular spirituality"—ethical behavior, concern for the weak, the discipline to resist childish impulses.

Here's my second big idea for handmaking America: To offset envy, selfishness, and the relentless pursuit of personal choice and self-invention, we must borrow from religion, shifting practices, ideas, and strategies from the sacred to the secular realm. For a time a few decades ago, I was married to a Salt Lake City Mormon, and I spent lots of time with practitioners of the faith. I never found Mormon doctrine especially compelling—Joseph Smith, golden plates, baptism for the dead, and so on—but the church encouraged real-world practices that are unquestionably useful in linking up communities and strengthening family ties. Latter Day Saints commit to a "family home evening" once a week. These Wednesdays are just what the name suggests. Face-to-face conversation, board and card games, and hobbies are fine; TV and video games, not so much. The Saints also contribute 10 percent of their income to the church, go off on two-year proselytizing missions, and maintain a vigorous non-judgmental welfare program for members who have fallen on hard times.

In *Religion for Atheists,* Alain de Botton offers a broad argument on behalf of lifting religious practices and recasting them in secular form. De Botton argues that our secular age should "look at religion and see what bits we can steal and place into the modern world." Everybody can "learn something from the ways in which religion delivers sermons, promotes morality, engenders a spirit of community, inspires travel, trains minds and encourages gratitude at the beauty of life." De Botton proposes "agape restaurants," where diners would sit with strangers and converse on prescribed topics for predetermined lengths of time. None of the usual small talk would be allowed. Instead, diners would ask, "'What do you regret?,' 'Whom can you not forgive?,' 'What do you fear?'"[229] I would move the author's bold ideas straight into American schools. Consider lunch hour. If students rotated through assigned seats, put social media devices aside, and discussed preset topics for an hour, there is little doubt that the school day would pass along not just math and reading skills but a significant measure of civility, empathy, and respect. America prides itself on separation of church and state. Fine. But there's nothing wrong with borrowing the social tactics of religion to enhance civil society.

What business wants from education is insufficient for democracy. We need a generation of citizens devoted to government, resistant to consumerism and careless debt, and committed to overarching values with a sense of action, intervention, and positive change. This is a form of humanism: "A progressive lifestance that, without supernaturalism, affirms our ability and responsibility to lead ethical lives of personal fulfillment, aspiring to the greater good of humanity."[230] We want to be happy, but we must learn to pursue pleasure as engagement and meaning, "an idea of happiness deeper than mere property-bound prosperity."[231]

We must connect with our children differently, placing the experience of nature and the outdoors in the "health" column, not "leisure," restoring discretionary time and self-directed play. And we must let schools and teachers do their thing while we work to bring citizenship, critical thinking, and ethical behavior into the curriculum. There may be bumps, bruises, setbacks, and failures, but we must accept that these constitute experiences that form resilient grown-ups. Paul Tough puts it this way:

> We have an acute, almost biological impulse to provide for our children, to give them everything they want and need, to protect them from dangers and discomforts both large and small. And yet we all know—on some level, at least—that what kids need more than anything is a little hardship: some challenge, some deprivation that they can overcome, even if just to prove to themselves that they can.[232]

CONCLUSION:
HANDMADE AMERICA

In mid-January 2011, speaking to the nation in the wake of a deadly attack on a member of Congress in Tucson, President Obama challenged Americans to "expand our moral imagination, listen to each other more carefully, to sharpen our instincts for empathy, and remind ourselves of all the ways our hopes and dreams are bound together." There it is again: our connected "hopes and dreams"—yearned for but undefined. The 2012 State of the Union address wrapped up on a similar note:

> This nation is great because we built it together. This nation is great because we worked as a team. This nation is great because we get each other's backs. And if we hold fast to that truth, in this moment of trial, there is no challenge too great; no mission too hard. As long as we are joined in common purpose, as long as we maintain our common resolve, our journey moves forward, and our future is hopeful, and the state of our Union will always be strong.[233]

This was encouraging. There's just a hint of a progressive, communitarian vision—investing time and energy in relations with each other—in these remarks, but we're still moving forward without destination, without maintaining a common resolve to secure a future that is not only hopeful but also offers a better way of life.

A "hopeful future" isn't enough. I recall a prominent physician in Nashville who defined hope as an especially dangerous sentiment because it was "nothing more than a longing for things to be different than they really are." Hope leaves the big questions begged: Are we wishing that we will again feel wealthy; hoping against hope that the future will magically restore our treadmill of consumption and envy; hoping that leaders will let the marketplace have its way and we will time-shift to fat mortgages, debt, and distracted tinkering with high-tech toys? Or is the dream of real change: digging in to actually define the "America we want for our children," restoring value to work and integrity to government while pushing back against the assumption that America can borrow its way to happiness and a high quality of life? It is a foolish conceit to believe—to hope—that America can "go back"; that we can return to the consumerist excess that defined quality of life in the first years of the twenty-first century. As Kishore Mahbubani wrote in the *Financial Times*: "No U.S. leaders dare to tell the truth to the people. All their pronouncements rest on a mythical assumption that 'recovery' is around the corner. Implicitly, they say this is a normal recession. But this is no normal recession. There will be no painless solution."[234]

Instead, as Richard Florida argues, we are caught up in a "Great Reset," a "broad and fundamental transformation of the economic and social order."[235] As financier Mort Zuckerman put it, "We are not enjoying the normal cycle of economic improvement."[236]

True recovery demands a renewed commitment to the core principles of our progressive democracy, but America's value space is empty. The Republicans got what they wanted, and here's what we got in return: an uninvolved government, weakened by constricted tax revenues and saddled with costly permanent war; a run-amok marketplace that subjects citizens to lonely stagnation in work and quality of life. Our economy has been undermined, the public sphere diminished. Our self-confidence and America's image in the eyes of the world are in retreat. In the Right's enfeebled state, good citizenship demands nothing more than (begrudgingly) paying taxes while staying out of jail.

Once upon a time, liberals owned the dream of an egalitarian democracy. Today, as the Baylor Religion Survey shows, it's conservatives who most believe in meaning and truth in life.[237] It is time for progressives to again outfit our frontline policy actors—our mayors, senators, and presidents—with a vision for the future, reframing America's value space with core beliefs that justify the reinvention of our democracy:

- You are not alone
- You can live with purpose through work, family, and community
- We are still a beacon on a hill
- We owe it to each other

The content of America's value space justifies and shapes the character of action. If we are not alone, all citizens will live in a society with a robust safety net, with ready access to health care and to a range of opportunities linking individuals with others in strong communities. Further, if Americans are to understand who we are as a people, we must possess ready access to cultural heritage, to the shared river of knowledge and memory that flows through families and communities. A life of purpose requires new attention to the restoration of meaning in work and a critical engagement with technology and the dangerous effects of the imposed efficiencies that define postindustrial capitalism. Purpose is also about values, personal responsibility, and the will to resist the allure of both consumerism and the endless distractions of modernity to bring intent to our links to family and friends. If America will again be a beacon on a hill, we must step back from permanent war, recapture the delicate balance that allowed the United States to be simultaneously inspiring, powerful, and nonthreatening, and restore the freedom and dignity that have been the hallmarks of our plural democracy here at home. We must repair things that have been broken and craft new policies that follow the arc of America's egalitarian dream.

A joke circulated in Russia late last century as the country transitioned away from state socialism toward an authoritarian version of a market economy: "Everything Marx said about communism was false," the one-liner went, "but unfortunately, everything he said about capitalism was true." And true here. Three decades ago, the ideology of the Right— small government, low taxes, reregulation, militarism—conquered and occupied America's value space. We came to assume that "companies would regulate themselves and be competently monitored for the public good. Nothing could have been further from the truth."[238] Today it's clear that David Scheffer's blunt assessment in the *Financial Times* is true: "Corporate self-regulation and public oversight have failed. We need to rethink how companies operate in a fragile world and how governments monitor them."[239]

But Americans have done more than simply acquiesce to market demands that regulation be reconfigured to favor corporations. We've not only lifted constraints on behavior in the financial sector, but America's legislators and courts have continually extended constitutional rights originally crafted to protect the interests of citizens to the inanimate, unfeeling, selfishly purposed corporation. Widespread confidence in markets and sycophantic reregulation of business unleashed every capitalist excess cited by Marx and some he couldn't have imagined. Gideon Rachman shorthanded the Reagan/Thatcher legacy this way: "privatisation, deregulation, tax-cutting, the abolition of exchange controls, an assault on the power of the trade unions, the celebration of wealth creation rather than wealth distribution."[240] After this past decade, we might add "continual war."

While what Marx said about capitalism was true, he went too far, not only in the dismal failure of communism but in the more pervasive and insidious Marxian idea of "economic man"—that human aspiration and accomplishment are exclusively shaped by evolving means of production. That argument has helped diminish the power of religion and culture, commoditized art, conflated success with wealth accumulation, and handed us the bleak discipline organized to observe behavior exclusively through the window of production and consumption: economics. The influence of economics in policy cannot be overestimated; it led Tony Judt to coin the term *economism*—"the invocation of economics in all discussions of public affairs." For Judt, economists are the enablers of market excess: "Behind every cynical (or merely incompetent) banking executive and trader sits an economist, assuring them (and us) from a position of unchallenged intellectual authority that their actions are publicly useful and should in any case not be subject to collective oversight."[241]

The discipline's unassailable standing within halls of power is remarkable. Economics has retained influence while proving time and again to be distinctly unhelpful. Not only were leading economists handmaidens and cheerleaders of America's recent financial misbehavior, but the practice remains, in reality, a numbers-crunching, predictive pastime that never quite manages sufficient warning when things are really turning bad. It is economics—macroeconomics in particular—that handed us the theories that markets are inherently efficient in allocating resources to the best destination and that pricing in the market is always rational because the market takes all information into account. But, as John Kay wrote, "The account of recent events given by proponents of these models was comprehensively false. They proclaimed stability where there was impending crisis, and market efficiency where there was gross asset mispricing."[242]

Policy actors are addicted to information that appears useful because it can be reduced to software-crunched numbers. It is a discouraging truth that the discipline of economics seems both undented and unbowed by the field's manifest failures of analysis and forecast over the past decade. But liberals must continue to dispute the assumed primacy of economics in public policy and note, among other things, that market capitalism is a *feature* of our democracy, not its essence. Capitalism is today the primary mode of production throughout the world, but frequently in settings—such as China, Russia, and Chile—where it has little connection with democracy. As Daniel Bell put it, "There is nothing that makes it theoretically or practically necessary for the two to be yoked."[243]

Unregulated corporations have directed earnings to the richest Americans. Between 2002 and 2007, 65 percent of all income growth went to 1 percent of the population; today, half of U.S. national income ends up in the hands of America's richest 10 percent. And these are not old-style profits from the sale of factory-produced goods. No, most of this wealth was generated by simply moving money around—buying and selling shares, reconfiguring financial instruments into mysterious bundles to be sold again and again at a profit. In fact, it's a sad truth that investment bankers and MBAs minted in the first decade of the twenty-first century have exhibited little interest in nuts-and-bolts business. It's no surprise that factories have emptied out. As Noam Scheiber wrote in *The New Republic*, "It's hard to believe that American manufacturing has a chance of recovering unless business schools start producing people who can run industrial companies, not just buy and sell their assets."[244]

As sky-high bonuses return to Wall Street, and as the financial establishment lobbies to blunt both the effects of Dodd-Frank regulation and specific features such as the Volcker Rule, designed to prevent excessive bank risk taking, confidence in the government's ability to rein in corporations erodes. Disparities in wealth and income are no longer mere features of healthy market competition but are instead viewed as symptoms of broad systemic failure within our democracy.

"Any inequality is corrosive if those with wealth are believed to have rigged the game rather than won in honest competition. As inequality rises, the sense that we are equal as citizens weakens."[245]

The marketplace has just laid an egg. We know the truth and know what must be done. Corporations are not people; they are not citizens. We must enact legislation to strip corporations of pseudocitizen constitutional rights, including First Amendment rights. We must retain current corporate tax rates while eliminating deductions and inducements to export labor and profits. We must prohibit banks from taking excessive risk with deposited funds. We must legislate an open Internet free of advertiser control. We must reverse privatization of public education and prisons. We must make the composition of bundled investment products more transparent. We must encourage labor organizations. We must assess the transforming effects of technology in the workplace, especially in such artisan careers as teaching, health care, law, and aviation. We must consider new laws defining the length of the workweek and the rights of employers to use smart phones and other digital devices to access workers outside the regular workday. We know what must be done but also understand that it won't be easy. As the important reforms of the Dodd-Frank bill began to kick in early in 2012, it became clear that Wall Street would do everything in its power to roll back restrictions on trading, disclosure, and the like.

We have just lived through the worst of what capitalism can deliver. We know it is time to reregulate markets to align business with public purposes. We must press forward through government, but business has so far offered nothing but determined resistance to all efforts to reconstitute a playing field that worked perfectly well before the 1980s.

As we have seen, the character of American politics has reconfigured the way government works. There is widespread dismay over Washington gridlock, the influence of special interests, the race-to-the-bottom, advertising-driven style of modern campaigns, but there is little agreement about what to do. We know that provisions of the Dodd-Frank Bill and reinstitution of the Volcker Rule will serve the public interest, but what will fix government?

There's wide agreement that money is the problem. Robert Reich, Clinton-era secretary of labor, is passionate: "Campaign contributions, fleets of well-paid lobbyists, and corporate-financed PR campaigns about public issues are overwhelming the capacities of legislatures, parliaments, regulatory agencies and international bodies to reflect the values of workers and citizens."[246]

Lawrence Lessig also believes it's all about money—that money has created a "normalized process" in which government itself has been transformed into "an engine of influence that seeks simply to make those most connected rich."[247] Lessig supports the ideas, and the presidential campaign, of former Louisiana governor Buddy Roemer, who through the primaries of 2012 committed to taking no more than $100 from anyone. (His campaign was not especially successful.) It feels as though Lessig has given up on the two-party system and conventional pathways to reform: campaign finance reform, restrictions on lobbyists, and so on. His assessment of money, power, and government is gloomy.

It's no surprise that Lessig's proposed solutions are dramatic, fanciful, and fraught with potential unintended consequences. Disappointed in the centrist, promarket, business-as-usual character of the Obama administration, he recommends nothing less than a reconfiguration of U.S. politics. For the Harvard prof, both Republicans and Democrats are beyond reform; only a new third party led by a (presumably charismatic) nonpolitician "supercandidate" will shake the corrupting influence of money out of the system. Lessig also proposes a constitutional convention to reform elections. But such an open-all-issues opportunity guarantees mischief; bring delegates together to reconfigure the Constitution to take lobbying in hand and you instead get the end of *Roe v. Wade,* a national ID card, and oil rigs in national parks. Our founding fathers relied on strong, widely shared enlightened ideas—a robust value space—when they forged the compromises enshrined in America's founding documents. In today's political environment, any attempted do-over is sure to end badly.

Tom Friedman and Michael Mandelbaum, in *That Used to Be Us: How America Fell Behind in the World It Invented and How We Can Come Back*, agree with Lessig. Wrapping up a trenchant discussion of our failure to engage the overarching issues of the twenty-first century—globalization, the IT revolution, government deficits, and energy demand—the public intellectual duet recommends a "shock therapy" that sounds familiar:

> The only way around all these ideological and structural obstacles is a third-party or independent candidate, who can not only articulate a hybrid politics that addresses our major challenges and restores our formula for success but—and it is a huge but—does this in a way that enough Americans find so compelling that they are willing to leave their respective Democratic and Republican camps and join hands in the radical center.[248]

A "huge but" indeed! Of course, there is little doubt that money, and the influence it can buy, helps submerge the public interest beneath mounds of legislation designed to do nothing but help technology companies, big-time farmers, defense companies, and nonprofit hospitals. And it's clear that our addled democracy has not been up to the task of taking on critical challenges that will shape our future. Money isn't the cause of bad policy, but it's a powerful accelerant; money makes systemic failure worse. But throwing out the bathwater and the baby, and dismantling the bathroom, is not the answer.

We can work with the tools we have. We can fix our ailing democracy by limiting the use of populist, direct-democracy tactics. Media must be reregulated to make it hard for single news outlets to pound away on the same ideological message day after day. We must demand that the use of polls be restricted to the few days before or after political events—the only period in which they are credible. And let's find a way to make campaigns less expensive. If we need less money in politics, money will have less meaning. It will be a tough fight against big media dependent on advertising bonanzas coming along every few years, but it will be worth the effort. As famed "vast wasteland" critic Newton Minow observed, "We are nearly alone in the democratic world in not providing our candidates with public-service television time."[249]

It will take serious rethinking and some heavy lifting to handmake our democracy, but it will be easier—and less dangerous—than putting our faith in the charm of a new third party or hoped-for communitarian outcomes in an entirely unpredictable twenty-first-century constitutional convention.

Technology

We can remake politics and the marketplace by rolling back Reagan-era probusiness antigovernment laxity. Technology is more difficult. Author Rebecca Solnit defines it this way: "A technology is a practice, a technique, or a device for altering the world or the experience of the world."[250] Today, digital technology is altering both experience and the world; it demands new thinking, a smart response. The Internet is alluring, accessible, and fun. But it is hardly benign. As media critic Douglas Rushkoff puts it, websites and social networks "have been constructed by people with real agendas. They want us to believe certain ideas, spend our money on certain things, and connect to other people in certain ways." For Rushkoff, we are no longer just watching a TV commercial; we're "living in a virtual one."[251]

By now it should be no surprise that I view the digital revolution with suspicion. It is not that technology is all bad, or that we can somehow step aside and return to a simpler, predigital age. Rather we have been too uncritical; too willing to accept the latest gadget, software, or online service without asking hard questions about the real cost, the true benefit, and the potential for unintended consequences that can make us not happier but more dependent, indebted, and miserable.

David Brooks, in his column "Cellphones, Texts, and Lovers," observes that online, "social scripts become obsolete." There's always another choice, and choice leads to "compartmentalization," "general disenchantment," an "attitude of contingency," and a "coat of ironic detachment."[252] Heather Havrilesky, in the online article "Digital Nation," is less cerebral but on point: "So the digital revolution led us all to this: a gigantic, commercial, high school reunion/mall filthy with insipid tabloid trivia, populated by perpetually distracted, texting, tweeting, demi-humans."[253]

We can argue about the good or bad effects of our new world of information and communication, but this much is true: The Internet environment is too commercialized, too superficial, and too caught up in gossip and games to function as an arena in which to craft a quality of life unburdened by the curse of consumerism. To the extent that the digital world is proffered as a replacement for real life, it is part of the same big lie that tells us that markets are trustworthy and our economy will soon get back to the delusional pseudoriches that collapsed housing and jobs.

Lurking beyond advertising and media hype, the truth of new technologies is that they benefit technology companies. The iPad 3 was introduced while I was sitting before my PC screen at work on this chapter. By the time *Handmaking America* is in hand, we'll have marched to the iPad 4. This is technology in service of consumerism, not quality of life. As Rushkoff points out, "The announcement of the next great 'iThing' provokes not eagerness but anxiety: Is this something else we will have to pay for and learn to use? Do we even have a choice?"[254] We have a choice, of course, but the power of advertising linked to the pronouncements of techno-pundits makes it hard to opt out of the newest device, the trendiest software, or the cloud.

Internet companies are also in it for profit, confirmed by the size of IPOs for Google, Facebook, and other online services. Google maintains a polished public image (books for everybody; "Don't Be Evil"). But in truth, as Net guru Siva Vaidhyanathan points out, "Once Google specialized in delivering information to satiate curiosity, now it does so to facilitate consumption. 'Search' as a general concept of intellectual query has mutated into a process of 'browsing' for goods and services."[255] In this sense, Google has extended the TV metaphor—it's there to place advertising in front of our rented eyeballs, albeit with prior knowledge of habits and interests unimaginable in the television age.

Lessig has reminded us that an old-time library or archive is almost entirely free of corporate intrusion: "The real-space library is a den protected from the metering of the market." Among other things, the library once offered a noncommercial commitment to content. "It was a way to assure that all of our culture was available and reachable—not just the part that happens to be profitable to stock." Today, the original artifact—book, film, photograph—has become disposable while its digital shadow is packaged, priced, and rented. "We're collectively engaged in a mass conversion of what we used to call, variously, records, accounts, entries, archives, registers, collections, keepsakes, catalogs, testimonies and memories into, simply, data."[256]

And because data can be combined, analyzed, crunched, and reconfigured, it has value to the companies that harvest it. Google lives to sell information about you to advertisers. Facebook goes further: Your personal contacts, ambitions, likes, and dislikes sustain the company's business model. Yes, much of this is free, but remember, if you're not paying for a service or product, *the product is you*. From online bullying to not-quite-surgical drone attacks in Pakistan, technology is empowering behaviors with profound ethical and moral implications, concerns that we are only beginning to address.

Education

Back in the early sixties, when I entered the University of Michigan on an ROTC scholarship, the navy required midshipmen to pursue an engineering curriculum. So I struggled with chemistry, physics, and especially first-year calculus. Facing failure in my second attempt at the course, I threw myself on the mercy of my math TA, Mr. Kaczynski. "I'll let you out with a D, Mr. Ivey," the future Unabomber said, "if you promise to never take another math class." To this day, I've kept that promise and have been just fine.

Few public policy issues have attracted more comment, more expert opinion, and more opinionated argument over the past decade than has American education. By consensus, we need more math, better reading, and more science—something like a good-for-all rendition of the navy's engineering courses. It's striking that so many thought leaders—most of them schooled in social science and the humanities—confidently assert that what America needs are mathematicians and engineers nurtured in schools that produce expert test takers. Joe Scarborough, facilitating an ongoing *Morning Joe* conversation about American education on MSNBC, argues for more math while disclaiming, "I'm liberal arts, all the way."[257] Tom Brokaw writes in *The Time of Our Lives*, "Fundamental math skills will be required at all levels of society." Two pages later he's just as firm: "When I encountered advanced algebra and trigonometry, I knew my future would be more rewarding with words and political events than with x, y, and cosines."[258] I had the same epiphany when I was off-hooked by the then-kindly Ted Kacyznski. But this doublethink—smart, humanities-trained public intellectuals shilling for mechanistic math training—is a striking and unhelpful feature of our current education debate.

As I thought about an America handmade—about work, government, consumerism, and personal responsibility—I returned again and again to what we teach our young people. Are we teaching them how best to live, how to make our democracy whole, how to connect with family and community? Or are we just teaching them how to work?

Proposed reforms have dodged these big questions. We've dug into process—standardized tests, class size, preapproved lesson plans, peer review—not substance. There's not very much talk about what is being taught. In fact, the belief that a focus on science, math, and reading skills will reboot our economy, spur innovation, and maintain America's position as world leader is expressed again and again, even by those leaders whose experience, like mine, hints at a different path.

What do Americans need to know? For the Dreyfuss Institute, it is "knowledge of, and effective use of, the tools of political power, of how to maintain and comprehend this democracy."[259] This is not math and science but fresh emphasis on civics featuring educational objectives more attuned to the demands of citizenship than the needs of our market economy. Martha Nussbaum—one of the few critics dedicated to learning in the humanities—is more expansive: We need to cultivate the kind of student who can become "an active, critical, reflective, and empathetic member of a community of equals, capable of exchanging ideas on the basis of respect and understanding with people from many different backgrounds."[260]

Americans need knowledge and skills that enhance citizenship and enable critical pushback against the allure of advertising and the demagogic projections of political power that have come to influence our very souls. And we need learning that advances quality of life by providing the tools of personal creative practice—music, writing, dance. We need to be educated to engage the world with competence and enthusiasm, armed with knowledge to encourage smart choices and empathy for those of different backgrounds, and the ability to sense when somebody is trying to sell us a bill of goods.

Even for those who do become scientists, mathematicians, or engineers, mere to-the-test technical knowledge won't be enough. As Lawrence Summers wrote in a *New York Times* "Education Life" supplement, today's student must know how to process and use information, work in collaboration with others, and analyze data "beyond simple reflection,"[261] exhibiting a cosmopolitan capacity to engage the outside world. And education is also about values. David Brooks has written about the need for "emotional education" advanced through an "emotional curriculum." The goal is what British literary critic Terry Eagleton calls "a robust sense of selfhood."[262] Again quoting Martha Nussbaum, we need "complete citizens who can think for themselves, criticize tradition, and understand the significance of another person's suffering and achievements."[263]

Math and science won't get us there. In fact, by itself, that kind of learning won't get us much of anywhere. Even if we accept the dubious proposition that education is about jobs and the needs of American business, "innovation," as John Kay put it, "is not about wearing a white coat." Instead, it is "understanding the needs of customers."[264] Remember, Steve Jobs failed as a computer technician; he succeeded because he understood how to use integrated design to create irresistible products that no one knew they needed. Jobs was an edgy perfectionist and a driven leader who dropped out of college, ingested considerable quantities of LSD, and pursued Eastern religion. If the American economy needs more of Jobs's brand of innovation, we're not going to see it in the products of standardized math and reading tests.

But business keeps trying to narrow content and privatize process. Those much-argued-over standardized tests are nothing except a market-comforting version of Taylor's old-time scientific management—standardization, measurements, discipline, customer satisfaction—enshrined in America's schools. In fact, regimented classrooms, administrative oversight, and numbers-based teacher rankings have a connect-the-dots political relationship to the push for charter schools, the sudden boom in for-profit colleges, and relentless Republican-led assaults on unions. What is astonishing is not that our entire public education system is being corporatized—that's par for the course in the "let's shrink government" era. The surprise is not the flaccid character of resistance but that progressives have far too frequently become cheer-leaders for a brand of reform that is nothing less than a market-driven transformation of education and our realm of public goods. Think of charter schools as a single, small example. Diane Ravitch couldn't have put it better: "For years, right-wing critics demanded vouchers and got nowhere." Now their attacks on public schools and support for private schools funded with public money "have become the received wisdom among liberal elites."[265]

The spread of technology into the classroom symbolizes the corpo-ratization of contemporary American education. In schools, computers promise to revolutionize learning, but there exists little evidence that knowledge on a screen, or information reconfigured as a digital game, affects the quality of education. The push to computerize the classroom is driven not by teachers but by "silicon valley titans and White House appointees."[266] There exists little proof that computers help, but the pres-sure to upgrade first and ask questions later is nearly irresistible. In 1997 President Clinton's science and technology committee issued a final report acknowledging that "research on technology's impact was inadequate" but saying that computers should be brought into teaching anyway.

Nothing has changed. In the fall of 2011, the Department of Edu-cation launched the Digital Promise initiative. "Championed by a coalition of educators and business leaders, Digital Promise will . . . help spur breakthrough learning technologies." Digital Promise will also circumvent "an outdated procurement system" in which start-ups find it "tough to prove that their services can deliver meaning-ful results." Digital Promise will instead foster "smart demand," and "new approaches for rapidly evaluating new products."[267] A between-the-lines read is easy: We're going to ignore the plodding process by which educational innovation is assessed and rush headlong into a market-driven, politician-enabled mass installation of computers in classrooms. But as Matt Richtel wrote in *The New York Times* in late 2011, "Schools are spending billions on technology even as they cut budgets and lay off teachers, with little proof that this approach is improving basic learning."[268]

What can we do? Let's begin by agreeing that the first responsibility of public education is to nurture informed citizens. The new civics proposed by the Dreyfuss Initiative is on the right track, but we must do more. Young Americans must acquire the skills necessary to interpret and at times deflect advertising. They must understand the difference between a fact-based policy argument and a politician's appeal to fear, anger, or suspicion. Students must learn that even something free and fun still comes with a price. Again, if an Internet search or online social connection costs nothing, then *you* are the product, and technology will mine and sell the deepest recesses of your private life. Citizens must have a basic understanding of the world and a capacity to engage difference in language and culture without automatically relying on stereotypes and prejudice. This requires a fresh commitment to humanities disciplines such as history, folklore, and literature. It demands that we provide young people with enough insight into their own passions and motives—basic psychology—to parse the strategies of advertisers and political manipulators. And we need to import useful practices evolved within the world's religions—practices that foster community, respect, contemplation, and ethical behavior. Schools used to provide this kind of education. E.D. Hirsch, writing in the *New York Review of Books*, observes that schools had a communitarian character until the 1950s. They were "institutions for inculcating democracy, designed to develop critical thinkers and able citizens in a setting of loyalty to the national common good."[269]

But there is no evidence that American employers want this kind of education or that the marketplace would value workers armed with the skills required to critique the demeaning character of the computerized white-collar cubicle or to discern the manipulative essence of an ad that equates freedom and a credit card spree.

We shouldn't be surprised that learning even at the highest levels has been reconfigured as job preparation and that classrooms increasingly resemble modern cubicle offices, with students silently staring at computer screens and teachers, like industrial supervisors, off to the side. Yes, the marketplace wants us to handle numbers and wants us to read enough to carry out our increasingly routine jobs, but that's where it stops. Garret Keizer, teaching low-income kids, was blunt. He told his students that "they were living in a society that value[s] people of their age, region, and class primarily as cannon fodder, cheap labor, and gullible consumers, and that education could give them some of the weapons necessary to fight back."[270] Keizer is right, but he meant a *real* education: critical thinking, politics, writing skills, historical perspective.

Every high school graduate needs to know how the digital world sells us things, how government shades the truth to stir support for sometimes dubious policies, and how impulse can create burdensome future obligation. Students need to know what the Koran and the Bible are about and where the nations of the Middle East can be found on a map or globe. They need to acquire a sense of courtesy, good manners, and self-discipline. Young people must begin to associate self-esteem with achievement and must understand that success requires resilience and determination: a kind of grit. "We should prepare youth to anticipate failures and misfortunes and point out that excellence in any discipline requires years and years of time on task."[271] Kids must ingest a reasonable measure of pessimism tied to the truth that quite often life doesn't work out as we wish. Learning of this kind requires a measure of the Socratic method—ideas challenged in open discussion. As Martha Nussbaum puts it, this kind of education, led by an "artisan teacher," can "produce a certain type of citizen: active, critical, curious, capable of resisting authority and peer pressure."[272] It is not available on a screen, and it's not only about jobs.

About one-third of adult Americans have been to college. That percentage will rise over the next decade, but our high schools are still producing millions of students who, for one reason or another, won't go further. Once good teaching assures that they're equipped to navigate citizenship and the economy, what else must these young citizens know?

Conventional wisdom has pointed toward skills that feed the digital world—computer programming, data management, IT services. But such jobs are risky; among other problems, they're as exportable as call processing centers. Instead we need advanced education that features "occupational certificates and other non-degree-based programs that prepare students for 'middle school' jobs—electricians, police officers, construction managers, health-care workers—jobs that are difficult or impossible to outsource."[273] The service economy, although plagued by low wages, also remains a source of jobs that can't be outsourced to India. In 2010 the Bureau of Labor Statistics forecasted, "Of the 30 jobs projected to grow at the fastest rate over the next decade in the United States, only seven typically require a bachelor's degree." And many of these jobs—framing carpentry, installation plumbing, mechanical repair of all kinds—preserve the kind of handmade artisan skillset that is everywhere threatened by technology and the organizational practices of postindustrial capitalism.

It's important to get this balance right. We need college graduates, of course, but popping out college graduates in excess of market demand simply creates a cohort of low-paid, well-educated workers. Matt Crawford, writing about the virtues of handwork, notes that once he had acquired a master's degree, he couldn't go back to his good-paying but blue-collar job as an installation electrician.

I promised to be practical. Here's the trade-off: If schools are going to offer a new kind of nonexportable vocational education, and if all young people will benefit from a reinvented civics curriculum that will equip them to craft good lives as engaged citizens, smart consumers, and dedicated community leaders, what will we drop from the curriculum? Well, math and science, of course. Not *all* math and science. We must service the passionate and capable few who really will turn into the inventors, lab researchers, and brain scientists of the future. But for most of us, we know what we need to know—how things work in the world; how to figure square footage, tips in restaurants, speed, distance, and mileage. Figuring percentages is critical, with an understanding of relative risk (a 50 percent increase in your chance of contracting flu does not mean that half the population will get sick), along with the ability to do basic addition, subtraction, and multiplication in your head (just in case you're without a device). By shortening up on the semesters dedicated to math and science, we can add the classes essential to citizenship and quality of life.

Expressive Life

The most radical idea in *Handmaking America* is a four-day workweek. In one sense I'm surrendering to the power of our technology-empowered Industrial Revolution 2.0; we will not reinvent our modern workplace as a space of accomplishment and satisfaction. On the other hand, I am optimistic that given the right opportunities and more time, our democratic vision of a good society—connected, rewarding, inspired, caring—can be realized. I am a cautious capitalist. Capitalism has done much good. It has afforded multiple societies, and millions of individuals, the opportunity to secure their stability and well-being. Markets have outperformed all attempts at centralized economic planning and have enabled third world nations to lift multitudes from grinding poverty. But unfettered capitalism tilts toward greed, inequality, and uncertainty. As the *Financial Times* editorial board opined in early 2012, "The excesses that drove the bubble and the breakdown that followed happened because leaders forgot that free enterprise requires rules. . . . Good ground rules are a public good; as such they are the responsibility of states."[274]

What can replace the hegemony of economic man and the resultant reconfiguration of quality of life into nothing more than material well-being? I think a communitarian vision—"a deeper and thicker involvement with the other"[275]—offers one alternative to the isolation of our envious consumer society. And we should also speak of "cultural vitality" as a public good—the notion that knowledge, art, and the capacity to engage creative practice, politics, and the world of ideas can provide a place where citizens can flourish through the pursuit of happiness and meaning.

But even if we can recalibrate education, politics, and the workplace to regain what has been lost, what do we want in the place of a society that has been allowed to corrode? How can we think about quality of life as something more than material well-being? Is there a way of advancing toward a happy, fulfilled society without endlessly pursuing the chimeric quest for validation through wealth?

The arts and crafts movement was led by a loose aggregation of nineteenth-century public intellectuals. The movement named itself in 1887, in "response to a century of unprecedented social and economic upheaval." Arts and crafts thinkers "tried to ameliorate conditions at the end of a century characterized by a dramatically accelerated rate of change."[276] Their ideas would inspire political action in England and Russia, some of it reformist, some of it sensational, revolutionary, and repressive. For Americans the movement was different—diffuse and not especially political. Hull House and other settlement houses worked with European newcomers to preserve their folk practices while at the same time introducing them to employment in modern factories. Utopian communities such as Ruskin, Tennessee, tried to put arts and crafts values into work, buildings, and civil society. But when Americans hear the term *arts and crafts,* we immediately think of dark-stained oaken

Stickley furniture or low-profile houses that blend into surrounding natural landscapes, not much more. However, even without an organized political or social movement, arts and crafts thinking produced profound and lasting effects in the American scene. The virtues of a vigorous, outdoor, physically energetic life; the value of an annual vacation in a remote natural setting; our regard for the family farm, small-town America, and gardening can all be traced to arts and crafts enthusiasm for a preindustrial life.

When we hang an Indian rug on the wall, reject the mass-produced product in favor of the lathe-turned bowl, admire a log cabin, or insist, against all practicality, that our suburban home must feature a (gas-powered) fireplace at its center, we are acting out an antimodernist vision. Antiques, homemade wine, the garage workshop, national parks, African folksongs around the campfire—all constitute exotic, slightly nostalgic tributes to our arts and crafts heritage. When the family gathers for a meal around a table, cell phones off, tablets set aside, we are seeking new meaning by replacing speed and complexity with old-fashioned directness. When we honor wood over plastic, rough-hewn more than factory-smooth, and we value labor in the pasture over work in a cubicle, we are channeling the old-time intellectuals who first questioned the social impact of capitalism and industrialization on society. While the legacy of arts and crafts thinking in the United States has not been especially political, it is pervasive. By embracing the lifestyles advocated by nineteenth-century antimodernists, we affirm that their concerns and values remain important today.

John Ruskin, founding father of what became the arts and crafts movement, advanced craftsmanship as a metaphor for a way of life devoted to community, tradition, and family—the handmade and homegrown. He was devoted to the idea that a craft-work engagement with life could introduce essential freedom and autonomy that was threatened by industrial production. Richard Sennett describes the dream this way:

> Ruskin sought to instill in craftsmen of all sorts the desire, indeed the demand, for a lost space of freedom; it would be a free space in which people can experiment, a supportive space in which they could at least temporarily lose control. *This is a condition for which people will have to fight in modern society.*[277] (my italics)

What must we do to be an artisan, a metaphorical craft worker capable of building a high quality of life in our postconsumerist democracy? Progressives are the legitimate heirs of the arts and crafts movement. If social democrats will deploy public policy to take back time, how will we fill the hours?

Consider "expressive life."

I started using the phrase five or six years ago, when I was working on a book about the U.S. arts scene and needed language unburdened by the assumptions and preconceptions that undermine *culture,* a term that, in its multiple meanings, was damaged goods. What ingredients comprise expressive life? How do they connect? Can expressive life be the place where Americans can craft our postconsumerist democracy, living with purpose?

The term had the virtue of being fresh—unburdened by the muddled preconceptions and hierarchical assumptions that have made discussions of creativity, artistry, culture, and entertainment enormously difficult. I tried to consider expressive life as a basic and essential component of the everyday—like "work life" or "family life." In that sense we could talk about the expressive life of an individual or a family, of a community, or even of a region or a nation. Is our expressive life vibrant or dull? Is it there for all to experience or restricted to a few? Is the policy frame that surrounds expressive life open and free of constraint, or is the landscape littered with toll booths and gatekeepers?

I divided expressive life into two components: *heritage* and *voice*. Heritage is history, community, family, and tradition; it is religious faith, neighborhoods, and the multiple connections to the present and past that give us a sense of belonging, an understanding of who we are. Voice, on the other hand, is who we are alone. What are our dreams and talents? What do we bring to politics, to community, and how do our feelings and insights find their way to the larger world? If heritage is about the comfort of belonging, voice is about adventure and the unknown. Others have observed the expressive life tension. David Brooks, in his incisive and funny *New Yorker* essay "Social Animal," argues that two sides of the debate about "what makes us happy" can be represented by Jack Kerouac's novel *On the Road* and the movie *It's a Wonderful Life*. As Brooks sees it, "the former celebrates the life of freedom and adventure. The latter celebrates roots and connectedness."[278] His distinction is exactly right. Every American (and all people) must continually choose between activities and engagements that connect them with family and community and those that enable them to "go inside," digging into personal expression, individual creativity, and idiosyncrasies.

Brooks nails the continual tension between community and autonomy in American life, but he jumps to the wrong conclusion. Brooks slides all his chips over to one side of the table: "What the inner mind really wants is connection."[279] But it's not either/or, family and home versus the wild frontier; it's both. For while connection, with its associated sensations of security, belonging, and continuity, is critical to human happiness and quality of life, independence and a sense individual meaning are just as important.

After all, community and connectedness can be overdone. Philosopher Anthony Appiah and others argue that the gravitational weight of belonging inherent in strong communities constitutes an anchor weighing down individual human development in an era in which our challenge is to craft a life on a flattened global stage.[281] There is something to this argument; the notion that one should be primarily defined as a Jew, a New Yorker, a Navajo, or a university professor can be profoundly limiting. In fact, Eastern religions—the ones that honor meditation and the monastic life—can be understood in part as responses to the overly constraining linkages that envelope individuals in family and community in India, China, and Japan.

It's all about balance. A vibrant expressive life *can* be a key to happiness and purpose in our post-consumerist democracy, but only if citizens have access to both the connective tissue of tradition and spiritual practice and the tools of political engagement and personal creativity. This is important because a balanced expressive life grounds America's sense of well-being in something more fundamental and affordable than envy-induced spending.

In his final book, Tony Judt observes that "democracies corrode quite fast. . . . They corrode because most people don't care very much about them."[282] While we must concern ourselves with policy, we must begin by taking care of our value space—the "American Idea."

Egalitarianism reflected in a reasonable standard of material well-being for all citizens is an important hallmark of America's democracy. If our vision for a progressive future asserts that "You are not alone" and that "We owe it to each other," America must maintain an active government, one that uses the collective power of legislation and regulation to secure public purposes—strengthening communities, reshaping education and work, reining in markets, while making certain that what is done in the name of the American people provides avenues to a high quality of life through initiatives that are aligned with humane democratic principles. If Americans will not be abandoned and lonely, we must tax ourselves, not grudgingly but in the spirit of mutual endeavor and shared accomplishment. If we are to live with purpose and meaning, we must reinvent education and work to restore pathways to achievement and autonomy. We must steer technology so it serves our vision of the future, not reshape ourselves to fit the demands of advertisers and machines. We must crack open the vaults that hold our cultural heritage and make real-world knowledge and an understanding of democracy a part of every citizen's tool kit.

If we want the smartest, most adept, most inspiring teachers to lead our classrooms, we must abandon the teach-to-the-test (or teach-to-the-machine) mentality that ignores the experiences that nurture "the rich underwater world where character is formed and wisdom grows."[282] This means walking away from No Child Left Behind and its progeny. It means putting art, civics, home economics, and, yes, a modern rendition of vocational training back into schools. If we want our young people to be inventive and adventurous—open to risk and adaptable to change—we must free them up to outdoor play. We must resist the temptation to exert control, to protect, to manage them.

In the same vein, we must expose the doublethink that enables us to assume that new technologies present pathways to saving time and enhancing quality of life when all they do is expand the workday. A Blackberry signal that interrupts a family meal or an iPad that lets you work on the beach while on vacation is not improving things. If corporate profits rise on the backs of ever-more-productive labor, remember that's at least partly because the iPhone and netbook have blown up the forty-hour workweek to something that resembles 24/7.

Although the Internet had its day as a free and open wild frontier, it is best understood today as something just like television—a powerful system dedicated to extending the reach of advertising into ever-growing chunks of everyday life. Work once done in a library is now completed with a few clicks of a Google/Wikipedia search. But there were no ads in the library, and even the ads in a newspaper or magazine lacked the power to jump up uninvited to fill up the space between our eyes and the printed page.

In addition to harboring an unshakable belief that America is somehow always "just fine," we maintain a sunny confidence in the idea of progress. Change is good, and change often arrives in the form of new consumer products, especially new gadgets that advertisers and cheerleading techno-pundits remind us are essential to a sense of personal satisfaction. Like American exceptionalism, these commonplace assumptions exert everyday influence powerful enough to keep even the truth from getting in.

The American Idea: Handmade

Where do we look to find the real America? Where is the uncorrupted value space immune from the corrosive power of carelessly deployed technology, wealth, and commerce? Can we come together to find a pathway to a stronger citizenry, a more-meaningful workplace, a functioning representative government? Tom Brokaw put the question this way: "What happened to the America I thought I knew? Have we simply wandered off course, but only temporarily? Or have we allowed ourselves to be so divided that we're easy prey for hijackers who could steer us onto a path to a crash landing?"[283]

In 2002, 60 percent of Americans believed that "our culture is superior to others." By 2011 that percentage had declined by more than 10 percent. As Tom Friedman and Michael Mandelbaum put it in *That Used to Be Us*, "America's exceptionalism is now in play. It is not an entitlement. It is not a defined benefit."[284] For Gideon Rachman, "The endless politicking in Washington reflects a certain complacency—a belief that America's position as number one is so impregnable that it can afford self-indulgent episodes such as the summer's [2011] near-debt default."[285]

"We want to be No. 1—but why, and at what?"[286]

Despite the disastrous failure of the right-wing assault on the American Idea, the 2012 Republican primary campaigns remind us that the lonely, every-woman-for-herself distortion of American values remains conventional wisdom. So our new path will not feel easy, especially at first, but change is critical—not only here but around the world. After all, America's position as an inspiration to the world can be sustained only if we are just, open, and fair at home. Zbigniew Brzezinski is clear:

> The continual attraction of the American system—the vital relevance of its founding principles, the dynamism of its economic model, the good will of its people and government—is . . . essential if America is to continue playing a constructive global role. Only by demonstrating the capacity for a superior performance of its societal system can America restore its historical momentum.[287]

President Bill Clinton, in an interview conducted while he campaigned for Democratic candidates in the run-up to the 2010 midterm elections, observed that Americans have trouble absorbing information that runs contrary to our embedded mythology. He said something like this: "We believe that America is exceptional—and we *are* a unique country—but that belief prevents negative truths from getting in. Our rate of poverty, infant mortality, the dramatic disparity of wealth between the richest among us and average citizens; the belief that we are special just keeps these ideas out of the conversation." I recall Clinton's clear, well-spoken, off-the-cuff political observations; he was right again. Our assumptions about the quality of health care, the talent of America's workforce, the capacity of our education system, and the reasonableness of the invasive presence of U.S. military forces around the world are all wrapped in a protective coating of American exceptionalism sturdy enough to deflect hard evidence that our society is not what it could or should be.

Is America's character manifest in the world only through wealth accumulation and the projection of military might? I don't think so. I had a surprising encounter with the real America last summer while rushing through Nashville's airport toward my flight to Washington. Coming toward me was a young couple—happy, hand in hand. Maybe married; clearly in love. I didn't look for rings. Instead, my gaze settled on the high-tech artificial limbs that extended to the concourse carpet from their shorts. They each had one—a left and a right—and it took little imagination to invent a story of love blossoming in a post-Iraq rehab facility.

What impressed me most was the forthright acceptance of disability and the ease with which the aluminum-and-steel substitute for flesh and bone was displayed and accepted. Through most of history, and today almost anywhere else, damaged bodies are hidden, and if a flaw becomes apparent, it is stigmatizing. America is more generous to our veterans than at times in the past; that's part of the reason there's no need to hide the lasting effects of a permanent wound.

But I give more credit to the Americans with Disabilities Act. This law, passed in 1990, forces schools, offices, shopping centers, and factories to accommodate the physical and mental impairments that challenge millions of Americans. Over the decades, mainstreamed disabilities have been drained of their ability to shock or disturb. This fact should be a source of great pride for Americans. And it is something we accomplished together, by empowering government to act on behalf of all of us to make damaged lives a richer part of the American experience. Rest assured that even given a thousand years, a deregulated marketplace would never have taken up the challenge of integrating disabilities into society. Only government, through law and regulation, could accomplish this important task.

In the spring of 2012, Ezra Klein published a smart piece in the *New Yorker*. In "The Unpersuaded," Klein argued that presidential speeches had no measureable effect on policy making. "Whether an Oval Office address on a single topic, or a monumental State of the Union, speeches don't move the needle when it comes to public policy, or public opinion. In fact, Presidential persuasion might actually have an anti-persuasive effect on the opposing party in Congress."[288] But are presidential speeches really about persuasion, or about inspiration and vision? Should we assess presidential communication on the basis of legislation, policy change, or quickly polled public opinion, or on how remarks fill, enhance, or inform our value space? When John Kennedy challenged us to "ask what you can do for your country," or when Dwight Eisenhower warned of a threatening military-industrial complex, were they seeking to persuade us to do something, or were they serving the underlying framework of ideas and insight that justifies law and regulation? Klein's conclusion—true as far as it goes—is merely evidence that presidential speeches have been taken down from their lofty perch of inspiration and deep meaning, transformed into mere arguments for one piece of legislation or another. Yes, our value space *has* emptied out.

Thomas Frank—the brilliant journalist and historian who wrote *What's the Matter with Kansas?*—is discouraged. Having stared hard into the barrel of the Right's messaging cannon, he's beginning to rethink the very character of our American idea. In a wan *Harper's* essay, he speculates that the arc of American progress may be an illusion. Perhaps the era of political inclusiveness, public interest regulation, and concern for the social safety net bracketed by the Great Depression and the Great Society were a temporary digression from the real American dream:

> Maybe the New Deal and its various reforms—a boring financial establishment, a secure retirement, a boring middle class—were . . . an exception to the rules of American history, instead of the norm they once appeared to be.[289]

Far from constituting America's overarching metaphor, our tilt toward an increasingly egalitarian society might have been nothing more than "a short-lived attempt by average people to defy the stern moral narratives of economic orthodoxy."[290] There's ample evidence to justify Frank's concern. The Right and the Republican Party have engaged in an ironic last-stage effort to remake our economy, politics, and social norms, doing their level best to drive down the most meaningful legacies of the New Deal, the Great Society, women's rights, the Environmental Protection Agency, and the Voting Rights Act. Congress has moved beyond debt reduction to debate contraception. The presumptive 2012 Republican candidate has promised to end funding for both Planned Parenthood and the National Endowment for the Arts. The Republican legislature in my home state, Tennessee, has cranked out bills allowing guns in workplace parking lots and on university campuses, menacing immigrants, and specifying how clothing must be displayed in schools, while at the same time empowering teachers to bring unscientific, religious-based theories into biology classrooms. One bill would have made it illegal to say the word *gay* in elementary school. And Tennessee, like dozens of other states, has enacted a voter ID law—a response to a nonexistent offense that by coincidence effectively suppresses Democratic votes.

This spasm of right-wing policy and political argument feels more like the death throes of a dying era than what Thomas Frank fears, a return to some dog-eat-dog, minimal-government American norm. Instead, the Right has, in show business terminology, "jumped the shark,"[291] going over the top in a doubled-down effort to recover from abject failure.

But Frank's alarm must be taken seriously. He understands that despite its failures, the Right remains poised to slide its small-government, big-defense, underregulated dream back into America's value space. We can't let that happen. They have held the ball for more than thirty years. They've fumbled, and now it's time for us to take it back.

The America we thought we knew is still in place. It's just a little hard to see. There's good reason for our discomfort; we're in the midst of a transition driven by technology and market forces every bit as profound as the global nineteenth-century Industrial Revolution. Wealth, debt, consumerism, and unhinged government have distracted and diverted us from our society's true nature. We must look to the edges of our daily lives for evidence that we remain a nation of "liberty and justice for all." The opportunity and responsibility are ours. If progressives can replenish the American Idea by advancing core values, challenging and overturning the false promises of the past thirty years, and crafting policies that can encourage a high quality of life tailored to the challenges of a still-new century, our nation will continue to lead the world.

I began my argument by quoting the final lines of a presidential Oval Office address. I was moved to write this book because the president's words told me something was wrong: Today our liberal vision lacks both destination and a way forward. Progressives have given up the fight in America's value space. It seems that even our most observant liberal commentators have surrendered. But we've seen we can do better. Let's return to the president's remarks and tweak them just a bit to *really* tell the American people where we are going and how we want to get there. At the conclusion of his first Oval Office speech, as an oil spill disaster was spreading across the Gulf of Mexico, President Obama could have said this:

> What has defined us as a nation since our founding is the capacity to shape our destiny—our determination to fight for the America we want for our children. America must be a nation in which every citizen can live with purpose through work, family, and community; where the elderly, helpless, and fearful are not alone; a society that stands proudly to the world as a beacon on a hill. This is where we are going and our government—your elected leaders—can help find the way. We will achieve this dream because as citizens of the greatest democracy in the world, we owe it to each other.

NOTES

1. Barack Obama, "Remarks by the President to the Nation on the BP Oil Spill," The White House, 6/15/2010, www.whitehouse.gov/the-press -office/remarks-president-nation-bp-oil-spill.
2. Peter Baker, "The Vision Thing," *The New York Times*, 4/10/2011, http://query.nytimes.com/gst/fullpage.html?res=9C06e1DC1039F933 A25757C0A9679D8B63&pagewanted=all.
3. Drew Westen, "What Happened to Obama," *The New York Times*, 8/7/2011, SR 1, 6–7, www.nytimes.com/2011/08/07/opinion/sunday/ what-happened-to-obamas-passion.html?pagewanted=all.
4. Jack Hitt, "This Party Sucks," *This American Life*, October 29, 2010.
5. Stanley B. Greenberg, "Why Voters Tune Out Democrats," *The New York Times*, 7/30/2011, www.nytimes.com/2011/07/31/opinion/ sunday/tuning-out-the-democrats.html?_r=1.
6. Tony Judt, *Ill Fares the Land* (New York: Penguin Press, 2010), 179.
7. George Soros, "My Philanthropy," *New York Review of Books*, June 23, 2011, www.nybooks.com/articles/archives/2011/jun/23/ my-philanthropy/?pagination=false.
8. E.J. Dionne Jr., "Why the Democrats Are Losing," *Truthdig*,

2/17/2010, www.truthdig.com/report/item/why_the_democrats _are_losing_20100217/.

9. Paul Krugman and Robin Wells, "Where Do We Go from Here?" *New York Review of Books*, 12/16/2010, www.nybooks.com/articles/ archives/2011/jan/13/where-do-we-go-here/?pagination=false.

10. John Plender, "Capitalism in Crisis: The Code That Forms a Bar to Harmony," *Financial Times*, January 2012, www.ft.com/intl/cms/s/0/ fb95b4fe-3863-11e1-9d07-00144feabdc0.html#axzz1kaFxtyem.

11. Lawrence Summers, "Current Woes Call for Smart Reinvention Not Destruction," *Financial Times*, www.ft.com/intl/cms/s/2/f6e8a7c 4-3857-11e1-9f07-00144feabdc0.html#axzz1kaFxtyem.

12. Chris Matthews, *Morning Joe*, MSNBC, 1/11/2012.

13. Martin Wolf, "The Big Questions Raised by Anti-Capitalist Protests," *Financial Times*, 10/27/2011, www.ft.com/intl/cms/s/0/86d8634a-ff 34-11e0-9769-00144feabdc0.html#axzz1kaFxtyem.

14. Jeffrey Sachs, "Time to Plan for Post-Keynesian Era," *Financial Times*, 6/7/2010, www.ft.com/intl/cms/s/0/e7909286-726b-11df-9f8 2-00144feabdc0.html#axzz1kaFxtyem.

15. *Handmaking America* draws inspiration from Arts & Crafts thinkers of the 19th century, but it is neither a history nor a critique of this diffuse and consequential movement. For more on Arts & Crafts in Europe and especially the US, see T.J. Jackson Lears *No Place of Grace*, or Wendy Kaplan's two collections of essays accompanying exhibitions of Arts & Crafts interior decoration, furniture, textiles, ceramics and glassware, *The Arts & Crafts Movement in Europe & America*, and *"The Art that is Life": The Arts & Crafts Movement in America, 1875–1920*.

16. Greenberg, "Why Voters Tune Out Democrats."

17. Richard Wilkinson and Kate Pickett, *The Spirit Level* (New York: Bloomsbury, 2009), 4.

18. "Harper's Index," *Harper's Magazine*, December, 2011, p. 15.

19. April, 2009 Pew Poll, cited in, Lubrano, Alfred, "Americans blame

poor in hard times." *The Philadelphia Inquirer*, published in *The Tennessean*, p. 8a, 2/28/10.

20. Al Gore, "We Can't Wish Away Climate Change," *The New York Times*, 2/27/2010, www.nytimes.com/2010/02/28/opinion/28gore. html?pagewanted=3&sq=al%20gore&st=cse&scp=2.

21. Richard White, *Railroaded: The Transcontinentals and the Making of Modern America* (New York: W.W. Norton, 2011), 516.

22. Virginia Heffernan, "The Old Internet Neighborhoods," *The New York Times*, 6/10/2011, www.nytimes.com/2010/02/28/opinion/28gore. html?pagewanted=3&sq=al%20gore&st=cse&scp=2.

23. Matt Crawford, *Shop Class as Soulcraft: An Inquiry into the Value of Work* (New York: Penguin, 2010), 12.

24. www.thedreyfussinitiative.org/index.php.

25. Matt Bai, "The Brain Mistrust," *New York Times Magazine*, 2/18/2010, www.nytimes.com/2010/02/21/magazine/21fob-wwln-t.html.

26. Judt, *Ill Fares the Land*, 183.

27. Jeff Madrick, *Age of Greed* (Toronto: Alfred A. Knopf, 2007), 124.

28. Tyler Cowan, "Innovation Is Doing Very Little for Incomes," *The New York Times*, 1/29/2011, www.nytimes.com/2011/01/30/business/30view.html.

29. Frank Rich, "In Praise of Extremism," 9/25/2011, http://nymag.com/news/frank-rich/bipartisanship-2011-10/.

30. Madrick, *Age of Greed*, 175.

31. George Soros, *My Philanthropy* (New York: Open Society Foundations, 2011), 54.

32. Gore, "We Can't Wish Away Climate Change."

33. Judt, *Ill Fares the Land*, 273.

34. Peter C. Whybrow, *American Mania: When More Is Not Enough* (New York: W.W. Norton 2005), 11.

35. Pico Iyer, "The Joy of Quiet," *The New York Times*, 12/29/2011, www.nytimes.com/2012/01/01/opinion/sunday/the-joy-of-quiet .html?pagewanted=all.

36. Juliet Schor, *Do Americans Shop Too Much?* (Boston: Beacon Press, 2000), 7.

37. For an insightful and imaginative explication of the impact of 19th century technologies on human perception see Rebecca Solnit, *River of Shadows: Eadweard Muybridge and the Technological Wild West.*

38. Jaron Lanier, *You Are Not a Gadget: A Manifesto* (New York: Vintage Books, 2010), 80–81.

39. Crawford, *Shop Class*, 156.

40. Harry Braverman, *Labor and Monopoly Capital: The Degradation of Work in the Twentieth Century* (New York: Monthly Review Press, 1998), 271.

41. Mary Billard, "A Yoga Manifesto," *The New York Times*, 4/25/2010, http://query.nytimes.com/gst/fullpage.html?res=9C06E7D71E30F93 6A15757C0A9669D8B63&pagewanted=all.

42. For an up-to-date take on advertising, including newer marketing strategies like product placement in films and TV shows, see Michael Sandel, *What Money Can't Buy: The Moral Limits of Markets.*

43. Judt, *Ill Fares the Land*, 168.

44. Daniel Boorstin, *The Image: A Guide to Pseudo-events in America* (New York: Vintage Books, 1992), xvii.

45. David Broder, *Democracy Derailed: Initiative Campaigns and the Power of Money* (New York: Mariner Books, 2001), 225.

46. John Avlon, *Wingnuts: How the Lunatic Fringe Is Hijacking America* (New York: Beast Books, 2010), 142.

47. Sunstein, Cass. *Going to Extremes: How Like Minds Unite and Divide* (New York: Oxford University Press, 2009).

48. Jonathan Guthrie, "Lunch with the FT: Biz Stone," *Financial Times*, 12/30/2010, www.ft.com/intl/cms/s/2/a5243058-0ee5-11e0-9ec 3-00144feabdc0.html#axzz1lBdIVnAt.

49. Judt, *Ill Fares the Land*, 176.

50. For a discussion of new approaches to cultural diplomacy see Joseph

Nye, *Soft Power*, and a 2007 report by the Center for Strategic and International Studies, Joseph Nye and Richard Armitage, *A Smarter, More Secure America.*

51. Zbigniew Brzezinski, *Strategic Vision: America and the Crisis of Global Power* (New York: Basic Books, 2012), 38.

52. John Le Carré, "The Art of Fiction No. 149," *The Paris Review*, www .theparisreview.org/interviews/1250/the-art-of-fiction-no-149-john-le-carr.

53. George Soros, "My Philanthropy," Quoted in Chuck Sudetic, *The Philanthropy of George Soros* (New York: Public Affairs, 2011), 52.

54. Chelsey "Sully" Sullenberger and Jeffrey Zaslow, *Highest Duty: My Search for What Really Matters* (New York: Harper Collins, 2010), 261.

55. James Salter, "The Art of the Ditch," *New York Review of Books*, 1/14/2010, 14.

56. Richard Sennett, *The Craftsman* (New Haven, CT: Yale University Press, 2008), 9.

57. Sullenberger, *Highest Duty*, 9.

58. Ibid., 149

59. Braverman, *Labor and Monopoly Capital*, 109.

60. Bruce Landsberg, "A Personal and Systemic Failure," *AOPA Pilot*, May 2010, 36.

61. Sullenberger, *Highest Duty*, 276

62. Robert Sumwalt, quoted in Christine Negroni, "As Attention Wanders, Rethinking the Autopilot," *The New York Times*, 5/17/2 010, www.nytimes.com/2010/05/18/business/18pilots.html.

63. Sullenberger, *Highest Duty*, 40.

64. See both Richard Sennett, *The Craftsman*, and Matthew Crawford, *Shop Class as Soulcraft.*

65. See: Frederick Winslow Taylor, *The Principles of Scientific Management*, 1911.

66. Braverman, *Labor and Monopoly Capital*, 136.

67. Project on Incentives in Teaching (POINT). National Center on

Performance Incentives, Peabody College of Education, Vanderbilt University, 2010.

68. Gardiner Harris, "Talk Doesn't Pay, So Psychiatry Turns Instead to Drug Therapy," *The New York Times*, 5/5/2011, www.nytimes.com/2011/03/06/health/policy/06doctors.html?pagewanted=all.

69. Braverman, *Labor and Monopoly Capital,* 330.

70. While Richard Florida was unable to convince sociologists that his "creative class" possessed the same intellectual coherence as "working class," during the first decade of the 21st century the author's phrase exerted a profound impact on the thinking of civic boosters, politicians, real estate developers, and arts advocates.

71. Crawford, *Shop Class,* 52.

72. Brooks, *Bobos in Paradise: The New Upper Class and How They Got There,* (New York: Simon and Schuster 2001), 136.

73. Crawford, *Shop Class,* 143.

74. Sennett, *Craftsman,* 34.

75. Susan Cain, "The Rise of the New Groupthink," *The New York Times*, 1/13/2012, www.nytimes.com/2012/01/15/opinion/sunday/the-rise-of-the-new-groupthink.html?pagewanted=all.

76. Ellie Winninghoff, "Book Review: *White-collar Sweatshop*," *Yes Magazine*, 1/31/2002, www.yesmagazine.org/issues/what-does-it-mean-to-be-an-american-now/book-review-white-collar-sweatshop-by-jill-andresky-fraser.

77. Susan Cain, "The Rise of the New Groupthink."

78. Richard Sennett, *Corrosion of Character: The Personal Consequences of Work in the New Capitalism* (New York: W. W. Norton and Company, 1998), 99.

79. Sennett, *Craftsman*, 34.

80. Daniel Bell, *Cultural Contradictions of Capitalism* (New York: Basic Books, 1976), 94.

81. Winninghoff, "Book Review: *White-collar Sweatshop*."

82. Lanier, *You Are Not a Gadget*, 8.

83. Clive Crook, "Monumental Job Losses in America," *Financial Times*, 5/23/2010, www.ft.com/cms/s/0/653d6036-6698-11df-aeb1-00 144feab49a.html#axzz1oMDJ90lp.

84. Tyler Cowen, *The Great Stagnation: How America Ate All the Low-Hanging Fruit of Modern History, Got Sick, and Will (Eventually) Feel Better* (New York: Penguin, 2011), 88.

85. Richard Florida, *The Great Reset: How New Ways of Living and Working Drive Post-Crash Prosperity* (New York: Random House Digital, 2010), 46.

86. Richard Waters, "Job-Devouring Technology Confronts US Workers," *Financial Times*, 12/15/2011, www.ft.com/intl/cms/s/0/1e12826e-27 0c-11e1-b9ec-00144feabdc0.html#axzz1oMDJ90lp.

87. Jackson Lears, interview by Edward J.K. Gitre, *Hedgehog Review*, Summer 2009, 39.

88. Robert Reich, "We Are All Going to Hell in a Shipping Basket," *Financial Times*, 1/16/2012, www.ft.com/intl/cms/s/0/2f0babbe-3e30-11 e1-ac9b-00144feabdc0.html#axzz1oMDJ90lp.

89. Matt Richtel, "Idaho Teachers Fight Reliance on Computers," *The New York Times*, 1/3/2012, www.nytimes.com/2012/01/04/technology/idaho-teachers-fight-a-reliance-on-computers.html?pagewanted=all.

90. Katrin Frye, "Firearms Industry Booms in Montana," *All Things Considered*, 1/16/2012, www.npr.org/2012/01/16/145309332/gun-makers-move-operations-to-montana.

91. Cowen, *Great Stagnation*, 51.

92. Crawford, *Shop Class*, 53.

93. Braverman, *Labor and Monopoly Capital*, 109.

94. Ruskin, John. *Complete Works*, Vol. 14, 206. Reuwee Wattly & Walsh: London, 1891, p. 8.

95. Sennett, *Craftsman*, 263.

96. Moisés Naím, "Take Note America: The Public Is Angry," *Financial Times*, 10/26/2011, http://blogs.ft.com/the-a-list/2011/10/26/take-note-america-the-public-is-angry/#axzz1oMOiWc3J.

97. "US Budget Impasse," *Financial Times*, 6/20/2011, www.ft.com/intl/cms/s/0/e0f57ee6-9b82-11e0-98f2-00144feabdc0.html#axzz1uIwEGl80.

98. Sullenberger, Highest Duty, 262.

99. *Perry v. Schwarzenegger*, 116.

100. Wallace, Chris. Interview with Ted Olson, *Fox News Sunday*, 8/8/10.

101. Broder, *Democracy Derailed*, 16.

102. Peter Baker, "Hip, Hip—if not Hooray—for a Standstill Nation," *The New York Times*, 6/18/2011, www.nytimes.com/2011/06/19/weekinreview/19paralysis.html?pagewanted=all.

103. Andrea Seabrook, "Health Summit May Enforce Partisan Divide," *Morning Edition*, 2/25/2010, www.npr.org/templates/rundowns/rundown.php?prgId=3&prgDate=2-25-2010

104. David Brooks, "Interview with David Brooks," *Booknotes*, 7/30/2000, www.booknotes.org/Watch/157392-1/David+Brooks.aspx.

105. Max Frankel, "The Elections: A Modest Proposal," *New York Review of Books*, 2/9/2012, 8.

106. Sean Condon, "Fighting for Air: An Interview with Eric Klinenberg," Adbusters, 6/27/2007, www.adbusters.org/magazine/72/Fighting_For_Air_An_Interview_with_Eric_Klinenberg.html.

107. Avlon, *Wingnuts*, 109.

108. Marvin Kitman, "Murdoch Triumphant: How We Could Have Stopped Him—Twice," *Harper's Magazine*, November 2010, 35.

109. Ibid.

110. Markus Prior, *Post-Broadcast Democracy* (New York: Cambridge University Press, 2007), 32.

111. Ibid., 244.

112. Ibid., 271.

113. Ibid.

114. Lanier, *You Are Not a Gadget*, 62.

115. Kitman, "Murdoch Triumphant," 29.

116. Elizabeth Drew, "Can We Have a Democratic Election?" *New York*

Review of Books, 1/24/2012, www.nybooks.com/articles/archives/2012/feb/23/can-we-have-democratic-election/?pagination=false.

117. Buddy Roemer on *Real time With Bill Maher*, HBO, 1/20/2012.

118. Mark Liebovitch, "The Man the White House Wakes Up To," *New York Times Magazine*, 4/21/2010, www.nytimes.com/2010/04/25/magazine/25allen-t.html.

119. Seabrook, "Health Summit."

120. Friedman, Thomas, *Morning Joe*

121. Nate Silver, "A Warning on the Accuracy of Primary Polls," *The New York Times*, 3/1/2012, http://fivethirtyeight.blogs.nytimes.com/2012/03/01/a-warning-on-the-accuracy-of-primary-polls/.

122. Howard Fineman on *Countdown With Keith Olbermann*, MSNBC, 5/18/2010.

123. Seabrook, "Health Summit."

124. Dan Frosch, "Professional Petitioners Aid Ballot Initiatives," *The New York Times*, 10/23/2010, www.nytimes.com/2010/10/24/us/politics/24petition.html.

125. Mike Frost, "Technology Can Return Democracy to the People," Letter to the editor, *Financial Times*, 1/20/2012, www.ft.com/cms/s/0/6c1f5b08-4205-11e1-9506-00144feab49a.html#axzz1rUhMJUdj.

126. Justin Wolfers on *All Things Considered*, NPR News, 10/30/2011.

127. Broder, *Democracy Derailed*, 225.

128. "Recall Threatens to make Officeholders ever more Spineless," *USA Today*, 1/26/2012, 8a.

129. http://www.youtube.com/watch?v=M0yY5wQZTaU

130. John Heilemann and Lawrence O'Donnell on *The Last Word with Lawrence O'Donnell*, MSNBC, 6/8/2011.

131. Chris Matthews, MSNBC, 2/26/2010.

132. *The Daily Show with Jon Stewart*, Comedy Central, 6/20/2011.

133. Max Frankel, "The Elections: A Modest Proposal," *New York Review of Books*, 2/9/2012, 8.

134. Ibid.

135. To view Magritte's "The Treachery of Images" online, see gaelart.net/pearseconnollylarkin.html.

136. Tom Scocca, "The Downward Spiral of Progress," *Boston Globe*, 5/31/2009, www.boston.com/bostonglobe/ideas/articles/2009/05/31/the_downward_spiral_of_progress/.

137. Amitai Etzioni, "Spent: America After Consumerism," *New Republic*, 6/17/2009, www.tnr.com/article/spent.

138. Whybrow, *American Mania*, 11.

139. Braverman, *Labor and Monopoly Capital*, 188.

140. In addition to Bell and Braverman, see more recent treatments of advertising and consumption by T.J. Jackson Lears, *Fables of Abundance*, Thomas Frank, *The Conquest of Cool*, and Michael Sandel, *What Money Can't Buy*.

141. See: Thorstein Veblen, *The Theory of the Leisure Class*, 1899.

142. Ibid.

143. This is a restatement of Thomas Frank's smart argument about the power of advertising to deflect or overwhelm anti-consumerist opinion and social movements.

144. Leslie Kaufman, "At 40, Earth Day is Now Big Business," *The New York Times*, 4/21/2010, www.nytimes.com/2010/04/22/business/energy-environment/22earth.html.

145. Adam Gopnik, "The Caging of America," *The New Yorker*, 1/30/2012, www.newyorker.com/arts/critics/atlarge/2012/01/30/120130crat_atlarge_gopnik.

146. Corrections Corporation of America, "2005 Annual Report," http://ir.correctionscorp.com/phoenix.zhtml?c=117983&p=irol-reportsannual.

147. Thomas Frank, *The Conquest of Cool: Business Culture, Counterculture, and the Rise of Hip Consumerism* (Chicago: University of Chicago Press, 1998), 229.

148. J.L. Powell Men's Clothing Catalogue. *The Sporting Life*, No. 15, Spring, 2010, p.76.

149. Crawford, *Shop Class*, 56.
150. Walter Kirn, "The Autumn of the Multitaskers," *The Atlantic Monthly*, November 2007, www.theatlantic.com/magazine/archive/2007/11/the-autumn-of-the-multitaskers/6342/.
151. Whybrow, *American Mania*, 243.
152. Ben Stein, "Avoid the Craziness and No One Gets Hurt," *The New York Times*, 8/26/2007, www.nytimes.com/2007/08/26/business/yourmoney/26every.html?pagewanted=print.
153. Michael Pollan, "Out of the Kitchen and onto the Couch," *New York Times Magazine*, 7/29/2009, www.nytimes.com/2009/08/02/magazine/02cooking-t.html?pagewanted=all.
154. Ibid.
155. Claire Cain Miller, "Santa via Cellphone: Shopping Online without a Computer," *The New York Times*, 12/17/2010, www.nytimes.com/2010/12/18/technology/18mobile.html.
156. Lanier, *You are not a Gadget*, 83.
157. Ibid.
158. James Gleick, "How Google Dominates Us," *New York Review of Books*, 8/18/2011, www.nybooks.com/articles/archives/2011/aug/18/how-google-dominates-us/?pagination=false.
159. Evgeny Morozov, "The Death of the Cyberflaneur," *The New York Times*, 4/10/2012, www.nytimes.com/2012/02/05/opinion/sunday/the-death-of-the-cyberflaneur.html?pagewanted=all.
160. Somini Sengupta, "Should Personal Data Be Personal?" *The New York Times*, 2/4/2012, www.nytimes.com/2012/02/05/sunday-review/europe-moves-to-protect-online-privacy.html?pagewanted=all
161. Morozov, "The Death of the Cyberflaneur."
162. Jennifer Van Grove, "Your Address Book is Mine: Many iPhone Apps Take Your Data," *VentureBeat.com*, 2/14/2012, http://venturebeat.com/2012/02/14/iphone-address-book/.
163. Lori Andrews, "Facebook Is Using You," *The New York Times*,

2/4/2012, www.nytimes.com/2012/02/05/opinion/sunday/facebook-is-using-you.html?pagewanted=all.

164. Lanier, *You Are Not A Gadget*, 112.

165. Scocca, "The Downward Spiral of Progress."

166. Carina Chocano, "The Dilemma of Being a Cyborg," *New York Times Magazine*, 1/27/2012, www.nytimes.com/2012/01/29/magazine/what-happens-when-data-disappears.html?pagewanted=all.

167. Etzioni, "Spent."

168. Richard Falkenrath, "Google Must Remember Our Right To Be Forgotten," *Financial Times*, 2/15/2012, www.ft.com/intl/cms/s/0/47 6b9a08-572a-11e1-869b-00144feabdc0.html#axzz1uIwEGl80.

169. Benjamin Barber, "The Pocantico Gathering," Curb Center at Vanderbilt University, www.vanderbilt.edu/curbcenter/files//HAPPINESS-REPORT_web1.pdf.

170. Diane Johnson, "Finish That Homework!" *New York Review of Books*, 8/18/2011, www.nybooks.com/articles/archives/2011/aug/18/finish-that-homework-tiger-mother/?pagination=false.

171. Daniel Akst, *We Have Met the Enemy: Self-control in the Age of Excess* (New York: Penguin: 2011), 69.

172. Harold Meyerson, "Without a Movement, Progressives Can't Aid Obama's Agenda," *The Washington Post*, 1/6/2010, www.washingtonpost.com/wp-dyn/content/article/2010/01/05/AR2010010502989.html.

173. Jackie Calmes, "Party Gridlock in Washington Feeds Fear of a Debt Crisis," *The New York Times*, 2/16/2010, www.nytimes.com/2010/02/17/business/economy/17gridlock.html?pagewanted=all.

174. Thomas Edsall, "What the Right Gets Right," *The New York Times*, 1/15/2012, campaignstops.blogs.nytimes.com/2012/01/15/what-the-right-gets-right/.

175. Gleick, "How Google Dominates Us."

176. Maureen Dowd, "Power to the Corporation!" *The New York Times*,

7/13/2011, www.nytimes.com/2011/08/14/opinion/sunday/Dowd-power-to-the-corporation.html.

177. "Lex on US unemployment, August 6," *FT Newsmine*, week ending Friday, August 12, 2011.

178. Madrick, *Age of Greed*, 284.

179. For the origins of lobbying see Richard White, *Railroaded*, and for a more-contemporary examination of globalized corporate influence and government, see Steve Coll's history of ExxonMobil, *Private Empire*.

180. White, *Railroaded*.

181. Andrew Leonard, "Apple's Cool Is No Liberal Triumph," *Salon.com*, 8/23/2011, www.salon.com/2011/08/23/apple_and_liberal_values/.

182. Ibid.

183. Edward Wyatt, "White House, Consumers in Mind, Offers Online Privacy Guidelines," *The New York Times*, 2/23/2012, www.nytimes.com/2012/02/23/business/white-house-outlines-online-privacy-guidelines.html.

184. Rachel Maddow, *Drift: The Unmooring of American Military Power* (New York: Crown Publishers, 2012), 176.

185. Richard Bruce Anderson, "Glimpse of the Apocalypse," *Adbusters*, 12/15/2009, www.adbusters.org/magazine/87/richard_bruce_anderson.html.

186. Lori Gottlieb, "How to Land your Kid in Therapy," *The Atlantic Monthly*, July–August 2011, www.theatlantic.com/magazine/archive/2011/07/how-to-land-your-kid-in-therapy/8555/4/.

187. Johnson, "Finish That Homework!"

188. Alina Tugend, "Family Happiness and the Overbooked Child," *The New York Times*, 8/12/2011, www.nytimes.com/2011/08/13/your-money/childrens-activities-no-guarantee-of-later-success.html?pagewanted=all.

189. Lewin, Tamar, "Children Watching More Than Ever." *The New York Times*, 10/25/11, p. A6.

190. Richard Louv, *Last Child in the Woods: Saving Our Children from Nature-Deficit Disorder* (Chapel Hill, NC: Algonquin Books, 2008), 67.

191. Steven Brill, "Super Teachers Alone Can't Save Our Schools," *The Wall Street Journal,* 8/13/2011, http://online.wsj.com/article/SB1000142405 31119039181045765005310664 14112.html.

192. Gottlieb, "How to Land Your Kid in Therapy."

193. Alan Sroufe, "Ritalin Gone Wrong," *The New York Times,* 1/28/2012, www.nytimes.com/2012/01/29/opinion/sunday/childrens-add-drugs-dont-work-long-term.html?pagewanted=all.

194. Gottlieb, "How to Land Your Kid in Therapy."

195. Jeane Twenge, *Generation Me: Why Today's Young Americans Are More Confident, Assertive, Entitled—and More Miserable than Ever Before* (New York: Simon and Schuster, 2007), 69.

196. Roy F. Blaumeister and John Tierney, *Willpower: Rediscovering the Greatest Human Strength* (New York: Penguin, 2011), 192.

197. Paul Tough, "What If the Secret to Success Is Failure?" *New York Times Magazine,* 9/14/2011, www.nytimes.com/2011/09/18/magazine/what-if-the-secret-to-success-is-failure.html?pagewanted=all.

198. Jane Brody, "Attacking the Obesity Epidemic by First Figuring Out Its Cause," *The New York Times,* 9/12/2011, www.nytimes.com/2011/09/13/health/13brody.html?pagewanted=all.

199. Joseph Epstein, *Envy: The Seven Deadly Sins* (New York: Oxford University Press, 2003), 1.

200. Ibid.

201. Susan Dominus, "Terrible Swift Tongue," *The New York Times,* 2/11/2011, www.nytimes.com/2011/02/13/books/review/Dominus-t.html.

202. Joseph Epstein, *Snobbery: The American Version* (New York: Houghton Mifflin, 2003), 116.

203. Epstein, *Envy,* xxiv.

204. Akst, *We Have Met the Enemy,* 46.

205. Tom Brokaw, *The Time of Our Lives: A Conversation About America* (New York: Random House Digital, 2011), 110.

206. Ibid.

207. Tom Brokaw, *The Time of Our Lives: A Conversation About America* (New York: Random House Digital, 2011), 110.

208. Greg Epstein, *Good Without God: What a Billion Nonreligious People Do Believe* (New York: William Morrow, 2009), xiii.

209. American Humanism Association, "Humanist Manifesto III," www .americanhumanist.org/humanism/Humanist_Manifesto_III.

210. Neil DeGrasse Tyson, "The Cosmic Perspective," www.haydenplan-etarium.org/tyson/read/2007/04/02/the-cosmic-perspective.

211. Richard Layard, *Happiness: Lessons from a New Science* (New York: Penguin, 2006).

212. Quoted in Steven Kurutz, "Pete Seeger's Guide to Surviving the Recession," *New York Times Magazine*, 4/26/2009..

213. David Cameron, "PM Speech on Wellbeing," HM Government, 2/25/2010, www.number10.gov.uk/news/pm-speech-on-well-being/.

214. Jean Twenge, "The Age of Anxiety? Birth Cohort Change in Anxiety and Neuroticism, 1952-1993," *Journal of Personality and Social Psychology, 79, no. 6* (2007): 1007–21, quoted in Wilkinson and Pickett, *The Spirit Level*, 33.

215. Seligman's three levels of happiness – pleasant sensation, engagement, and deep meaning – are outlined in Bill Ivey and Paul Kingsbury, *The Pocantico Gathering*, proceedings of a Curb Center/Vanderbilt University conference on the role of art in happiness and quality of life. Seligman has written about happiness a number of times, and has tweaked his argument frequently. For more see, *Authentic Happiness* and his most-recent volume, *Flourish*.

216. The term "Flow," used in this sense, was defined by psychologist Mihaly Csikszentimihaly. It refers to a mental state characterized by complete absorption with the task at hand – a notion distinctly compatible with the way Arts & Crafts thinkers viewed artisan work.

217. While political scientist James Q. Wilson is best remembered for his

"broken windows" theory of police work, he also studied factors leading to citizen engagement in community.

218. Anderson, "Glimpse of the Apocalypse."

219. Tyler Cowen, "Self-Constraint Versus Self-Liberation," *Ethics*, 101
(January 1991): 360–373.

220. Steve Ratner, "Don't Just Blame the Capitalism, Blame the Regulators," *Financial Times*, 2/9/2012, www.ft.com/cms/s/0/6ec998ec-53
11-11e1-8aa1-00144feabdc0.html#axzz1r0AclD9z.

221. Kishore Mahbubabi, "Western Capitalism Has Much to Learn from
Asia," 2/7/2012, http://blogs.ft.com/the-a-list/2012/02/07/western-
capitalism-has-much-to-learn-from-asia/?Authorised=false#axzz1r
0BQctYV.

222. Akst, *We Have Met the Enemy*, 242.

223. Steve Ratner, "Don't Just Blame the Capitalism."

224. Seelye, Katherine Q. "What Happens to the American Dream in a
Recession? *The New York Times*, 5/8/09, citing a NY Times/CBS News
poll from spring, 2009.

225. Alan Wolfe, "Joy to the World," *The New York Times*, 2/16/2010,
http://www.nytimes.com/2010/02/21/books/review/Wolfe-t
.html?pagewanted=all.

226. Ibid.

227. John Ruskin, *Seven Lamps of Architecture* (New York: J. Wiley Press,
1849).

228. Ibid.

229. Alain de Botton, *Religion for Atheists: A Non-believer's Guide to the
Uses of Religion* (New York: Pantheon, 2012).

230. "American Humanist Association, "Definitions of Humanism," www
.americanhumanist.org/Humanism/Definitions_of_Humanism."

231. Ibid.

232. Tough, "Secret to Success."

233. Barack Obama, "State of the Union Addresss," The White House,

1/24/2012, www.whitehouse.gov/the-press-office/2012/01/24/ remarks-president-state-union-address.

234. Kishore Mahbubani, "Gaddafi's and the West's Love of the Big Lie," *Financial Times*, 9/4/2011, www.ft.com/intl/cms/s/0/9b5907da-d4 cc-11e0-a7ac-00144feab49a.html#axzz1r1cb7mca.

235. Florida, *The Great Reset*, 5.

236. Mort Zuckerman, "The Jobless Recovery Remains Issue Number One," *US News and World Report*, 5/28/2010, www.usnews.com/ opinion/mzuckerman/articles/2010/05/28/mort-zuckerman-the-jobless-recovery-remains-issue-number-one.

237. *Baylor Religion Survey*. Institute for Studies of Religion. Baylor University: Waco, Texas, 2008.

238. David Scheffer, "BP Shows the Need for a Rethink of Regulation," *Financial Times*, 5/27/2010, www.ft.com/intl/cms/s/0/919f37fe-69 c1-11df-8432-00144feab49a.html#axzz1uIwEGl80.

239. Ibid.

240. Gideon Rachman, "The End of the Thatcher Era," *Financial Times*, 8/27/2009, www.ft.com/intl/cms/s/0/98ef04fe-3357-11de-8f1b-00 144feabdc0.html#axzz1r1cb7mca.

241. Judt, *Ill Fares the Land*, 105.

242. John Kay, "Economics: Rituals of Rigor," *Financial Times*, 8/25/2011, www.ft.com/intl/cms/s/0/faba8834-cf09-11e0-86c5-00144feabdc0 .html#axzz1r1cb7mca.

243. Daniel Bell, *Cultural Contradictions*, 14.

244. Noam Scheiber, "Upper Mismanagement," *The New Republic*, 12/18/2009, www.tnr.com/article/economy/wagoner-henderson?page=0,1.

245. Martin Wolf, "The Big Questions."

246. Robert Reich, "Insatiable Consumers are Undermining Democracy," *Financial Times*, 1/16/2012, blogs.ft.com/the-a-list/2012/01/16/ insatiable-consumers-are-undermining-democracy/?Authorised=f alse#axzz1r1kls400.

247. Lawrence Lessig, *Republic, Lost: How Money Corrupts Congress—and a Plan to Stop it* (New York: Twelve, 2011).

248. Thomas L. Friedman and Michael Mandelbaum, *That Used To Be Us: How America Fell Behind in the World It Invented and How We Can Come Back* (New York: Farrar, Straus and Giroux, 2011).

249. Newton Minow, address to National Association of Broadcasters, 5/9/1961.

250. Rebecca Solnit, *River of Shadows: Eadweard Muybridge and the Technological Wild West* (New York, Viking Penguin, 2004), 114.

251. Douglas Rushkoff, "Digital Nation: Living on the Virtual Frontier," *Frontline*, 2/2/2010, www.pbs.org/wgbh/pages/frontline/digitalnation/etc/synopsis.html.

252. David Brooks, "Cellphones, Texts, and Lovers," *The New York Times*, 11/2/2009, http://www.nytimes.com/2009/11/03/opinion/03brooks.html.

253. Heather Havrilesky, "Digital Nation: What Has the Internet Done to Us?" *Salon*, 1/30/2010, www.salon.com/2010/01/31/frontline_digital_nation/.

254. Rushkoff, "Digital Nation."

255. Siva Vaidyanathan, *The Googlizaiton of Everything: (And Why We Should Worry)* (Berkeley, CA: University of California Press, 2011), 201.

256. Carina Chocano, "The Dilemma of Being a Cyborg," *New York Times Magazine*, 1/27/2012, http://www.nytimes.com/2012/01/29/magazine/what-happens-when-data-disappears.html?pagewanted=all.

257. Scarborough, Joe. *Morning Joe.*

258. Brokaw, *The Time of Our Lives*, 73.

259. The Dreyfuss Initiative, www.thedreyfussinitiative.org/.

260. Martha Nussbaum, *Not for Profit: Why Democracy Needs the Humanities* (Princeton, NJ: Princeton University Press, 2012), 141.

261. Lawrence Summers, "What you Really Need to Know," *The New York Times*, 1/20/2012, www.nytimes.com/2012/01/22/education/edlife/the-21st-century-education.html?pagewanted=all.

262. Terry Eagleton, *The Meaning of Life: A Very Short Introduction* (New York: Oxford University Press, 2011), 16.

263. Nussbaum, *Not for Profit*, 2.

264. John Kay, "Innovation Is Not About Wearing a White Coat," *Financial Times*, 2/15/2009, www.ft.com/intl/cms/s/0/f5b07a10-e9af-11de-9f1 f-00144feab49a.html#axzz1r1cb7mca.

265. Diane Ravitch, "The Myth of Charter Schools," *New York Review of Books*, 1/11/2012, www.nybooks.com/articles/archives/2010/nov/11/ myth-charter-schools/?pagination=false.

266. Matt Richtel, "In Classroom of the Future, Stagnant Scores," *The New York Times*, 9/3/2011, www.nytimes.com/2011/09/04/ technology/technology-in-schools-faces-questions-on-value. html?pagewanted=1&_r=1.

267. "Digital Promise Factsheet," The White House, www.whitehouse.gov/ the-press-office/2011/09/15/fact-sheet-digital-promise-initiative.

268. Matt Richtel, "In Classroom of the Future."

269. E.D. Hirsch Jr., "How to Save the Schools," *New York Review of Books*, 5/13/2010, www.nybooks.com/articles/archives/2010/may/13/how-save-schools/?pagination=false.

270. Garret Keizer, "Getting Schooled: The Re-Education of an American Teacher," *Harper's Magazine*, September 2011.

271. Tough, "Secret to Success."

272. Nussbaum, *Not for Profit*, 72.

273. Christopher R. Beha, "Leveling the Field: What I Learned from For-Profit Education," *Harper's Magazine*, October 2011, http://harpers .org/archive/2011/10/0083639.

274. "Ruling Capitalism," *Financial Times*, 1/26/2012, www.ft.com/intl/ cms/s/5e02ce70-4826-11e1-a4e5-00144feabdc0,Authorised=false .html?_i_location=http%3A%2F%2Fwww.ft.com%2Fcms%2Fs%2F 0%2F5e02ce70-4826-11e1-a4e5-00144feabdc0.html&_i_referer=htt p%3A%2F%2Frefererned#axzz1r1cb7mca.

275. Etzioni, "Spent."

276. Wendy Kaplan, *The Arts and Crafts Movement in Europe and America: Design for the Modern World 1880–1920*, (Los Angeles, CA: Thames & Hudson, 2004), 11.

277. Sennett, *Craftsman*, 114.

278. David Brooks, "The Social Animal," *The New Yorker*, 1/17/2011, http://www.newyorker.com/reporting/2011/01/17/110117fa_fact_brooks.

279. Ibid.

280. David Brooks, "The Social Animal."

281. For a strong argument against the influence of tradition and community, see Kwame Anthony Appiah, *Cosmopolitanism*; for a good argument on the opposite side, see *Cultural Democracy* by folklorist Bau Graves.

282. Tony Judt, "On Intellectuals and Democracy," *New York Review of Books*, 3/22/2012, www.nybooks.com/articles/archives/2012/mar/22/intellectuals-and-democracy/?pagination=false.

283. Brokaw, *The Time of Our Lives*, ix.

284. Thomas L. Friedman and Michael Manlebaum, "America Really Was That Great, but That Doesn't Mean We Are Now," *Foreign Policy*, November 2011, www.foreignpolicy.com/articles/2011/10/11/america_really_was_that_great.

285. Gideon Rachman, "America Must Manage Its Decline," *Financial Times*, 10/17/2011, www.ft.com/intl/cms/s/0/0c73f10e-f8aa-11e0-ad8f-00144feab49a.html#axzz1rV8F0eyb.

286. David J. Rothkopf, "Defining the Meaning of No. 1," *The New York Times*, 10/8/2011, www.nytimes.com/2011/10/09/opinion/sunday/gdp-doesnt-measure-happiness.html?pagewanted=all.

287. Brzenzki, *Strategic Vision*, 35.

288. Ezra Klein, "The Unpersuaded," *The New Yorker*, 3/12/2012, www.newyorker.com/reporting/2012/03/19/120319

289. Thomas Frank, "Easy Chair: Debt, Be Not Proud," *Harper's Magazine*, March 2012, 9.

290. Ibid.

291. The concept of "Jumping the shark" was developed in the late 1970s by comedian/radio personality Jon Hein when Hein and University of Michigan friends spotted something no one had noticed: whenever a long-running television series began an inevitable and inexorable decline, writers and producers often employed increasingly-outlandish, "over-the-top" plot devices in an attempt to maintain viewer interest. The term itself is derived from a scene in the fifth season of the "Happy Days" telecast, when Fonzie—the featured character played by Henry Winkler—and the cast of the show decamped to California to film an episode in which Fonzie jumped over a shark on water skis. Hein noted a radical departure from the normal, east-coast interior format of the show, and he and his associates began to mark the point at which other programs had jumped the shark—reacting to impending failure by doubling-down on increasingly-outrageous plot elements. The useful new idiom escaped the show business lexicon and is today applied to desperate, excessive responses to failure or decline. When cracks appeared in the small government, low tax, big military Republican argument, the party doubled-down by attacking Planned Parenthood, increasing the defense budget, and hinting at a debt-ceiling government shutdown. They had jumped the shark.

BIBLIOGRAPHY

Akst, Daniel. *We Have Met the Enemy: Self-control in the Age of Excess.* New York: Penguin, 2011.

Andersen, Kurt. *Reset: How This Crisis Can Restore Our Values and Renew America.* New York: Random House, 2009.

Armstrong, Karen. *Twelve Steps to a Compassionate Life.* New York: Alfred A. Knopf, 2010.

Avlon, John. *Wingnuts: How the Lunatic Fringe Is Hijacking America.* New York: Beast Books, 2010.

Bacevich, Andrew J. *Washington Rules: America's Path to Permanent War.* New York: Metropolitan Books, 2010.

Barber, Benjamin R. *Consumed: How Markets Corrupt Children, Infantalize Adults, and Swallow Citizens Whole.* New York: W.W. Norton, 2007.

Baumeister, Roy F., and John Tierney. *Willpower: Rediscovering the Greatest Human Strength.* New York: Penguin, 2011.

Bell, Daniel. *Cultural Contradictions of Capitalism.* Basic Books, 1976.

Boorstin, Daniel. *The Image: A Guide to Pseudo-events in America.* New York: Vintage Press, 1992.

Braverman, Harry. *Labor and Monopoly Capital: The Degradation of Work in the Twentieth Century*. New York: Monthly Review Press, 1974.

Brockman, John, ed. *Is the Internet Changing the Way You Think?: The Net's Impact on Our Minds and Future*. New York: Harper Perennial, 2011.

Broder, David. *Democracy Derailed: Initiative Campaigns and the Power of Money*. New York: Mariner Books, 2001.

Brokaw, Tom. *The Time of Our Lives: A Conversation About America*. New York: Random House, 2011.

Brooks, David. *Bobos in Paradise: The New Upper Class and How They Got There*. New York: Simon and Schuster, 2001.

Brzezinski, Zbigniew. *Strategic Vision: America and the Crisis of Global Power*. New York: Basic Books, 2012.

Carr, Nicholas. *The Shallows: What the Internet Is Doing to Our Brains*. New York: W.W. Norton, 2010.

Chua, Amy. *Battle Hymn of the Tiger Mother*. New York: Penguin, 2011.

Citizens United v. Federal Election Commission, U.S., (2010).

Cowen, Tyler. *The Great Stagnation: How America Ate All the Low-Hanging Fruit of Modern History, Got Sick, and Will, Eventually Feel Better*. New York: Penguin, 2011.

Crawford, Matt. *Shop Class as Soulcraft: An Inquiry into the Value of Work*. New York: Penguin, 2010.

De Botton, Alain. *Religion for Atheists: A Non-believer's Guide to the Uses of Religion*. New York: Pantheon, 2012.

Drucker, Peter. *The Practice of Management*. New York: Harper Collins, 2006.

Eagleton, Terry. *The Meaning of Life: A Very Short Introduction*. New York: Oxford University Press, 2011.

Eagleton, Terry. *Why Marx Was Right*. New Haven, CT: Yale University Press, 2011.

Edsall, Thomas Byrne. *The Age of Austerity: How Scarcity Will Remake American Politics*. New York: Doubleday, 2012.

Epstein, Greg. *Good Without God: What a Billion Nonreligious People Do Believe*. New York: William Morrow, 2009.

Epstein, Joseph. *Envy: The Seven Deadly Sins*. New York: Oxford University Press, 2003.

Epstein, Joseph. *Snobbery: The American Version*. New York: Houghton Mifflin, 2003.

Florida, Richard. *The Great Reset: How New Ways of Living and Working Drive Post-Crash Prosperity*. New York: Random House Digital, 2010.

Fogel, Robert William. *The Fourth Great Awakening and the Future of Egalitarianism*, Chicago: University of Chicago Press, 2000.

Frank, Thomas. *The Conquest of Cool: Business Culture, Counterculture, and the Rise of Hip Consumerism*. Chicago: University of Chicago Press, 1998.

Frank, Thomas. *Pity the Billionaire: The Hard-Times Swindle and the Unlikely Comeback of the Right*. New York: Metropolitan Books, 2012.

Fraser, Jill Andresky. *White-collar Sweatshop: The Deterioration of Work and Its Rewards in Corporate America*. New York: W.W. Norton and Company, 2002.

Friedman, Thomas L., and Michael Mandelbaum. *That Used To Be Us: How America Fell Behind in the World It Invented and How We Can Come Back*. New York: Farrar, Straus and Giroux, 2011.

Garon, Sheldon. *Beyond Our Means: Why America Spends While the World Saves*. Princeton, NJ: Princeton University Press, 2012.

Harkin, James. *Lost In Cyburbia: How Life on the Net Has Created a Life of Its Own*. Toronto: Alfred A. Knopf, 2009.

Heffernan, Margaret. *Willful Blindness: Why We Ignore the Obvious at Our Peril*. New York: Walker & Company, 2011.

Ivey, Bill. *Arts, Inc.: How Greed and Neglect Have Destroyed Our Cultural Rights*. Berkeley, CA: University of California Press, 2008.

Ivey, Bill, and Paul Kingsbury. *The Pocantico Gathering: Happiness and a High Quality of Life: The Role of Art and Art Making.* Nashville, TN: The Curb Center, 2008.

Johnson, Steven. *Where Good Ideas Come From: The Natural History of Innovation.* New York: Riverhead Books, 2010.

Judt, Tony. *Ill Fares the Land.* New York: Penguin Press, 2010.

Judt, Tony. *The Memory Chalet.* New York: Penguin Press, 2010.

Judt, Tony, and Timothy Snyder. *Thinking the Twentieth Century.* New York: Penguin, 2012.

Kaplan, Wendy. *The Arts and Crafts Movement in Europe and America, 1880–1920: Design for the Modern World.* Los Angeles: Thames & Hudson, 2004.

Kaplan, Wendy. *The Art That Is Life: The Arts and Crafts Movement in America, 1875–1920.* Boston: Museum of Fine Arts, 1987.

Lanier, Jaron. *You Are Not a Gadget: A Manifesto.* New York: Vintage Books, 2010.

Layard, Richard. *Happiness: Lessons from a New Science.* New York: Penguin, 2006.

Lessig, Lawrence. *Republic, Lost: How Money Corrupts Congress—and a Plan to Stop it.* New York: Twelve, 2011.

Louv, Richard. *Last Child in the Woods: Saving Our Children from Nature-Deficit Disorder.* Chapel Hill, NC: Algonquin Books, 2003.

Luce, Edward. *Time to Start Thinking: America in the Age of Descent.* New York: Atlantic Monthly Press, 2012.

Maddow, Rachel. *Drift: The Unmooring of American Military Power.* New York: Crown Publishers, 2012.

Madrick, Jeff. *Age of Greed: The Triumph of Finance and the Decline of America, 1970 to the Present.* Toronto: Alfred A. Knopf, 2011.

Morgenson, Gretchen, and Joshua Rosner. *Reckless Endangerment: How Outsized Ambition, Greed, and Corruption Led to Economic Armageddon.* New York: Times Books, 2011.

Morozov, Evgeny. *The Net Delusion: The Dark Side of Internet Freedom.* New York: Public Affairs, 2011.

Morris, Desmond. *The Nature of Happiness.* London: Little Books, 2006.

Murray, Charles. *Coming Apart: The State of White America, 1960–2010.* New York: Crown Forum, 2012.

Nussbaum, Martha. *Not for Profit: Why Democracy Needs the Humanities.* Princeton, NJ: Princeton University Press, 2012.

Perry v. Schwarzenegger

Platt, David. *Radical: Taking Back Your Faith from the American Dream.* Colorado Springs, CO: Multnomah, 2010.

Podesta, John. *The Power of Progress: How America's Progressives Can, (Once Again) Save Our Economy, Our Climate, and Our Country.* New York: Crown Publishing Group, 2008.

Prior, Markus. *Post-Broadcast Democracy: How Media Choice Increases Inequality in Political Involvement and Polarizes Elections.* New York: Cambridge University Press, 2007.

Reich, Robert B. *The Future of Success.* New York: Alfred A. Knopf, 2001.

Reilly, James Marshall. *Shake the World: It's Not About Finding a Job, It's About Creating a Life.* New York: Portfolio/Penguin, 2011.

Rushkoff, Douglas. *Program Or Be Programmed: Ten Commands for a Digital Age.* Berkeley, CA: Soft Skull Press, 2011.

Ruskin, John. *Seven Lamps of Architecture.* New York: J. Wiley Press, 1849.

Sachs, Jeffrey D. *The Price Of Civilization: Reawakening American Virtue and Prosperity.* New York: Random House, 2011.

Schor, Juliet. *Do Americans Shop Too Much?* Boston: Beacon Press, 2000.

Seligman, Martin. *Flourish: A Visionary New Understanding of Happiness and Wellbeing.* New York: Simon and Schuster, 2011.

Sennett, Richard. *Corrosion of Character: The Personal Consequences of Work in the New Capitalism.* New York: W.W. Norton and Company, 1998.

Sennett, Richard. *The Craftsman*. New Haven, CT: Yale University Press, 2008.

Solnit, Rebecca. *River of Shadows: Eadweard Muybridge and the Technological Wild West*. New York: Penguin Viking, 2004.

Sudetic, Chuck. *The Philanthropy of George Soros: Building Open Societies*. New York: Public Affairs, 2011.

Sullenberger, Chelsey "Sulley" and Jeffrey Zaslow. *Highest Duty: My Search for What Really Matters*. New York: Harper Collins, 2010.

Sunstein, Cass. *Going to Extremes: How Like Minds Unite and Divide*. New York: Oxford University Press, 2009.

Turkle, Sherry. *Alone Together: Why We Expect More from Technology and Less from Each Other*. New York: Basic Books, 2011.

Twenge, Jean. *Generation Me: Why Today's Young Americans are more Confident, Assertive, Entitled—and More Miserable than Ever Before*. New York: Simon and Schuster, 2007.

Tyson, Neil deGrasse. *Space Chronicles: Facing the Ultimate Frontier*. New York: W.W. Norton, 2012.

Vaidhyanathan, Siva. *The Googlization of Everything, And Why We Should Worry*. Berkeley, CA: University of California Press, 2011.

Van Buren, Peter. *We Meant Well: How I Helped Lose the Battle for the Hearts and Minds of the Iraqi People*. New York: Metropolitan Books, 2011.

Wilkinson, Richard, and Kate Pickett. *The Spirit Level: Why Greater Equality Makes Societies Stronger*. New York: Bloomsbury, 2009.

White, Richard. *Railroaded: The Transcontinentals and the Making of Modern America*. New York: W.W. Norton, 2011.

Whybrow, Peter C. *American Mania: When More Is Not Enough*. New York: W.W. Norton, 2005.

Wu, Tim. *The Master Switch: The Rise and Fall of Information Empires*. New York: Alfred A. Knopf, 2010.

INDEX

ACKNOWLEDGMENTS

Many colleagues and friends have helped shape *Hand-making America*. Journalist-educator Nicholas Lemann provided helpful advice when the project was just getting started. My agent, Sarah Lazin, and Counterpoint's legendary Editor-in-Chief, Jack Shoemaker, expressed confidence in a barely-finished first draft. Counterpoint's cohort of professionals—Charlie Winton, Liz Parker, Lorna Garano, Jodi Hammerwold, and Kelly Winton—were enthusiastic about *Handmaking* from the beginning. I am grateful for their encouragement. Editorial assistant Cameron Barr corrected many errors and made valuable contributions to the structure of my argument. Copyeditor Peg Goldstein greatly improved the manuscript by, among other things, cutting it down to size. My Vanderbilt colleagues, Heather Lefkowitz and professors Richard Lloyd, Dan Cornfield, and Bruce Barry provided encouragement leavened by smart, critical conversation. Professor Steven J. Tepper, associate director of our Curb Center at Vanderbilt, remains the best tag-teamer to have in the ring when the challenge is to wrestle a fresh idea to the ground.

Handmaking would not exist without the dedication of others, and I am grateful to the many writers and scholars whose work sustained progressive values through difficult times, and who today are restoring the liberal vision of a better America to its rightful place in our national conversation—Richard Sennett, T.J. Jackson Lears, E.J. Dionne, Rachel Maddow, John Podesta, Lewis Lapham, Thomas Frank, Chris Hayes, Jason DeParle, Frank Rich, Wendell Berry, Steve Coll, Tony Judt. And special thanks to my irrepressible partner, Susan Keffer, who again and again asked the frightening question that kept me going: "When can I read it?"

Photo credit: Leslie Rodriguez

ABOUT THE AUTHOR

Bill Ivey is a writer, teacher, and experienced nonprofit executive, and is a principal in Global Cultural Strategies, an online policy consortium. He was founding director of the Curb Center for Art, Enterprise, and Public Policy at Vanderbilt University and is senior consultant to the University's Office of International Relations. During his long tenure in public service, he served as Senate-confirmed chairman of the National Endowment for the Arts in the Clinton-Gore administration, and in that capacity is credited with both increasing the agency's budget and restoring good relations between the NEA and Capitol Hill. He is a trustee of the Center for American Progress, and was a Team Leader in the Barack Obama presidential transition. He is the co-editor of *Arts, Inc. How Greed and Neglect have Destroyed our Cultural Rights*, and *Engaging Art: the Next Great Transformation of America's Cultural Life.* As past president of the American Folklore Society, he today serves as China Liaison for that group. He makes his home in Nashville, Tennessee.